M000309822

Captain Jolly's Do Over

By

JR Ingrisano

Cover Art by:
Chrissy Shanahan

Edited by:
Veronica Castle

Published by:
Crimson Cloak Publishing
All Rights Reserved
Copyright © 2015

ISBN 13: 978-1-68160-279-0

ISBN 10: 1-68160-279-2

Publishers Publication in Data

Ingrisano, John

Captain Jolly's Do Over

   1. Ficrion 2. Lifestyle 3. Adventure 4. South Seas Islands

To Susan:

my wife, my muse, my reality, my myth,
and, yes, my do over.

As the details of even our strongest memories fade, it's easy to wonder if any of it ever really happened.

– Aaron Gilbreath ("Leaving Tatooine")

All characters in this book are fiction. If you see yourself or someone you know on the following pages, you are paranoid.

FOREWORD

The fact is, we all really have only one story, though details may vary: Grew up in the States, got married (and figuratively, if not literally, lived in a house with a white picket fence) to a spouse who forgot how to have sex in the backseat (or who discovered how to have sex in the backseat with someone else), got bored, got dumped, or just got greedy, read one too many Hemingway stories or heard one too many stupid Jimmy Buffett songs, and fled to the Caribbean to drink margaritas. Resume in full.

We were lost by choice. We had no plot, no purpose, and could imagine no clear-cut, happy-ever-after ending to our vague beginnings. And that was fine. We weren't heroic or even tragic, at least in that ironic, bittersweet way of a good tragedy. We were leftovers looking for a do over. No, actually, we weren't so hopeful that we imagined anything resembling a do over.

Again, we had no plot, no purpose, as we picked through the debris of lives we never really understood. Like the lives of most of us (and unlike the formula novels sought by editors who have never howled during sex or done anything more risqué than get stoned and pee in the country club pool), there is no plot. People come, people go, and all too often, when they just begin to be interesting, they wander off.

Like in those romantic movies about the guys who joined the French Foreign Legion, we came down to the islands to forget or to be forgotten. Nothing noble about it. We'd strip off our change-daily-stain-free shirts, put a match to the excuse-me-you-can't-do-that-in-here rule book, and take jobs that bore no resemblance to our back-home lives. (Someone, I think it was Black Mike, once said that Calabash, who spends his days drinking Green Label and snagging crabs off the piers in the lagoon, he'd been a pediatrician, back in the States. More on that later.) We lived in cheap shacks too in disrepair to rent to the *touristas*, furnished with throw-away stuff and a padlocked frig. Ice, beer, whiskey, and aspirin were the most treasured commodities.

The funny thing was that we had all once been normal, or at least not especially noticeable for being too abnormal. Until that day when something snapped and we either figured it out or knew that we would never figure it out. Didn't matter. So, we jumped – or got pushed – out of one chapter into another. Like Alice, we ended up down the rabbit hole.

Squint, who I can't stand, claimed to have once been a stockbroker on Wall Street, and these days did a pretty good job of pretending to be a photographer. French Tony, who was once cornered by a back-homer who asked why he had given up the noble, make-a-difference life of a middle-school teacher back in Mount Pleasant, Michigan, cranked out lewd T-shirts, 3–4–$10. Penny, once a gated housewife feigning satisfaction, and Lea, once a Fortune 500 VP with a six-figure income, did glass art and pretended, God knows why, not to be lovers.

It was a pleasant life in its way, if only because none of us expected anything from ourselves or anybody else. And even when it was unpleasant, well, as one of Tony's T-shirts reads, "Even a lousy day in Paradise is better than a great day back home."

We are considered to be unreliable, ignore our bills (which is probably why we are considered to be unreliable), live in casual need of a clean pair of clothes and a good shower, drive drunk, never even think about buckling up a seat belt, and try to concentrate on little more than running out of cigarettes or where, and with whom, we're likely to wake up in the morning. The girls don't shave their legs; neither do the men, well, except for Daisy, the cross-dressing police chief.

Mornings tend to be a bit fuzzy, and days can be monotonous, spent answering the same old questions from the same old, squeaky clean *touristas*, and telling the same old, totally bullshit exotic tales on the same old, half-day snorkeling excursions, day after day after day … after day.

I remember one slightly sunburned wife gushing, "This is paradise!" and I had shrugged. "Yeah, well, sometimes it's just home," I'd said, stuffing Bonita's shorts into a laundry bag.

MANGROVE COVE

I guess this is the end of the story, so I might as well tell it first. I figured Kid was dead. He had to be. The last I'd seen of him, he was doing some stupid King Kong pose on the bow when a fifteen-foot wave ripped over what was left of the boat. "Could have been worse," I said aloud now, and, for no reason, started laughing. The silence echoed back and shut me up. I hadn't bothered to tell anyone except Kid where I was going, and I had adamantly told him he could not come along.

The radio was under water. My phone, though water-proof wrapped, wasn't picking up any signal.

I was lying on my back on the broad roof of *The Do Over*. That was all that was above water. Hurricane Olive had passed, and if it hadn't been for the fact that my boat was sunk – sleeping like a submarine on the bottom of the shallow channel – it really was a beautiful, blue-sky day. One Problem: Snugged into a mangrove thicket off the leeward side of the island, I was totally alone. I wondered if the rest of the island was even there. I was sure Bonita was fine; she's a survivor, though I was glad – well, kind of – I had said no to her coming along.

I sat up and dangled my feet in the water and looked around. A small barracuda swam restlessly out of the cabin beneath me. "Hey, Barry," I called to the cuda as I peered into the water, "see if that last bottle of whiskey is still down in my cabin." Though I'd quit wearing jewelry years ago, when I'd plunked my wedding ring into Connie's coffee, I checked my hands out of habit. When cudas see something shiny, they swim in fast for a swift, flesh-shredding meal. They don't nibble. They don't circle. They rip, tear, gulp. One of my half-day snorkeling customers had lost an earlobe because she'd ignored the instructions to remove all jewelry before going in. (Down here, girls who play dumb usually learn real fast that nobody's gonna carry their school books home or save them from themselves.) Her husband had been outraged about that severed earlobe. It probably hadn't helped that I'd said, "Good thing your wife wasn't wearing a nipple ring."

A small bottle of water stood beside me on the roof of the cabin. How it got there, I had no idea. I'd long since given up trying to figure out the why or how of even the simplest things. I guess that put me on the same level as Rocky, my old Boxer. When he used to walk into a room, tail all a waggin', I'd say, "Hey, Rock, whadaya know?" Then I'd answer for him in a Bullwinkle voice. "Uh, Dad, I'm a dog. I don't know nuttin."

So, now you know, I'm no great freakin' intellectual.

Anyhow, sitting on the roof of *The Do Over*, I snapped off the cap and flipped it in front of the barracuda. As the cap wobbled downward, the cuda darted in, grabbed it, mashed it a bit, and then spit it out and zigzagged his way like a shot out into the channel.

At the mouth of the channel, I saw a fin cutting back and forth. Agitated and restless, by its long tail it looked like a harmless Thresher shark, probably hungry after the storm. Even if it was a great white, sharks didn't bother me.

The only folks who gave more than a passing thought to sharks were landlubbers who had watched way too many goofy death-in-the-water movies. Anyone who lived around the ocean ignored sharks, and it was almost always mutual. They ate maybe three people a year; odds were it wouldn't be you.

How had Black Mike put it? Interrupting two couples from the States who were sitting close by at the bar and debating the shark question, he'd said, "Excuse me. Listen, the odds are greater that you'll get a good Eggs Benedict breakfast in a hotel restaurant, find a woman over the age of 40 who still thinks sex is about love, *and* see the legendary green flash at sunset over the Caribbean, all in the same day, than that you'll ever, ever be attacked by a shark." I remember watching the two couples as they grew silent, each chewing over his or her own part of what Black Mike had just said. Finally, one of the wives looked at him challengingly and demanded, "Well, where can I get a good Eggs Benedict?"

But myths are stubborn critters. They have lives of their own.

"Any danger of sharks, Captain Jolly?" at least one snorkeler every excursion would ask before stepping off the stern platform into the water.

"Not a chance," I'd say with a confident smile. "Just please be sure to take off any shiny jewelry."

***

Kid and I had discovered this little channel inside Mangrove Cove about a year earlier, and had slowly motored inside. The nice thing about these wide catamarans like *The Do Over*, with their two pontoon hulls, is that they draw very little water. I could slip her over a reef where a canoe would scrape bottom. But she could also weather a hurricane, or at least most hurricanes. That had been my hope.

About fifty yards in, the channel cut sharply to the left, protected from the Caribbean on all four sides. What I like about mangroves is that they defy reality, like a lot of people I know. The ones here in the islands – the mangroves, and, well, maybe a lot of the people, too – were all gnarly root, with little green. They were as hard as steel and made oak trees feel like balsa. They thrived on brackish and salt water. It made no sense to me, but like I said, I had long gotten used to things that made no sense.

It was those steely roots that had made me think then that this would be a terrific place to sit out a hurricane. Not so sure Kid, who'd agreed at the time, would agree now. His body was probably wrapped around one of the roots like a ragdoll. The bait fish and gulls would love him. So would the crabs. Gave a whole new meaning to the idea of crab dinner.

My throat was scratchy from the salt water, so I took a long pull from the water bottle, then tipped it in a brief toast to Kid, out there somewhere, and looked at the soggy head of the stuffed monkey still lashed to the submerged base of the mast.

"Well, Jocko, looks like it's just you and me again, Buckaroo."

Yeah, I thought, and shrugged. Kid, who loved defying reality, would have approved.

Suddenly, feeling nauseous, a bit dizzy, and bone-sinking weary, I dropped back down slowly onto my back on the roof of the cabin. Before passing into peaceful oblivion, I remembered to pull my legs up out of the water. No sense tempting any passing cudas with a fresh toe-food snack.

THE ISLAND
Topless Women Drink Free

I confess that I love the islands. They are comfortable, with just enough edginess.

I was looking out over the sea, past Jason the bartender, who was pouring shots for the three topless blondes. Though the sun was almost down, it was still warm, sultry warm, just-pull-on-a-pair-of-ragged-shorts-and-go warm. Like always.

I studied the western horizon and waited for the mythical green flash. Some say they've seen it pop when the sun sets into the Caribbean. Some lie, too.

I don't know exactly why, but if I had a favorite spot on the island, I guess this would be it, staring off the beach to the west at Sunset Bar as the late afternoon sun disappeared. It's something I did the first evening I'd arrived on the island three years earlier, and I still liked to position myself and just look at the sunset at least once a week.

I lit a cigarette and raised my whiskey – cheap, rail liquor – in a toast to Jason. He glanced at me as he worked his way comfortably along the round, open-air, thatched-roof island of the Sunset Bar. That's what a good bartender did; he always knew where his customers were and what they needed.

The Sunset sat on the edge of the beach, like all the money-making bars on the island. The heavy, slab-wood tables and chairs rested solidly on the sandy tile floor; others, flimsy plastic ones, were planted precariously out on the beach. Over the course of the day and night, they were moved and clustered and reconfigured as individuals, couples, and groups gathered, drank, ate, and then drifted off into the night. The chairs, cheap and not worth stealing, remained.

Behind Jason was the sign: Topless Women Drink Free.

Around the other side of the bar, a young couple, honeymooners from the States by the well-scrubbed, optimistic look of them, were pointing at the sign and giggling. Finally, with a look that said, what-happens-in-the-islands-stays-in-the-islands, right Honey? she slowly, nervously shrugged out of her bikini top. The way she hunched over and folded her arms across her chest, I suspected that this was the first time those babies had ever been set loose in public. And they were nice looking: firm, full, supple. The three topless blondes raised their glasses and smiled in … what? Sisterhood? Solidarity? Invitation? No idea. I never could tell what women were thinking. The only thing that makes me smarter than other guys, at least in my opinion, is that I no longer tried.

Jason quickly poured the wife a drink. Watching Jason and noticing that I was also looking and paying more than passing interest in admiring his wife's breasts, the husband became a little uncertain regarding his suggestion about how they could cut their bar bill in half. The wife had come to the same conclusion, even with the support of the three blondes.

She turned and looked at hubby as if to say, "Okay, I did it." Then she quickly dipped her breasts back into the bikini top and hooked it in place. The couple giggled and relaxed. Now they could go back home and brag to friends for years about their risqué, honeymoon island adventure. And that really was what it was all about.

"What, no photo for the folks back home?" Jason joked, reading their thoughts. He picked the husband's phone off the bar. "Okay, we'll skip the topless version. Smile."

Heads together, the couple grinned broadly. Jason took a few quick, loving-couple-on-honeymoon pictures and put the phone back on the bar.

"So, where you folks from?" he asked, chatting them up.

Ka-ching, I thought. That'll be good for a ten dollar tip.

***

I admired Jason. He had the true bartender's gift; I thought of it more as an intuition. Anybody could pour drinks, given a few hours of training, though some people never really did get the hang of it. Jason, though, he understood people. He had a feel for them; he could read them. I'm not sure if it's because he loves people or thinks they're all idiots.

Still, Jason was likeable. Even Chicago Mike liked Jason, and Mike liked almost no one. "If you have a good bartender," he'd growled on one occasion, staring down at the drink on the bar under his nose, "you'll never need a psychiatrist."

And just between you and me and the rest of the world, I didn't think there was a psychiatrist in the world who could ever help Mike. He was what I think of as a brilliant moron.

"Yeah, but if psychiatrists could pour drinks, you wouldn't need a bartender," Squint had added sagely, as he had looked around the bar through his camera lens.

Still, I thought, for once Mike might be right.

Topless Women Drink Free. Most couples just laugh and point at the sign. Then there are the ones who see it as a challenge, others as an invitation, still others as an opportunity, or just something silly and fun they couldn't do back home. The point was that it generated a lot of talk and drink orders, Jason had explained.

Jason understood people. He even seemed to understand women. Me? I was batting zero on all counts, but I was getting used to the idea.

THE STATES
Home Office Part I

Touristas would almost always ask how I got here, on the island. I'd just smile, keep it light. They loved a good romance story, with a little mystery and bullshit mixed in. I had several versions, none of them having anything to do with the truth. Sometimes I'd say something like, "Two things: Wanderlust and ladylust. Oh, and whiskeylust. I guess that makes three things. Hmmm." But seriously, I used to be way too give-a-damn serious back then, back in The States.

I guess that all has to do with how I got here.

***

When I'd first started my business back in the States, I'd worked out of the spare bedroom in our home. It was neat, efficient, and very cost-effective. But there's a general rule about men in business. Think about it. If things are good, we can always make them better, and that means bigger. We don't open up shops; we build businesses, envision empires. Never satisfied. I saw that as a good thing.

So, naturally, I went from having a nice, profitable, one-man consulting/marketing business to expanding, growing, learning how to be the boss. At first, it was like a perpetual orgasm – the thrill of bursting out of bed each morning at 5:30, hitting the floor running, giving it everything I had each and every day, so full of energy that I howled at the moon with lustful drive, and then dropping into bed at night exhausted, spent, worn out, drained. At first. Even Connie thought it was good because she saw that it consumed me in a happy kind of way. At first.

Then, gradually, it just got to be … well, a business. I brought on employees, spent a lot of time either developing SOPs or being pissed because my staff wasn't following the SOPs. I began to believe that line I'd once heard: "If it wasn't for the damn customers and the stupid employees, business would be a breeze." Well, it's true. Budgets. Payrolls. Taxes. Confabs with CPAs, meetings with ChFCs. BFD! Boring. Boring. Boring.

So much for the pure joy and ecstasy of climbing and clawing my way upward, hand over hand, from rung to rung to rung. That stupid cliché – the business I started out owning was now owning me – was becoming a truth, maybe a truism.

Plus, right on schedule, at least if there was a plot line to follow, I began to lose track of Connie. But there was no plot line. A key piece was missing: Boy meets girl. Boy loses girl. End of story.

***

Well, I have a theory about that. Essentially, I blinked. I got way off script by asking the most dangerous question: Why?

Never ask that question. Marriages, businesses, whole civilizations depend on nobody ever asking that question. Ever. Why should I take that promotion and transfer to the home office? Why do we think we need to be the leader of the Free World? Why in God's green earth did I ever marry that person?

That question assumes that things make sense, have a purpose. They don't. So when you ask that one question, it blows the lid off the rabbit hole and sucks you through.

As for the business, I was growing disillusioned and toying with the idea of downsizing even before Connie gave me the boot. I think we both asked that question. I tripped and stumbled down the rabbit hole; I think Connie dove in head first. She was gone long before she left. Me? I didn't have the sense to know when to quit, at least for a while. Besides, what else would I do? A man works. That's what he does. He gets up every morning and races to fight the traffic or catch the 7:24 commuter train into the city every day. If he ever asks "Why?" he's done. Finished. Nothing changes, if only because he has no backup plan, no alternative. He's just miserable rather than blissfully illusional and delusional. Never, never, never ask "Why!"

So, when things fell apart, with my attention half focused on saving an abandoned marriage and then on surviving the divorce, the business started to suffer without any help from me. Customers were leaving, and I didn't give a shit. Why? Why bother? Why not?

Finally, my once roaring enterprise was down to a small group of suites and a handful of employees with more loyalty than sense. Plus, the office was doubling more and more as my home, or at least my crash pad for sleeping. It was probably a bad idea. But like I said, I had no backup plan. I couldn't bring myself to rent an apartment. That would have meant it was over, something I wasn't quite ready to admit at first. Not yet.

***

So, there I was, sleeping, or just trying to sleep, in my office. Deep into the night was the toughest. I hated the night. During the day I could keep busy and avoid thinking. I could work. But at night …

I would stretch out on the couch in my office and, after several attempts to order myself to sleep, eventually, always, I would give in and let my mind go wherever it wanted, no matter how much it hurt. I had tried rejecting the pain, ignoring the pain, embracing the pain. In the end, it was still pain. And it was there, always. I still hadn't gotten from "Why?" to "Stuff just happens." It may seem like a small step, but in reality it's a life shifting leap through the darkness into the abyss. That was probably how it was the day Dave the police chief decided to become Daisy the transvestite while on vacation down in the islands, not exactly a minor realization or decision for a macho officer of the law from a small redneck town.

I was a long way from asking why to accepting that stuff just happens. That leap would come later.

In the meantime, I had heard somewhere that it was unhealthy to face the pain, better to ignore it, to just bull your way through. I think that's how a lot of guys bound into a rebound marriage, all the while telling themselves and anyone who will listen, "I'm fine. I'm fine. It's great." And then, two years later, they file for divorce number two. Yeah, real fine.

I had also been told – though I wasn't all that sure about all these supposed experts with their brilliant advice – that I would live, that I would survive, and that life would be good again.

I even bought a book called *The Civilized Divorce* because I liked the optimistic title. It took me three pages in to realize it had been written by the "leaver," and the entire purpose was to help other "leavers" ease the guilt of trash-canning their former spouse, children, life. The advice: all the exes were supposed to try to get along, to do holidays together, to stress the exceptional value of giving the kids multiple Dads and multiple Moms. It taught the children character and flexibility, and helped prepare them for real life. Hard to argue with self-righteous stupidity, I'd thought, flipping the book into the trash.

So I had decided I'd do it my way: I'd sprint through the gauntlet, face it nose to nose, lead with my chin, let the pain just wash over me, endure that cathartic drubbing that would beat me about the emotional head and shoulders as I ran through the pummeling of each day, so I could get out the other side that much sooner.

About that "other side": I took it on faith that there just might be an *other* side someday.

In reality, I wondered if the wound would never heal. Maybe I needed to stop picking at it, but I couldn't. So, I would just lie there with my desk lamp and the radio both on low. I liked the nightlight, and I needed the background music. It made the strange empty-office sounds of the building seem a little less lonely, a little less like an eerie crypt at midnight.

Even so, I could hear things. Phones ringing in dark offices at the other end of the building. Machines starting up somewhere by themselves and then subsiding. Eerie. Spooky. The whole building of office suites, with half a dozen small businesses as tenants, was meant to be active by day, filled with people, all in a hurry. At night, yes, it was like a tomb, halls lit by powered-down shadow lighting and hushed sounds coming from where no one was.

You Don't Get It

So, yes, before I ran away to the islands, I spent a lot of time rattling around in my old life, kicking through the debris, trying to make sense of it. It wasn't fun. I began to lose sight of who I was and where I fit in anywhere.

Perhaps the hardest part was sleeping at the office, mostly because I rarely slept. Instead, I'd think and think, running and rerunning episodes of my life and my thoughts – imagined, real, hopeful, fearful, rarely ever helpful – over and over in my head, and trying to figure out what happened.

The most popular one on my Men v Women playlist was the you-don't-get-it series. From my experience, when a woman says, "You don't get it," I think she's right. We don't. At least I don't. Now, that's not news. Men and women do not understand each other. However, I do think that men just accept it. Women take it personally, like we're not trying hard enough.

I sometimes felt like I was being given a pop quiz without having seen the assignment. I know it's not true – no, I only suspect it's not true – but that's how it felt sometimes. I know I pretty much suspected that Connie had a big measuring tape in her hands all the time, and everything I did was gauged by some mythical, perfect Prince Charming she had been told about growing up. When it became increasingly obvious that I was just a clay-footed yahoo, more frog than prince, that tape measure began to shrink closed, slowly, bit by bit, as expectations lowered and lowered and lowered. At first it wasn't even noticeable. She'd smile that patient, you-don't-get-it smile. Then she'd look at me quizzically, with a puzzled frown. That frown eventually became a purse-lipped shake of the head. Finally, one day she said it; "You don't get it."

All along, that tape measure kept getting shorter, inching closed, until one day it just snapped shut. With a bang that said, "Okay, we're done here." I think I know that day. No, not the exact date, but the time she didn't so much decide to go hunting for a new man as being open to the possibility of letting one hunt for her, of kissing another frog, and of seeing if this new one had any prince potential in him.

No, she didn't do it overtly. I don't think she even did it knowingly. You see, any guy married to a woman with a half-way decent ass has uninvited guys waiting in the wings. They're hovering there – sometimes almost invisible, sometimes sitting at the same poker table week after week at the Thursday night game – just waiting to fill the void if he doesn't work out. When the main man gets booted, they begin to show up, like sharks attracted to fresh meat, very fresh meat, and she pretends not to pick the one she wants, but pretends to let him pick her. It's a rigged game.

All I saw at first, however, was that Connie was growing increasingly disappointed in me. That will drive a guy crazy, if he can no longer make her smile, giggle, get excited about something he's excited about. I know it drove me crazy, all the while wondering what had changed, why I was being held to an impossibly high standard in which the increasingly common outcome was disappointment. Mostly, though, I began to feel exhausted trying to figure out just what to do about it.

Isn't that why guys buy girls flowers, because they have no ideas what else to do? Oh, sure, it means, "I love you," but it also means, "I can't think of anything else that might please you."

So, I began trying to second guess Connie, to think of ways to bring that once-adoring smile back to her face. I think in the end I just ended up confusing her, too, and we wandered around like two dazed idiots who could talk about little more than things like, "So, how would you like your eggs this morning?" or "I need to change the cat's litter box today."

Whatever the reason, I ended up flailing around like a puppet in the hands of a six-year-old, dancing to a tune that I don't think she even knew she was playing.

Seriously, in all fairness, I don't think she probably had any idea she was even doing it, measuring me by some impossible standard. That's what, looking back on it from the miserable comfort of my office couch, annoyed and scared me the most. It's like we were both puppets.

Mars v. Venus

So, that's what I did. Lying on that lumpy couch each night, I selected what I wanted to think about, though usually I had no say in the selection. My other favorite was Mars v. Venus. I liked that one; it was different from the you-don't-get-it tape. It let me off the hook.

The main theme was that men and women just see life differently. Take sex, for example. All the women I've known really seem to get off on all that knight-in-shining-armor stuff (another version of Prince Charming). Even the heel-clicking female execs who've shattered the glass ceiling, they can act tough, but I seriously suspect it's just an act. Send her a dozen roses (if only because you can't think of anything else to do) and she's back in high school, pinning a strap up, hoping the dress works, praying the acne medication hides the blemish, all the while breathlessly waiting for awkward Martin to pick her up for the prom, and praying that he used Listerine before he tries to kiss her.

Or take cut two from that CD: shoes. Like most men, I think of shoes as something to put on my feet. There are work shoes, running shoes, office meeting shoes, sandals, and slippers. That's it. I don't have summer shoes and winter shoes or shoes for each outfit; just brown and black, depending on the color of the suit.

For women, well, I've seen Connie get excited and call a friend when the flyer arrived announcing a shoe sale. I'm not knocking it. I just don't understand it. Women talk about shoes, some collect shoes, and some even share shoes with their friends. Can you imagine a guy doing that? (Hey, Bob, can I borrow that really cute shirt and those to-die-for loafers tomorrow night?)

Now, in all fairness, let's look at the flip side of the coin. I've seen guys pause, fall into heavy-breathing silence, and stare lustfully when some sleek, hot sports car roars down the street. Hell, I used to refer to mine as "sex on wheels." The only thing that Connie noticed was that it was black ... and that I looked at that car the way I used to look at her.

I mean, if men and women can't even understand how the other feels about shoes, it's no wonder we can't figure out how we feel about important things. (I said that once to Connie, and she corrected me: Shoes are important things. I rest my case.)

Anyhow, my point – oh, yeah, my point – is that during twenty years of marriage I got to know how Connie would react, what she would do, and how she would respond in most situations. But I admit that I didn't ever know why. Ever. I just took it on faith and blamed it on estrogen.

And here's what drove me nuts: When I got it wrong, it stayed wrong. And that damn tape measure kept getting shorter and shorter. I could hear it. I could see it. And I felt helpless. Snap!

THE ISLAND
Cap'm Jolly

A nother end-of-day. The *touristas* were all safely back in their hotels or onboard their cruise ships and steaming out of harbor. *The Do Over* was securely moored, the salt rinsed off, and I could stop being the charming, semi-mysterious skipper of the boat.

Ah, the first sip was always the best. Another sunset at The Sunset, wondering about that green flash and if I would ever see it.

"Here ya go, Jolly." Joanie had long, wispy hair and an afraid-to-look-at-you way about her. That was like a double dose of pheromones shot-gunning an aura of vulnerability that made guys circle and their nostrils flare. It was more powerful than the smell of blood to sharks. I got a twitch just the way she put my drink on the bar. I don't know what she had, but, boy, did she ever have it. She was wholesome, very blonde, very sweet, very trim. And very vulnerable.

Guys are attracted to vulnerable, but we're not always sure why. Do we want to be noble and protect vulnerable women or turn them into sweaty, moaning sex slaves? Both, I think.

These were the women you didn't tip. Or at least I used to think that way, back when I used to listen to everyone else's stupid ten-things-you-need-to-know rules. Treat 'em good, they'll start expecting stuff, like that you should close the door when you take a piss or go outside to fart. Treat a Joanie like shit, she'll love you forever. Worked for French Tony and Blah Blah Brenda. On the flip side, it also worked well for Patti the Beast and Chicago Mike.

She treated him like garbage, and he seemed to love it, well, as much as Mike could be said to love anything.

Then Jason the Bartender appeared beside Joanie and pinched her butt. She giggled and wiggled and gave him a kiss, along with a pathetically open smile that said she trusted him. I gave him that same furrow-browed frown he would give me when I talked to the topless blondes during working hours. "Hey, Mon. Dat bad fo business," I said, mimicking Black Mike.

They grinned back, two dopey kids who were still at least a few months away from the pretend phase of their relationship.

"You two deserve each other." More grins. These two idiots almost made me want to believe, the way old folks try to believe when attending the wedding of a couple of fresh-faced kids, even though they know the odds are that they'll end up just like them in a decade or two – bored, miserable, or, the worst option, just together.

"Bah, humbug," I added, stone faced, then threw a ten on the bar. Jason poured me another free drink.

Joanie gushed. "Thanks, Jolly."

So much for not tipping.

***

Jolly. That's me. Grammatically, I know, that should be, "That's I." Funny about names. Down here, I'm Cap'm Jolly. Names are important. As a kid, I was Jimmy, except when in school or in trouble with my mother or the nuns; then I was James Robert. It was Jamie in high school. That was rakishly cool. Then Jim. Simple. Plain. Finally, for years it was Joth; that was after I'd renamed myself based on some Viking name I'd heard – or invented, I now forget which – years ago. That stuck through college and even after I'd started working, tearing up the turf, building what I thought then was my dream. I'd answer the phone hard, fast and tight: "Hello, Joth here. Can I help you?"

I was still Joth back in the States when my accountant had called to tell me the business was in the red … deep in the red. ("Sell it. Burn it. Give it away," I'd reply patiently. "Just don't let The Bitch have it." More on that later.) So, I was Joth to those who knew and loved me, Asshole (with a capital A) when Connie had found me down here on the islands and called to say that Natty was graduating in a month. I wasn't welcome, but I was invited. That was like when she once told me that she loved me, but wasn't in love with me. I chewed on that one for a long time … and came up empty. To her, though, that explained everything. To me? Not a clue. "I love you, but I'm not in love with you." So, I was invited to Natty's graduation, but I wasn't supposed to come. Maybe I did get it.

Oh, well. In the islands, I'm Cap'm Jolly. Usually. I got the name Jolly the night I first officially met both Jason and Black Mike, the night Black Mike put a knife to my throat. I was chatting with that year's latest arrival of topless blondies when this big black man came over and, snarling and breathing like an angry bull with nasal congestion, leaned in real close and made me a threatening offer I wasn't the least bit interested in accepting.

"Why don't you go pound sand up your ass?" I'd suggested in response.

Out of the corner of my eye, I saw the bartender jolt, then freeze. "Yo one smartass," the bull of a black man warned, looking around to make sure there were no *touristas* in The Sunset. I just shrugged and laughed. I was new on the island, and I really didn't give a shit. Even when that knife was suddenly at my throat and Black Mike was trying to lift me onto my toes, nice and easy now, I refused to budge. There we were, nose to nose, and he was giving me a deadly, threatening evil eye. Slowly, staring back at him steadily, knowing that with one swipe he could slit my throat, I blinked and raised an eyebrow, inviting him to do whatever he felt compelled to do. That kind of unnerved him, and he slowly lowered his knife.

"Do me a favor," I explained matter of factly, "I am not in the mood. So, kiss me, kill me, or walk away, but do not waste any more of my time." Then I smiled.

He paused. "You one jolly dude, Mon," he said, studying me carefully and putting away his knife. He was looking at me curiously, like I was a dog with two penises. Then after a long pause, he said, "Come on. I buy you a Green Label." He turned his back on me and headed back to his stool.

I stood where I was, feeling both pissed and joyful. I started chuckling. I could feel blood trickling down my neck, but I refused the urge to wipe it away.

"Green Label? Shit! Where I come from, friend, when a man threatens another man with a knife, he usually buys him a whiskey, not some piss-water, buck-a-bottle beer." (In truth, where I came from, the country club, they never expressed their threats. They just let them hang in the air, and there were never any knives in sight, though they could stab you just the same. Still, it sounded good.)

He paused and turned. A big grin slowly crossed his face. That was before I started carrying my own knife, but he wouldn't have known that. So, not taking his eyes off me, he gestured to where Jason was standing. I expected him to snap his fingers, but that was before I knew Black Mike. He wasn't the finger-snapping kind of guy.

"Deal, Mon. Jason, please gi me and my jolly new fren here shots of dat high price stuff you sell to da tourists."

"Jason," I interrupted, keeping my eyes on the man with the knife, "since my black new friend is buying, make mine a double, lots of ice. Oh, and pour one for yourself, too, Jason."

I could see Jason, his right shoulder lowered to where I later learned he kept his billy club, watching alertly from behind the bar. Black Mike frowned briefly, still trying to read me, still studying me for a weapon. Then he burst into a big, toothy grin. Still not taking his eyes off me, he glanced at Jason and nodded.

Jason poured the drinks, a poker-player expression on his face. He also gave me a napkin to wipe the blood from my neck.

Finally, Black Mike released the tension by letting go and letting out a laugh so broad and deep and loud that I couldn't help but join in. "Jolly good!" he roared, almost choking as he downed his shot. "Ma friends, dey calls me Black Mike." He flashed pearly white teeth against his midnight black face and stuck his hand out. "And you be Jimbo, folks tells me."

I nodded. "That I be," I said, still laughing and not even realizing how I sounded.

"Captain Jolly Jimbo," he roared again, spilling my drink as he slapped my back and took the whiskey bottle out of Jason's hand to pour us another round. I liked this guy.

That's all it took on the islands, I learned that night – a little knife play, a little whiskey, and I had two new best friends. Beat the shit out of playing golf with the lizard-shirt boys at the Northbrooke Country Club back in the States.

THE STATES
Routines

Safely back behind the walls of my office, lying on the couch under my blanket, I would go through my nightly ritual. Night after night I would try to figure out what had happened. Roll that damn tape, boy! Tonight, the topic started out as "marriage" before slipping into "home." I don't know who picks the topic. I sure didn't. Didn't matter.

I actually like marriage. I think most men do. Getting married – that wedding day stuff with all that hoopla and dressing up – that doesn't do much for most guys, but we do like marriage. Scott once told me that men don't like getting married, but most of us do like being married. I had to agree.

I think what I loved most about marriage is the routine, the steadiness. I loved building a history, a tradition, right down to where we all sat at the table to eat, always in the same seats. It's not complicated. But it has a natural, silent rhythm. Everybody belongs, everybody knows his or her place, and everything moves smoothly. Everything makes sense. Everybody knows what everything means.

For example, I knew exactly what Connie meant when she'd say, "Fine." With one inflection, it meant that the world was right. But with just a slightly different tone, it meant that everything was anything but fine. Just like she and the kids knew never, never, never to approach me with anything but happy news before dinner. Still, everything made sense. Everything worked. Everybody knew the rules.

I used to wake at exactly five-thirty each morning, and while Connie slept for another thirty minutes, I'd get up and find my robe on the hook on the back of the bathroom door. As I headed down the hallway, Rocket would fall in at my left side, and I'd tug on his shaggy ear as we rounded the corner and I let him out the front door. Every day. Everyone knew the rules. Not my rules. The rules. The way things worked.

I loved knowing I'd find the paper at the same spot on the porch and knowing that I could read the front section before going to the door and whistling for Rock to come back in. He knew he had that much time to do his business and check out any good yard smells that had showed up during the night. I loved finding my same coffee cup in the same place every morning, and knowing that, by the time I got through the sports section, I would hear Connie's footsteps entering the kitchen.

I also loved the sounds of the house, which is partly why I hated sleeping at the office. At night, I could tell it was 1:30 because I would stir to hear the water softener run through its cycle; 3:15, when the morning paper would hit the front porch (except on Sundays, when the heavier edition slammed on the porch 20 minutes later); 5:15, when the coffee started to brew automatically.

Or I could tell by the sound, down the hall and two bedrooms away, whether one of the kids had the window open when a night shower hit. Or how I could tell someone was at the front door before the bell rang because of that oh-so-slight click the person's shoe would make on the loose brick on the top step.

I loved the order and routine.

Like I said, I liked marriage. A lot of women suspect that men don't like the way things are today, with women having more of a voice than their grandmothers did. And maybe there are some men who need and like to be in control. Me? I loved the idea of a partnership, and I think most other men do, too. Two people yoked together, side by side, totally opposite, totally the same, and sex thrown in, to boot. We like the feel of shoulder-to-shoulder, smooth-as-silk routine.

Actually, that's not totally true, at least the way Connie explains it now. She says I am a total control freak and everything either has to go my way or get run by me for my approval. I guess so. I know I micromanaged things at the office. I'd tell myself that my employees aren't paid to like me, but they do respect me. Do they? Hell, I'm the boss. I run things. It's not about equality. It's about making things work. It's about business. Routines.

THE ISLAND
The Theory of Breasts

"You can tell," Jason had told me a few months later, "how happy a couple is by how the woman takes off her top." No, this is not something I obsess over, well, at least not any more than any other guy; it's just something that comes up at the Sunset Bar a lot, especially when customers see the sign: Topless Women Drink Free.

Calabash, who had been sitting, hunched over, beside me at the bar, just nodded.

I had looked from one to the other. "What do you mean by *how*? You mean in here?"

"Yeah, or at the nudie beach over on Turtle cove. In public." Jason paused to collect his thoughts. "Okay, if she's a bit shy and uncertain, but also trusting about letting her ta tas loose …"

"She believes in her man and trusts him," finished Calabash. He dragged deeply on his cigarette, and I thought for a second he would singe his stained, whiskbroom of a once-white mustache.

"Exactly. They have a relationship. They're both in it together."

"Both?" I asked.

"Yeah, both. See, they're invested in each other; they own and share each other. I say that in a positive way. They're partners."

"Okay, like the guy who tells his friends, '*We're* pregnant?'" I suggested, trying to catch on.

"Exactly." Jason and Calabash looked at each other like there was hope for me yet.

"For this couple, when she takes off her top, it's a playful, almost innocent dare. They're still in love, at least for now."

"Okay," I offered and thought about how, back when Connie and I were newlyweds, back in the days of innocent trust, I used to get her to pose for nudie shots. I wonder whatever happened to them? Hmmm.

"Then there's the one who does it obediently."

"Obediently?" I asked, pulling my mind, reluctantly, back to the island. I was enjoying thinking about Connie and those boudoir shots.

Jason looked for the right words. "Yeah, pretty much. Look at her eyes. She has an uncomfortable look, a mask of bravery to cover up fear or lack of trust. She's trying to keep this guy happy, even though he's likely to never, ever really be happy about her. She loves him, or at least maybe thinks she needs him. Him? Not so much her. He holds all the cards, and he knows it. Deep down, she does, too. Maybe it's a control thing. So, she goes along, mostly because she thinks it will please him, or keep him from acting disappointed."

I thought of a couple I'd once seen in a bar filled with football fans. He was maybe fifty-five, and people said he owned a string of hair salons. He was charming, loud, and, at the same time, threatening looking. He was one of those guys who, no matter where they are, they command the center spotlight. He was a finger snapper. She was maybe twenty-five, cute as a bug, and seemed to think he was awesome. Or maybe she just enjoyed how he spent his money on her or liked being close to the spotlight. Anyhow, every few minutes, in this bar filled with fans, he'd be holding court about football or politics, and he'd abruptly stop, turn to her and – snapping his fingers, of course – say, "Hey, Maureen, show us your tits." And like a trained monkey, grinning, she'd hike up her blouse, flash her breasts, and wiggle them. Everybody would applaud. At one point, I remember, he said, "Do you know what I heard Maureen's name was in high school?" We all waited.

"Skippy … because she was easy to spread." Everyone laughed, including Maureen. That whole episode bothered me, probably a whole lot more than it did Maureen.

"Down here, vacationing in paradise," Jason added with a grandiose gesture, "he's sweet, charming, romantic. So, she starts hoping – eagerly, desperately – that things will be better now. Him? He's wondering why he'd bothered to waste the money on this trip, but at least he gets to watch the girls on the beach through his sunglasses. He's the one, other than you, Jolly, who likes to strike up a conversation with Black Mike's topless blondies."

I nodded, smiling at the playful dig. I was thinking about those desperate-eyed women. I'd seen them too many times, not just at the bar. These are the couples who head out to the islands for a week to start over again, to put the past behind them. But it's not going to work. The past comes with them. You can tell just by looking at them. Their smiles are just a little too broad, like they are painted on. They're trying; well, at least one of them is. They'll get into their next fight within a few days after returning to the States, perhaps on the flight home.

"It's as if," said Jason, pausing, a little uncomfortable with the role of being talker rather than listener, "she's trying desperately to please her guy. They're in trouble. He's already half way out the door. She definitely loves him, or needs him, more than he does her. But a lot of guys get off on that, too. Keeping their cuties off balance, uncertain, under their thumb. It's a control thing."

I frowned. I'd seen it. I'd done it. It's something that works early on in many marriages, before she figures out he's a putz. But I guess some don't ever figure it out. Feeling like shit about themselves, they cling to the very guy who makes them feel that way.

"And she's just trying to postpone what she already knows in her heart," added Calabash.

"But she does not want to admit or acknowledge any of this, especially to herself."

"The funny thing is, the guy usually overplays his hand. And then, one day, snap, she realizes she has nothing to lose, that he's not worth it."

Hmmmm, I thought, but not out loud. In my mind, I heard the sound of the tape measure closing with a snap. Had I been that way? Yeah, maybe a little. Maybe a lot.

Calabash nodded. "Those are the women, at least the ones in their 30s and 40s, who end up talking to Mike."

"Mike? You mean Chicago Mike?" I asked, confused, referring to the burned-out industrialist who bunked in with Patti the Beast.

"Black Mike," corrected Jason, as if that explained everything.

"Black Mike?" I thought about the topless blondes who worked for Black Mike. It almost made sense.

Jason paused to light my cigarette, as any good bartender would.

"Then," he'd continued, his face turning dark, "there's the woman who can't wait to strip to the waist, as if she has something to prove to herself. If she's with a bunch of female friends, dollars for donuts she's just coming off a bad breakup and pretending she's having the time of her life. She's not."

I nodded. I'd seen this one, too. "And if she's with her husband or boyfriend?"

Jason and Calabash waited, letting me figure it out for myself

Slowly, I spoke: "She has an attitude, or a grudge. She's looking to make her husband look foolish," I'd suggested, starting to understand.

"Or maybe she caught him cheating on her, or at least slopping his way one night through one of those hardcore porn sites. That stuff really upsets women, more than we realize."

"So, her flashing the family tits is part of the forgiveness revenge."

"Sometimes it's just revenge. No forgiveness to it. And the guy looks on nervously while she struts her stuff and tries to smile. This gal is one opportunity away from bedding the pool boy. If she stays, it's for the money or just to keep exacting revenge, twisting the knife. Or maybe it's because *she* enjoys being in control, pulling his chain, publicly whipping him every chance she gets. Some women do love control. And some guys get off on it, too."

As any man would, I compared these ladies to the women I'd known in my life, focusing first on Connie, the ex-wife back home. She had always been modest in public. Even once, when we'd found an isolated beach in Bermuda and I had stripped naked, she had refused to go along. Still, she did run off with a bass guitar player after twenty years of marriage. I guess all theories do have their exceptions. Where were those bedroom photos?

"Okay, what about Black Mike's girls?" I'd asked.

"Ah, the topless blondes? Surprisingly, most of them tend to be fairly modest off the job," Calabash had said, then added, "You wouldn't recognize them in church."

"Church?" I'd asked, but neither Jason nor Calabash had anything further to add.

THE STATES
Sundays

I'm not sure who invented church, but the one who did must have hated people, at least teenage boys.

I had nothing against God. I just wasn't sure I liked the way He did business. So, for about the last 30 years or so, we had not been on speaking terms, at least on polite speaking terms. Now and then I'd close a low-odds business deal and offer up a perfunctory, "Thank you, God." Or, more likely, a screw would strip and I'd skin a knuckle, I'd lose a file I had just had in my hand a minute earlier, I'd have to put down an old-friend dog, or a wife would decide to leave and say that I needed to get on with my life. That would be when I'd offer up a very abrupt prayer: "God dammit!" But for the most part, God left me alone, and I tried to steer clear of Him. That meant I didn't visit Him at His house.

A lot of that goes back to my Roman Catholic upbringing and how the good sisters had worked hard to beat the love of God into my thick skull. Maybe I missed something, but I suspected this faith stuff should have had more about it than the basic rules of calisthenics: sit down, stand up, shut up, kneel, stand, sit, rise. I felt like a dog being trained: "Sit! Stay! Roll over!" Or maybe the whole thing should have been done to the tune of "The Chicken Dance," along with the clap-clap-clap-clap. Some of the old-school nuns even had clickers that signaled when we were supposed to sit or stand. Of course, by the time I was in eighth grade, all I could do in church was wonder whether Kathy Mancini, kneeling in the row ahead of me, was wearing panties. If so, what color. It helped the time pass.

The girls were taught to be demure and virginal, not wear make-up, to be sure the hems of their skirts touched the floor when they were ordered to kneel, and to keep away from us tongue-dragging boys who, everyone knew, wanted one thing and one thing only. French kissing was out of the question, as was any touching above the knee or below the neck. The most interesting real estate was fenced off. Those were the days when just a micro-second glimpse of a black, lace bra strap could send a boy's dick into a full erection.

Oh, and by the way, ladies, the typical teenage boy gave his penis a name and referred to it obliquely in locker room conversations. "Yep, old Buford the One-eyed Snake had a good time with Mary Beth last night." One guy called his Joy, and thought it was borderline hysterically funny when he'd say, "I wanted to share my great Joy with her," or "I filled her with Joy." (Yes, ladies, I agree: There really is nothing quite as disgusting as a teenage boy ... well, except for maybe a full-grown man. We really don't change much as we get older.)

The primary role of the nuns, as I look back on it, was to protect those poor, supposedly defenseless girls from us deviant boys. The girls who took all the hocus pocus rules seriously eventually grew up to be orderly, obedient, joyless, well-organized, sexless wives, with washed-out hair they cut themselves. They were afraid of their own hidden passion. Some, however, grew up to have raging volcanos of sexual desire smoldering below the surface. They played the game and learned that they could do the exact opposite of what the good sisters taught. And speaking of Kathy Mancini, later, in high school, she once bent over, hiked up her skirt, and showed me the Winnie the Pooh tattoo on the right cheek of her panty-free backside. That split-second scene kept me awake at night for months. Actually, I still visit it now and then, Buford and me.

The boys had it pretty good by comparison. There was no double standard. We were taught – and told over and over and over – that we were bad. Period. Talk about liberating. The nuns expected the worst from us, so we tried not to disappoint them. It was like a game of cops 'n robbers. Obviously, smoking was forbidden, so we all smoked. And once a week, the nuns would rummage through our lockers for cigarettes and other contraband, like "dirty" magazines or condoms that all of us had but none of us really knew what to do with.

The only thing we were sure of was that if we died with a mortal sin on our souls (and that had something to do with sex, regardless of whether it was with a girl or the underwear section of the JC Penney catalog), we were heading straight to hell. So, we did our biggest and best stuff, like trying to cop a feel from Susan Helm at a party or breaking into Old Man Evans' garage to steal beer – we did that stuff on Friday nights. Always Friday nights. That way, as long as we didn't die in our sleep, we could go to confession on Saturday afternoon, admit everything to the invisible priest behind the screen, get our slate wiped clean so we could march up and do Communion on Sunday morning, and never did anything worse than drink and smoke and look at the lingerie pages of the Sears catalog the rest of the week … until Friday night came along again.

We had also been taught/trained that we were supposed to arrive at church for Sunday mass at least five minutes before the service began, to keep our feet off the kneelers, and to stay for the entire service, until the long, very bitter end, when the priest said, "Go in peace to love and serve the Lord," and we'd all respond, "Thanks be to God" (but most of us mumbled under our breaths, "Thank God"). The challenge was to try to sneak out after communion, shaving eight minutes off our Sunday Obligation time. It was the job of the burly, God-fearing men of the Knights of Columbus to prevent our escape. They served as ushers, and positioned themselves at the back of church by the main doors during the service. With folded arms, they looked more like bouncers than God-fearing men of God. One of the guys, usually Steve Fitzgibbon, because he was fast and ended up as quarterback of the varsity football team, would go up first to the altar to take communion. Then he would do an about-face and, hands folded like a steeple, eyes piously down, make a brisk bee-line for the main exit. As the men of the Knights of Columbus, those guardians of good, stepped forward to intercept him, he'd begin to bob and weave toward the side doors, finally breaking into a full sprint. It was a quarterback option play. Sometimes he'd make it out a side door, sometimes the main entrance, and sometimes he'd give it a good shot and then let himself be caught, buying precious time for us. That was when the rest of us made our moves and broke for the other doors like roaches splitting from a pre-heating oven. On a good Sunday, only one or two of us got caught. Then we'd meet at the Jewish deli down the block, snarf down bagels, Ho Hos, and Yoo Hoo, and brag about our exploits, offering up a moment of silence for the ones who hadn't made it. No wonder a lot of us loved Steve McQueen in *The Great Escape*. We were all trying to escape our good and righteous upbringing.

Then, by the time we were juniors in high school, it just wasn't as much fun, so most of us just shrugged and walked away, and stopped going to church. Sad, really.

MANGROVE COVE
Island Time

We'd loaded up *The Do Over*, my 38-foot sailing catamaran, putting in enough emergency gear and sealed food and bottled water for one person for a week. Every report – from the monster swirls on the satellite radar; to breathless, leggy Stateside television reporters predicting the storm of the century (always and again); to nesting birds abandoning their eggs and skittering fast and low across the water and heading west; to a swelling, restless tide, even in a place that barely had a tide; to an angry sky that everybody kept watching – everything said that Hurricane Olive was going to hit us dead on, and it was going to be one vicious piece of snotty weather.

I knew – actually, I didn't know shit, but it was more like a deep sense beyond knowing – that the boats that stayed in the lagoon would not survive. I was heading out to Mangrove Cove. If the storm was bad enough and boats started breaking free of their moorings or docks, they'd be banging all over each other and end up either on the bottom of the lagoon or piled up in a jumble on the docks, maybe all the way out to the road and half way up the mountain.

I'd take my chances outside. I guess this was because I didn't want to lose *The Do Over*. She was like my last stand, all I had left. And I'd be damned if I was going to just sit in the lagoon and see if we survived. Maybe we'd go down, but we'd sure as hell go down fighting, giving it all we had, *Do Over* and me.

It was a risk. I'd be alone. I'd told my first mate, Kid, and Bonita, my bunkie, to head up the mountain for high ground. Kid scowled and then quietly said okay before skulking off. Not even a good-bye. Bonita, on the other hand, had put up a fuss. She'd shouted and stomped her feet on the dock and kept saying, "No, Jolly, no!"

This had caught me by surprise. Sweet, easy-going, all-smiles, sometimes pungent Bonita had never shouted or complained about anything before. I ignored her as I checked lines and debated leaving my mast at the marina and just motoring around to the mangrove stands growing out onto the salt water on the wild side of the island. "Any thoughts, Jocko?" I asked my stuffed friend lashed to the base of the mast. He was neutral. That's what I liked about Jocko. He was a go-along kind of guy.

The wind was picking up.

Screw it. I needed to get moving. I'd drop the mast flat, but keep it on board. I fired up the engine and dashed for the bow to cast off.

Gloria, the marina's head housekeeper, appeared and did the lines for me. She was moving fast. An islander, she had been through hurricanes before, and she knew that what wasn't tied down and secure would be gone.

Still, she paused and grinned. "Where you go'n, Cap'm Jolly?" she called as she gave me that special smile before unwrapping the line from the cleat and expertly throwing it into my waiting hands at the edge of the cockpit.

"To hell, Gloria!" I called for no reason and laughed. I felt like John Wayne straddling his prancing horse and waving his hat to the townsfolk. "To hell!"

She laughed back, wagged a cracked black finger at me and shoved *The Do Over* away from the dock. "No way, Cap'm Jolly. You and me, we go'in to heaven. But first we go'in ta church dis Sunday."

"It's a date, Gloria," I called. Maybe I'll see Black Mike's girls there, I thought. Or maybe I'd be dead and have an excuse for not showing up. Jocko and I were neutral on which one was better.

"What day is today?" I called.

"It be Monday, Cap'm."

I hit the throttle hard and motored out toward the drawbridge.

More and more, I had less and less sense of time. All the memories swirled together. Things that happened twenty-five years ago, like Sam, lovely, first-love Sam, were like yesterday. And when it came to yesterday, well, that sometimes seemed like twenty-five years ago. No, it wasn't the whiskey. That wasn't much of an answer, but that was all I knew for sure. Time really meant nothing, and life didn't go in a convenient, neat, straight line, with a plot that wrapped up loose ends by the last page. I couldn't tell my endings from my beginnings anymore. All I knew for sure were my todays, and even then I wasn't all that sure.

Every week, Gloria invited me to Sunday church. Maybe this Sunday for sure. If I got back. And if there was an island to get back to. And if I felt like it.

Then I turned my thoughts to more important things. Would three bottles of whiskey, some trail mix, a case of Ho Hos, and a carton of cigarettes be enough to weather Hurricane Olive?

THE ISLAND
Family Dinner at the Sunset Bar

The Sunset on the west side of the island was sort of my *Cheers* bar. Actually, it was kind of a toss-up between the Sunset and Iggie's down by the loading docks across the island. I think what fascinated me about The Sunset were the *touristas* that changed each week. Most reminded me of why I was glad to be down here and not back in the States. Plus, there was that annoying collection of expatriates that may have been friends, depending on the day and who was buying.

I stood at the bar and touched my ribcage. That was my barometer. Life was lean in the islands. My ribs stood out. No more roly-poly, fat fingers pushing in to find my skeleton. Even though I drank too much by State-side standards, I felt good, healthy, alert. And I had to admit, I looked pretty good – tanned, toned, and down 40 pounds since I'd first put toes to sand on this rock.

Island life did that to you, made you look good on the outside. Throw on a pair of dark sunglasses, and I was hell on wheels ... even if I did say so myself.

There's something comforting about the islands. I think it's because I didn't feel so alone, or maybe just less lonely. Not much posturing down here, at least from the locals or ex-pats. The *touristas*? Hell, they were all about posturing, pretending they could afford that Mercedes they were leasing back home, pretending they had somehow earned and owned that big-boobed babe on their arms, pretending they were swell fellows, both loved and feared, pretending they were having fun in paradise. Most were wrong on all counts.

I glanced around for a mirror. For some reason, bars on the island don't have them. No idea why. Then again, I did. Someone would either steal them or smash them. But mostly, I think it had to do with the islands being fantasy. Mirrors reflected too much reality. People here were on vacation from reality.

I sauntered to the quasi-reserved ex-pat table with my drink and sat down. I leaned back in my chair, bare feet planted on the sandy, tile floor, and listened to my good friends, a friend on the island being just about anyone you'd shared a drink with. So, these were very good friends.

I thought of this Monday evening gathering as family dinner night. A far cry from Connie and the kids passing the Mexican carry-out after reciting thanks back in the States. Instead, it was rum, whiskey or beer with this bunch of mixed sots, washing down a burger or nachos or a fresh catch of the day, which Kid and I sometimes provided.

Other nights we tended to gather at Iggie's, a tin-roof dock bar on the windward, commercial side of the bay. With rusting machinery and derelict boat hulls rotting in the mud, Iggie's wasn't one of those squeaky clean tourist bars, just a place where you could relax, get a meal and not pay gouge-the-guest prices. The first time I saw that hole, I thought it was romantic. That was a while ago. Now it just felt like home.

But it was Monday, ex-pat family night at the Sunset. Samuel, the cook, was splitting lobster and nestling them on the big grill out front.

Jason only charged us a few bucks for these dinners, while the *touristas* paid much, much more. We sometimes thought Jason owned the Sunset. Actually, I don't think Jason even knew for sure who owned it. He ran an orderly house, kept things level and safe, and about once every month or two wet his pants when four black guys from somewhere down off one of the southern islands came in, sat down, and, peering over their sunglasses, even at night, beckoned Jason over. We all made a point of looking away, except Black Mike, who nodded and seemed to know them. When these guys showed up, Joanie understood it was best that she steer clear. We all thought there was a chance she might end up as a deal maker or deal breaker with these guys. Best if they didn't know she existed.

Bonita

B onita came into the Sunset, care-free, hips swinging like a
tight-bodied lesbian athlete. I liked Bonita. Every time I
saw her, I couldn't help but smile. She was easy on me.

"Hello, Cap'm Jolly," she announced with a broad smile and
a casual salute. This was her always greeting for me, which I think
she still thought was funny, even though we'd been together for
nearly a year: "Permission to come aboard, Sir?" she asked loudly.
Then she swung an arm around my shoulder and a leg over my lap,
straddling me, and stuck her tongue halfway down my throat. Ah,
now, there's a woman. Permission granted.

"Welcome aboard, Bonita," I said when she finally came up
for air and I caught my breath.

This may have been her routine whenever she greeted me, but
the folks at the table never tired of it, responding with hoots,
laughter and applause. I had to admit I kind of liked it, too.

As she sat beside me and took a sip from my drink, Kid got
up and moved to the other side of the table. It wasn't that Kid
didn't like Bonita. They were buds, like bro and sis. It was just
that he didn't always like being too close to her before she'd been
dragged by me into the lagoon to ease the pungent aroma of day-
old fish that tended to emanate from her body. What I liked best
about her is that she didn't give a shit about anything … and that
also just happened to include bathing.

I once asked her about her story, how she'd gotten to the
island. She had shrugged and thought for a long time before
answering. "Well, I was born in Muncie, moved to California for

a time, then came down here." With that, she shrugged again, as if to say, that's it.

Awesome. Decades of life summarized in one vague sentence. It made me think about some of the fifteen-page, bullshit resumés I'd read from tight-collared, tight-assed executives looking for jobs back in the States. But that was just about the best part about the islands. People got to create their own histories, write their own resumés. Actually, that wasn't much different from most of those tight-ass executives, now that I think about it.

Lifting my glass, I caught a whiff of her. That made me smile. The scent of a woman. The scent of Bonita. The scent of a good day on the island. It all blended in.

The fish aroma didn't bother me anymore. Bonita either, though I still sometimes wondered what pool of alien organisms I was plunging into with her. It was that first moist cloud that escaped when I'd peel down her shorts that always took my breath away.

Eventually, well ... I guess you can get used to anything ... eventually. Actually, there's something about the aroma of sun-dried bait. If you like Asian fish sauce ... well, it's an acquired taste. That was Bonita.

Still, after our first night, I'd sometimes include a skinny dipping plunge in the lagoon as part of foreplay. I sometimes wondered if she might attract sharks, but figured it was worth the risk. I called it my margarita theory: Salt makes everything taste better. So does booze.

Even though the sun was long gone now, we were all staring out over the sea. Then French Tony shrugged as if on cue, and we all turned again back to our drinks. No green flash. Not tonight. Not ever. Never. We always pretended to expect to see it, but we knew we never would, that it really didn't exist. Island myths.

Still, weirdest thing. Each evening together, right before sunset, we'd shut up, swing westward with our drinks in our hands, watch the horizon and wait in hopes of seeing the legendary green flash as the sun disappeared into the ocean. I'd never seen it. I knew of no sober man or woman who had. Some *touristas* even produced videos to prove they'd seen it. Sorry. I'd seen those videos. Nothing. Sorry, no flash. Still, we watched. Most people at the westward bars or walking along the beaches paused and watched, too. It separated something. Yeah, day from night, myth from more myth.

Those who claimed they had seen it usually had half a bottle of rum in their bellies or their heads stuck squarely up their asses. They thought it was important, that it meant something, that seeing it was like being tapped for entry into some elite, exclusive club. It didn't and it wasn't. And most days, when we were on the west side of the island and it wasn't overcast, we all looked for it, too. Still, it seemed important, giving some kind of bragging rights, right up there with saying you'd bumped shoulders with Jimmy Buffett standing at a urinal or being able to say you were a local, that you lived here.

People loved that shit. "Man, this place is paradise," the *touristas* would proclaim.

"Yeah, you bet, and we live here."

That always impressed the *touristas*, who visited paradise to swim, tan, fish and drink for a week to ten days, or even just to race through a quick, four hour layover on a cruise ship. Some of them even had license plates on their cars back home that said dopy things like Island Life1, or they used IslandGirl as their Email or Facebook names. Sad, really, like watching Jimmy Buffet concert goers in Topeka tossing around colorful beach balls and pretending that they were part of the island-life dream that Buffet sold by the margarita-ful. Somehow, they seemed to think it made them special. Sad, really.

Still, hearing that you lived on the island always impressed the *touristas*, and they wanted to hear more.

So, we made it up as we went, often alluding to mysterious legal or financial or personal troubles back home. The basic theme was always pretty much the same: Life had been stressful, demanding, overwhelming back in the States. It was free and easy down here in the islands. Ah, the good life.

I reached across the table and uncapped a bottle of hot sauce. Then, head back, I shook a few drops into my mouth. Bonita watched and laughed.

"You're such a guy," she said, taking a sip of my drink and then handing it back to me.

I grinned. "And, you, dear Bonita, are such a girl!"

"Amen!" The rest of the table agreed, pretty much concluding grace before dinner.

I raised my drink in a silent salute to nothing in particular. The others joined in. I always got a little morose around sundown. Bonita always helped chase that away. That was perhaps the best reason I liked Bonita. She was my antidote.

"How was your day, my beautiful Bonita?" I asked, once again smelling fish and wondering if we'd play rock the boat tonight.

Chicago Mike picked up a cigarette and cupped his hand across his face as he lit it, concealing his smirk. He knew Bonita. The match lit up his bare, gray-haired chest, and I looked at the vertical scar that ran all the way down. A member of the Zipper Club, he'd once told me, referring to his open-heart surgery. Though he'd never said, I got the impression that his heart attack and his decision to leave his wife of twenty-seven years were somehow connected. If not now, when? He said that a lot.

Or maybe one day, a screw had just fallen out of his head. It doesn't always have to be complicated. Sometimes it's as simple as that. You get tired of caring and pretending ... and most of us just keep pretending long after we quit caring.

I looked over at Patti the Beast. Mike had to be nuts to be with her. Last month he'd had to barricade himself in their shack after she'd tried to run him down with the car and threatened to cut off his balls.

Still, Chicago Mike was another person who I guess just didn't care. Most guys back in the States with a bum ticker would go on a seaweed diet, monitor their blood pressure three times a day, never, never, never smoke, faithfully go to the gym three times a week, checking the bio feedback gizmo on their wrists the whole time, and allow themselves one shot of whiskey on a Saturday night. Not Mike. He smoked too much, drank too much, exercised only when he had to make a fast escape from Patti when she lost it.

"I never saw a runner with a smile on his face," he once snarled and then held court: "Most of these fitness freaks are an anal bunch of idiots. They talk about quality of life, but they measure that quality in terms of a decent bottle of wine or an aged cheese from some town in France nobody had ever heard of. Whoop-dee-doo! Longevity is wasted on them. Once you get used to the fact that life hurts like hell, and you're wasting your time trying to escape that pain, it gets a lot easier. Live fast; die young; and have a corpse that looks beat to shit." Not often, but every once in a while, Mike got it right.

***

"It was fine," Bonita said casually, in a soft, gentle voice.

"What was fine?" I asked.

"My day, silly. Didn't you just ask?"

"Oh, yeah." I admit I had trouble keeping up sometimes, probably because I really didn't care. That's where women get it right. Men don't listen. Let's just leave it at that. "What made it fine?" I asked.

She stared at me for a long time, as if the question was odd. "I don't know. It was just … fine."

Every day was fine for Bonita. Though she was smart as a tack, she didn't waste her time on deep thinking. She just enjoyed – or at least seemed to enjoy – every day.

Searching, she finally decided to tell me: "Good customers. No complainers. No whiners. Good tippers."

I thought about it. Yep, I realized, that was pretty much all it took for Bonita to have a good day. Even without any of that, she always had a good day. What a gal!

"And Sajid took the day off, which is always nice," she added by way of a bonus. "I don't mind him undressing me with his eyes, but he drools on himself while he's doing it."

Everybody at the table laughed. They knew Sajid, and they knew that he was disgusting, but harmless. Besides, Bonita could take care of herself. Once, a *tourista* with a few drinks in him made a grab for her breasts. Before I could stand up and rush to her protection, she clasped his hand, did a graceful underarm swing through, put him face first on the tile floor, and jammed a foot into his armpit. The thought crossed my mind that she may have once, in a long-ago life, been a street cop. When she let him go and helped him up, she put her face up close to his and, as sweet as can be, seriously, with no rancor or anger, said, "Please don't do that. It's not nice."

Sajid, the day manager at the Giggling Gecko, is a lecherous Pakistani who hires his beach-bunny waitresses because of the length of their hair, the size of their tits, and how their hips swing as they cross the beach. The Giggling Gecko is a beach bar that serves overpriced drinks and crappy food to guests who burn themselves to a bright and painful crisp on the beach in rented lounge chairs, sipping rum punches and telling each other, "Man, this is the life." The Gecko's marketing twist is simple: There is a three-foot tall flagpole beside each chair. When guests want another round of drinks, they hoist the blue flag, and Bonita or one of the other girls comes prancing over. When the guests are ready for their bill, they hoist a red flag. Stupid? Maybe. But the *touristas* ate it up. Doesn't take much.

Bonita was cheerful and good with the customers and loved working outside all day. Sajid's stares and occasional comments never fazed her. Just as important, between the open air and the steady island breeze, nobody noticed her body odor. (Thank God we were on one of the Windward Islands, which always had a light, steady breeze blowing. She might have struggled to keep a job on one of the Leeward isles.)

Other days, she was second mate on *Outrageous*, a 28-foot deep sea charter boat. She was pretty good at it, Captain Ronnie had told me, and she handled the bait fish and the catch like a man. "Sorry if she comes home at night smelling like fish," he'd said with an inside-joke smile. I just raised my eyebrows.

I was proud of her, something I'd never been able to say about any other woman.

"So, you didn't have to deal with that old letch Sajid staring at your breasts?" I confirmed.

Everybody, including the women, looked at Bonita's breasts, the topic of the moment. And there they were, right where they were supposed to be, nipples up, nestled behind her Life is Good T-shirt.

Personal hygiene aside, Bonita must have once been something. She was still something, but she looked a bit worn around the edges. Nonetheless, compared to some of the long-time expatriates like John/Candy (either one, take your pick) she looked fresh, like a firm-fleshed virgin. (Now, there's a line I need to remember for cocktail parties and high school graduations.) Parading up and down the beach in a bikini all day, tray in hand, taking drink orders from *touristas*, or bending over in her shorts baiting a hook on board *Outrageous*, she had a firm, sunbaked body and straw-blonde hair that drew men like flies. Best of all, with the exception of one night, she almost always seemed like she was having fun.

On occasion, I would study her eyes, an old habit. It was mostly her eyes that gave away her age, and a few years more, but nothing else. Her eyes were always bright, almost laughing. Nothing seemed to bother her. Only once had I seen her sad, and that was the night she'd cried after we'd made love. I guess I could do that to women.

"She's a nation," Squint had once said, "a walled city state, with armed guards, ever vigilant, manning the parapets. She's hard as nails inside, Jolly. Trust me."

I never trusted Squint. I couldn't stand him. So, I hadn't bothered to answer him. Still, I had thought about what he had said, the prick.

My conclusion: No, Bonita isn't hard. She had survived all these years, and whatever history had been dumped on her, by being ... by being what? Soft and flexible? Maybe. All I knew was that she was easy as silk to get along with. And joyful. I think she was the only person I'd ever met who had absolutely no attitude, no agenda, no smoldering resentment bubbling close beneath the surface.

I suspected that once, perhaps in a past life back in the States, she had been afraid, perhaps beaten down, emotionally, if not physically. She had come out of it, according to my totally clueless theory, totally free. Blessed be those who expect nothing for they shall not be disappointed.

And that's something else about people I'd picked up over the years: We absolutely had to find a category for people. Even when we knew nothing at all, we had to come up with a fucking theory. Not just a theory, but a fucking theory. The bottom line: Bonita was and is Bonita. Period.

What had intrigued me about her at first was that at 45 or so – her age, as near as I could guess; I never asked and she never offered – and after being adrift on the islands for perhaps a decade or longer, she had a natural, lean tightness to her body that kept her borderline beautiful. That was what had intrigued me at first.

I also tried once to categorize her at first, to pigeon-hole her, calling her Maggie May, but everybody liked Bonita better. And she didn't seem to give a shit what I called her. She didn't give a shit about much of anything, as far as I could tell. She had no story, no history, no background. She just was. That was what I loved about her, even if I didn't love her.

She was the total opposite of Blah Blah Brenda, who had a story about everything and just had to tell it – to everyone and anyone – who would listen.

I suspect that, in her heart, Bonita was still someone's princess. Maybe her father had called her that long ago (maybe he was still alive; I hoped he was), and she'd believed him, still waiting today for her prince to come. Or maybe she finally figured out that Daddy had just been trying to be nice. I suspected that if a guy was lousy to her, she'd just leave. No big drama. No big scene. No big woof. The prince would show up, eventually. Or not.

I think that's why she stayed with me, like a cat that adopted the people in its home. By island standards, I was a prince. I never hit her, physically or emotionally abused her, or asked for kinky, hold-her-down-till-she-choked sex. I think she knew she had a hygiene problem, but I also think she didn't see it as a problem. Instead, I sensed that it was her way of keeping other guys at bay.

She was easy and didn't try to change me. She kept her promise. And she didn't have any of those non-verbal cues designed to let me know she was disappointed or annoyed or disapproved. She didn't carry an emotional tape measure. If I poured myself a stiff whiskey at seven in the morning or said I was heading over to *Iggie's* or even Yvonne's Place, or said I just preferred to be alone today, she never batted an eye. No commentary. No negative body language.

One day I figured out that she liked being with me for the same reason I liked being with her: I didn't give a shit. What a pair!

As with all of us ex-pats, her past was her business. It didn't take me long on the island to learn that you just didn't ask "Where are you from?" except with the *touristas*, or "What brought you here?" If people want to talk, they talk. If not, they lie or just leave out a few decades of their stories.

THE STATES
Oneness

Life with Bonita was a lot different than life with Connie and the kids back in the States. Bonita didn't have a tape measure. Connie sure did, and it just kept getting shorter.

Take Father's Day. Connie had always thought it was important to make a big stink over me on Father's Day. I never told her, never, that I hated Father's Day, just like I hated Valentine's Day. I always thought they were set-ups, days when people got you junk you didn't want, and you were expected to act like you cared. Really love me? Then give me something on a day that has no holiday. Just don't spend too much money. Better yet, never mind, I'll just buy it myself. If you really love me, give me the world's best, fifteen-minute back massage. Don't even care if it turns into foreplay. That's love. Or make sure there's the backup roll of toilet paper in the bathroom. That's really love.

Father's Day had always reminded me of the story of an older-than-dirt, wrinkled up old lady you'd see on local television news on one of those slow-news-day, human-interest stories: She had just turned a hundred or a hundred and ten; doesn't matter, I guess. Though she could barely remember her own name, her family would show up and put a paper party hat on her head, help her blow out a firestorm of candles, and then clap like she'd just swum (or is it swam?) the English Channel. Everybody wore patient, fake smiles and probably got the hell out of that disinfectant-and-urine smelly old nursing home two minutes after the camera shut down, leaving old granny alone with that shiny paper hat on her head, probably still smiling, having no idea what the hell had just happened. And while nobody had had a good time, all the kids and grandkids and great grandkids felt like they had done something important. They felt good about themselves for having honored the old gal. They also marveled at how turning a hundred and ten was something special, though I've never been sure why. But then again, people got medals just for surviving. Why not?

Anyhow, that's Father's Day to me, a day in which people are made to pay some imaginary debt that makes them feel good. And Mother's Day, too, I guess. People don't so much honor you as they feel obligated to do something ... and then feel pretty good about themselves for doing it. That's sort of like the do-gooders who all flocked to New Orleans a few years ago in the wake of the big hurricane. They'd announce they were going to help the storm survivors recover, get someone to do fundraising so it didn't cost them a nickel, fly down and spend three or four days saving a few puppies or pounding a few nails, go home ... and then, wine swirling in the glass, modestly brag for years about how appreciative the people were for all that they had done. Gag me!

But I guess that crap about Father's Day was really all my fault. I guess. Connie knew how I would react, that I would act pleased and honored. She probably never suspected that I was faking it. Just like I suppose there were times she faked an orgasm. I did it to make her feel good. Ditto for her, I guess. I think that's what makes a marriage work – the ability to fake it convincingly. It is an art form.

The fact is that she had no better idea how I felt about stuff than I did about how she felt. Nobody had given her a user's manual either. It's like punching that button on the computer or turning the key in the ignition. We don't know why or how it works. It just does.

***

The point? I don't know. Oh, yeah: Stuff just works. Until one day, it just doesn't. Someone says, I'm done faking and pretending. That's the day it just doesn't work anymore. That's the day someone asks, "Why?"

Until that day comes, you get to thinking you're living in some great, unified yin and yang Oneness. Most of all, you're best friends. You have to be; it's what puts the capital M in Marriage. Even if it's a lie.

That's why you have secret codes. It's all about that Oneness. The slightest lift of an eyebrow or brush of a hand at a party means this person I'm talking to is an idiot or why don't we get out of here? "I wonder how Aunt Mary's doing?" one asks the other. Even though good old Aunt Mary has been dead for 20 years, that's the code that it's time to beat feet for the door.

You communicate beautifully with a look, a nod, a squeeze of the hand. But you really have no idea who that person beside you on the mattress really is. And that's okay, as long as you don't think otherwise, as long as one day, someday, one of you doesn't suddenly decide who you or she or he really is. That's the day you stop faking it ... not just with each other, but with yourself, as well. That's worse than the "why?" question.

THE ISLAND
Rainy Days at Home

Ah, rainy days. My favorite. Sure, I made no money, but I also didn't have to perform like a dancing bear or wear underwear for the snorkeling excursion *touristas*. When the cruise ships hung in port on rainy days, the shops would do good business; the beach kiosks wouldn't. The bars always did okay, both ashore and on board the liners, since some passengers never got off. On sunny days, on the other hand, the sand-sun-n-sea businesses bustled, and the island shops were often empty. That was also when I'd pick up my cargo, 16 tourists, for a half-day snorkeling adventure.

"Watch your step," we'd say gently as we offered a hand to the women who'd unsteadily descend the ship gangway or excursion pier onto *The Do Over,* and wait until everyone found a spot he or she could claim as their home space for the rest of the four-hour trip.

No, today was fine with me. The weather had settled down from stormy to just threatening, and now just an overcast drizzle. The hurricanes? They were at least six days out. I watched as the liners slowly steamed out to sea, heading for their next port of call. I raised my glass of iced tea and said, unconvincingly, "Bon voyage." It was good to have a day off.

Connie and I had once taken a cruise. I loved it. The best part was unpacking just once and yet waking up each morning in a new place. Home away from home. That was how we had discovered the islands. Or how I had discovered the islands. I think she had enjoyed the exotic aura. Me? I fell in love ... hard. I resurrected my old dream of living on a boat and living the island life, whatever that really meant. So, when the last debris of our marriage had finally been swept up and deposited in the dumpster, and the lawyer letters had slowed to a trickle of about one or two a week, it just had seemed natural. I headed to the Caribbean.

And now, here I was, Captain Jolly, skipper of *The Do Over*, my own 38-foot sailing catamaran, with a contract to take cruise line tourists on half-day snorkeling excursions. And only one employee, Kid, my first mate.

I watched Kid, who was hunched down beside a bin half filled with bleach water and sorting the masks and snorkels. He was out in the drizzle, wearing only a pair of shorts, seemingly oblivious to the warm rain.

Bonita, a whiskey in her left hand, was working the hibachi under a tarp at the stern, sizzling three steaks.

I glanced around *The Do Over*. Home. Office. Perpetual vacation.

"Hey, Bonita."

She turned and marched over to where I was sitting and decisively threw her left leg over my lap and plunked down hard, as if testing to see if I had an erection. Looking down into my eyes, she wrapped her arms around my neck and assaulted me with her tongue like she was trying to climb down my throat. Then she settled onto my lap and just smiled at me.

"Let's get a baby sitter for Kid and go out dancing tonight," she said.

"Let's just throw him overboard and drown him."

Kid looked up and wiped the rain from his eyes. "I can tell when I'm not wanted," he announced.

"Smart boy," I said and watched as he jumped up and, as if doing a backward high jump, tossed himself overboard with a loud splash into the lagoon.

Bonita tried to get up to see how he was, but I held onto her. "He'll be just fine," I said.

"That's what I'm afraid of," she said. "I want to toss him the anchor, just to make sure he doesn't come back."

At that moment, like a shaggy, wet sheepdog, Kid came up the stern ladder and, doing an arms-outstretched monster walk, staggered onto the deck. He had attached a red foam clown ball to the tip of his nose.

"Did you miss me?" he asked, wrapping his arms around both of us to get us good and wet.

Then, abruptly, he stood up and stepped back, holding his red nose. He never did seem to get used to the aroma of Bonita.

To me, something I never shared, I was partial to the smell of day-old bait fish in the hot sun. Seriously, just like some people love the odor of gasoline. I think it reminded me of lazy summer days as a boy fishing on The Great South Bay off the South Shore of Long Island. So, I had no complaint about Bonita's scent, though foreplay usually involved a swim in the lagoon.

Not all that strange, really, I thought. I know people who love the combo of peanut butter and chocolate. Me? It almost makes me throw up, though I like them both separately. Or raw seafood; I could just gobble up that stuff by the handful – clams, oysters, and anything sushi. Other people? Some gag at the mere thought of it. But then there are some folks who think red meat is disgusting.

I guess it's the same when it comes to sexual tastes. Though I know a few guys who are gay, I could not imagine ever kissing a man in passion or having sex with one. And I know a guy who knew a woman who only wanted anal sex. Some like being tied up; some like being spanked. Some like …

So, I guess that I don't have a problem with – even kind of like – Bonita's pungent, fishy odor. I don't find it all that strange.

"Hey, Cap'm," Kid asked, still dripping on the deck, "you want me to throw Bonita overboard for you?"

Bonita rose, smiled at Kid in a way that indicated she knew she could take him any time, and swung her hips as only she could as she went back to check on the steaks.

"Careful, boy," I warned Kid with a smile.

Out of the corner of my eye, I saw the cabin door slide open on the hulking, 95-foot mega-yacht in the slip next door. The *She Monster* towered over my single-story catamaran. The cruiser and its owner, a slack-jawed, round-faced fellow named Gary, came down at the start of the high season. Actually, Gary and his wife flew down. They hired a crew to bring the boat down. Once safely moored in her slip, *She Monster* never left the dock the rest of the season, and except for the sound of the air conditioner running full time, it was shut up tight and seemed to be abandoned.

But once in a while, I'd see a curtain shift. Sometimes a badly aging woman – Gary's wife, I assumed – would come on deck in a flowing robe, barely nod to one of us, and, squinting in the sunlight, look cautiously around like she wasn't sure how she had gotten here, and then go back below deck again.

Gary came out and looked down on *The Do Over*. He had on his blue, shiny-visored captain's hat, with a gold-braid anchor on the front.

Kid looked up, then lowered his eyes in mock submissiveness. Then he looked up again at Gary. Gary, his thick, pasty white jowls hanging, stared blankly down at Kid.

"Sorry if we bothered you, Your Lordship," Kid said in what could have passed, if just barely, for a cockney accent. "The cap'm and me, and his wench here, we was just engaging in a bit of tom foolery. We'll keep 'er quiet, eh, Governor."

Gary said nothing for a long time, and I began to think we might have some trouble. Steer clear of the money-bag fat cats, I'd told Kid just this morning, as I pretty much did almost every morning. Then I realized that was exactly why he was pulling this tiger's tail. Kid always seemed drawn to the hornets' nests.

Then Gary said, very softly, sadly, "I heard the splash, and I wanted to make sure everybody was okay. Have a good evening."

Then he went back inside and closed and latched the door.

THE STATES
Night Sweats

I woke up to the gentle sound of the harbor and Bonita beside me, whispering, "Jolly? Jolly?"

I had been dreaming again.

I kissed her, said, "Go back to sleep, Babe," and went on deck to watch the stars and let the old memories wash over me. In my office back in the middle of winter back in the States or down here, where there was no winter, just memories, it all sometimes still caught up with me.

***

I had become an entrepreneur, a meat-eating business owner. And I'd had a ball. I'd loved it, logging long hours – though I always took off Friday and Saturday evening and all day Sunday because, after all, I was a family guy – and becoming the best "marketeer" in my industry. I remember that bumper sticker I'd once seen on the BMW in front of me in the left turn lane: "Unless You're the Lead Sled Dog, the View Never Changes." I'd read it, drew a blank for a moment, then visualized Huskies tethered in a row, pulling that sled. Finally, I'd burst out laughing when I was able to visualize the view of the dogs behind the leader. Yes! As soon as the light changed and we made the turn, I'd zoomed in front of the BMW, waving in a half-assed salute as I went by. Lead dog or nothing.

I had had plenty of competitors and plenty of enemies, but being real honest, I had to admit: I was good at what I did. Of course, looking back now from the deck of *The Do Over*, I realize I had paid a high price. In the end, I had only one friend, Scott, and he was from the days before I had gone into business and become a big shot. Just as bad, I had thought that this was the way it was supposed to be. Men may have once hunted in packs, back in the days of the mastodons. Today, we were lone hunters. We were supposed to make a full commitment to building our empires, alone. Total commitment. Full metal jacket. Eat or be eaten. Business is war, and war is a bigger thrill than sex. It wasn't at all about money or even power. That's where the liberals and the losers got it all wrong. It was about winning. Just winning. The money and the power were bonuses.

That was why, when Connie finally left me, it wasn't that I decided to keep it to myself. I just had nobody to tell.

I had done it all for Connie and the kids ... or that was what I had told myself. Really? Actually, I think I did it because I could think of nothing better to do. I think that's why men become successful entrepreneurs and nations go to war: boredom and/or lack of imagination. I remember the time my brother, never my biggest fan, had called me an asshole. I'd smiled and thanked him.

Either you're the pigeon or the statue, I used to tell people, the lead sled dog or the one that ran along with its nose up the lead dog's ass.

Not exactly a deep philosophy, but it worked for me. And, no, it wasn't about stuff. I thought the clowns with the T-shirts that read, "He who dies with the most toys wins," they were shallow morons. No, I was a business man – tough, agile, making big bucks by living by wit and grit. It's like an athlete who wants to be the best at the game. Or like a military commander. I was Julius Caesar conquering Gaul and breaking all the rules. Business was a sport. Competition. It was also war, and I loved it … at first … kind of. Why was it so important to win?

Sitting in the darkness of the Caribbean aboard *The Do Over*, I tried to remember. I came up blank.

I had gotten to be more like Chicago Mike than I'd ever have admitted back then. Someday, I had to thank Connie for ending that delusion. Her leaving me was the best thing that had ever happened to me. "Yep, that's my story, and I'm sticking to it," I said aloud to the Caribbean night, and didn't laugh. In truth, I think we were both miserable, but she had the sense to do something about it. Me? I was like that frog that starts out in a pot of cold water just swimming around and having a helluva good time. But then, someone turns up the gas. As the water gets hotter and hotter, he just sits there, barely noticing it, until he gets boiled alive.

I think that's why I started thinking about Sam, my high school sweetheart. She had a gift for seeing right through my bullshit bravado. "You're a gentle boy, Joth," she had once said to me. "That's why I love you. That's why I'll always love you."

And that's probably the main reason I walked away from her – too much truth in those eyes. It's hard to be an asshole when somebody thinks you're not.

THE ISLAND
Job Interview

Tropical storms were starting to build out in the Atlantic, which meant more rainy days on the island. As I'd said, these were my favorite days. I sat in one of the deck chairs just under the cabin roof and listened to the sound of the rain. It was overcast, with just a slight breeze cooling the lagoon down just enough that I put on a light hoodie. Excursions had been cancelled because of the snotty weather. The cruise lines hated it when a customer fell overboard and drowned. Bad for business. Didn't do anything for tips, either.

I remember the day I signed the excursion contract with the Company. A tall, fit, bouncy, sharp-eyed blonde with white shorts, a pony tail and a pink cap nimbly stepped aboard *The Do Over* with a clipboard in hand. Excursion director. Though she was all cheer, charm and smiles, her eyes scanned me and the boat like a sniper searching for a target, as she was going to make damn sure we were fit to carry her cruise line's customers on half-day snorkeling excursions.

I had shaved that morning and put on a clean pair of shorts and shirt, which I actually buttoned. I also had on my deck sliders, no socks, and a cap with the cruise ship's name on it.

"Okay," she said, unclipping a half-inch thick contract from her clip board, "this is for you. Now let's see the life vests first. Oh, and lose the cap. That suggests you work for us, which creates implied liability. You are an independent contractor, not an employee."

I took off the cap, nervously bounced from one foot to the other, and almost said, "Yes, sir." Almost.

Also, without looking up, she pointed to the top of the mast. "And lose the skull and crossbones flag. You're not a pirate."

I nodded and kept my expression blank. This could be a long day, I thought.

For some reason, I wondered if she was wearing underwear. Yes, I concluded. It was probably on page 66 of the employee handbook. All employees must wear underwear, white or light pink (no thongs), which must be changed at least once a day. Suddenly, I realized I'd forgotten to put my own underwear on this morning. Shit! I wondered if she'd notice. I wondered if she'd ask and then, shaking her head, mark a great big X in that box. No underwear. Contract denied.

I took the contract and pointed to the life vest compartment. She squatted down and, her back to me, began rifling through the neat stacks of vests, counting them and inspecting them for rot. Yep, definitely wearing underwear, I observed, and looked away just in time.

Standing up, she glanced at me (I swear women can tell) and frowned as she made a note on her clip board. Then she snapped on her best cruise-ship smile again as she turned and asked, "Alrighty, then, fire extinguishers?"

I pointed them out. I decided I did not like this lady. As she roamed about and touched everything on my boat, I felt like she was giving me a proctology exam with cold hands. Still, I kept my best day-cruiser grin plastered on my face, matching her, mindless smile for mindless smile.

I hated job interviews. The best, most charming liar always got the job, I remembered, as I signed the cruise-line contract without even bothering to read it and handed it back to her.

THE STATES
The Story of Men

It had been winter, it was dark, and the wind was howling. I was in my office and lying on the couch, my left arm across my eyes. Gradually, it was becoming clear that I needed either to kill myself or move on down to the islands. And all the while, those damn memory tapes kept playing over and over and over in the background. Tonight's topic, for your listening pleasure, we have story of men. Enjoy.

Men? What are we like? I thought, trying to explore a new thought. Well, I concluded, we feel most comfortable when we go out and hunt down a mastodon, gut it, skin it and drag it home. We're providers. No matter what anybody else says, that's what we feel best doing. Winning, conquering, toppling things, besting the other guy in a sport or business deal – that's the stuff that turns us on. Even losing, as long as we know we gave it our all. We're proud of our scars. They mean we got into the battle and gave it our best.

That's what ran through my head the time Rocket tripped a squirrel in the driveway and killed it in a snap. Connie was horrified and grossed out. But Rock straddled his kill and looked back at us with his head held high. He was so proud he damn near howled. He strutted with a special bounce in his step for a week. I was as excited as he was. "Go, Rocket!" I'd shouted, and wanted to get my gun and go hunting …

except that I didn't own a gun. Connie had looked at me blankly and then, without saying a word, turned away and went back into the house.

Still, that's how most men think. That's why we love action movies. That's why we go out and kill ourselves for our families. We feel like warriors, hunters. Or at least that's how we would love to feel. Then when we get home? Hail the conquering hero.

That's why my heroes growing up were swashbuckling buccaneers – the old-time ones like Errol Flynn and the macho Stallone characters like Rocky and Rambo, but especially the real men of history who discovered the world in sailing ships in the great Age of Exploration. I marveled as a child at the story of how the Spanish Conquistador Hernando Cortez in 1519 led 600 Spanish soldiers and sailors against the Aztec empire. In an all-in gesture, Cortez gave the order, "Burn the ships!" marooning himself and his men on the Mexican shore halfway around the world from home. This was fewer than 30 years after Columbus had discovered the New World. No phones. No mail service. Win or die. Within two years, he had conquered the Aztec Empire and started the Spanish Empire ... without a single moral misgiving or second thought.

I also loved the stories of the British merchantmen who sailed from England to places like Hong Kong and set up trading companies, making their fortunes.

They returned home, if they made it home, with riches and power. Yes! Was it too late, I thought, to chuck it all, head to the islands, and become a skipper of my own pirate ship? Probably. Still ...

Those myths kept me alive. Even so, I realized, that if I had owned a gun ...

***

I'd spent a lot of late-night couch hours thinking about my father and his father – tough, unemotional, rather unpleasant men. During the Great Depression, a good man was a good man because he was a good provider. That meant he provided. Period. He worked all day, came home most every night, and only got drunk once in a while. He didn't have to be sensitive to his wife's feelings or worry about damaging his children's fragile psyches. He was a good dad and a good husband if he put food on the table. Today? I don't have a clue.

It was easier, I think, for men back then. Probably for women, too. Their role was to take care of the house, cook, clean, do laundry. They didn't have to worry about whether their husbands were happy. I suspect they did not lose sleep about being five pounds overweight or feel offended about being asked to make coffee for the boss. I also suspect nobody was really happy, but nobody ever really thought about it. As my mother once explained to me, "The man provides the house; the woman provides the home." The older I got, the more sense that made.

I sometimes wonder if everybody else finds this stuff as confusing as I do.

THE ISLAND
Between Two and Four Drinks In

I had to admit that life on the island was easier; so were the people.

Take Chicago Mike, for example. It was rumored that he'd gone to the University of Chicago and MIT. He had been some kind of wunderkind who built a $15 million a year techno-biz by the time he was twenty-five, had a mind like a computer, which explained why he won regularly at the poker table. Then one day, he just left. He walked away from his catwalk wife to run away with Patti the Beast – foul-tempered, fat Patti the Beast.

Patti? No history. No story. Nobody cared enough to want to know. She was a mistake that vaguely resembled a human being … barely. Just a scowl, though people said she had left behind a five-year-old son to come with Mike down to the island. Lucky boy, we all agreed.

John/Candy had been lifers, or at least had been on the island longer than anybody else. They had what in the islands is known as Rock Fever. No, not a rock band or an infectious disease, Rock Fever down here is loosely defined as either love for the freewheeling island life or a kind of claustrophobia that makes people desperate to get off the island. John/Candy had it both ways. She kept calling this place Devil's Island. He just drank. Well, so did she. That was what they had in common.

They had been on the island for decades. They were known collectively as John/Candy. It made sense when they were together, but island life didn't always make sense. Even if she showed up alone, she was known as John/Candy.

Even after he'd committed suicide ... or perhaps, I should say, finished committing suicide.

He'd learned that his mother, ancient at 98, was dying. His brother had said he had to come home; no more excuses. He pretended to make plans, but then he realized that he couldn't leave. He had said that it was because he hadn't been off island in decades.

"I haven't been home in 30 years," he had told Blah Blah Brenda, who was always sympathetic toward anyone who would talk to her. "I don't have a driver's license. I haven't seen my passport since Carter was president. Even if I went to the States, they wouldn't let me back on the island again. My last visa ... well, I think it's somewhere with my passport."

So, both stressed and relieved at the impossibility of leaving, John/Candy stayed. But something wasn't right after that. It was like they had lived in a cage with the door unlocked all those years. Suddenly, they found that there was a big padlock on the bars. It did something to them.

That's kind of how it is with couples who simply live together as bunkies for decades. Then one day, for whatever reason, they decide to make it official, to get married. They're divorced within two years.

As for John/Candy, Calabash had pointed out that something had changed. Normally, though they drank all day, they weren't stinko drunk until six in the evening. But these days, they'd both be staggering by lunchtime. "He can't run his boat like that," Calabash had offered. "He's gonna go for a long swim some night," he'd added sadly, recognizing that some things had to run their course and the end result could not be altered.

Nobody argued. The tragic part is that he didn't invite her to swim with him. She ended up an island ghost. More on that later.

***

Then there's Bonita, one of my favorite people. Sitting next to me at the Sunset on Monday night, Bonita glanced at the sign over the bar, shrugged, and peeled off her T-shirt. Free drinks are free drinks, even though Jason almost always poured her drinks for free anyway. Everybody liked Bonita.

Bonita didn't seem to fit any of Jason's definitions of why women take off their tops. I think Bonita did it for the free drinks, or maybe because she knew I liked it. Or maybe she just liked going topless, just like I liked wearing cutoff shorts.

Lea smiled appreciatively at Bonita's tits.

"No girls allowed," Bonita said, smiling back and snugged closer to me. "And your day?" she asked like a mother after school. "How was your day?"

"We did great," chimed in Kid at the other end of the table. "Las a tits ... I mean tips." He dug into his pocket and pulled out a handful of bills, mostly ones and fives, and a few tens.

Bonita looked at me. I nodded. "We paid the bills today, Darling." Meanwhile, I mentally calculated how many excursion days we had left, especially if one of those hurricanes stacking up east of us decided to come plowing across the island.

"Chicago, how was your day?" I asked, just to stir up the conversation, and everyone paused to listen.

Patti the Beast snorted and growled and answered for Mike. "I guess when you hook the ass of the guy who's paying for the charter, you don't generally get a big tip, do you, Sweetie?" she said sarcastically, scowling, shaking her head, and spitting out the last word like a chaw of tobacco.

The table cheered and congratulated him. Chicago Mike, who probably had the highest IQ on the island, would have starved if it weren't for Patti. Of course, Patti was the reason he had no money in the first place.

He was hapless. He may have been a multi-million-dollar entrepreneur back in the States, but he had few – okay, no –

marketable skills down here in the islands. For the moment, he worked as a hand on John/Candy's boat, the *Tor Helga*. Even with rummies like John/Candy, his screw-ups on board the *Tor Helga* were almost legendary. His worst was cracking open the wrong fill cap in harbor and pumping 70 gallons of diesel fuel into the boat's fresh water tank. It took a while to live down the nickname Dumb Ass, especially in front of the well-heeled *touristas*, who usually decided by the time they passed through the drawbridge and out into open water that he was more idiot than savant.

***

Just then, side by side, John/Candy came marching unsteadily into the Sunset, looked around and came to the table. He was a foul drunk, and had gotten even fouler since hiring Chicago Mike as his mate. Rock Fever didn't make him any more cheerful. She, on the other hand, was a sweet, dull-eyed drunk. They went well together.

He stopped and stood unsteadily in front of Mike.

"You're fired!" he snarled, pointing a finger in Mike's face for emphasis. As I said, John/Candy owned the *Tor Helga*, and they barely made a go of it. He was a burly man with a Texas accent that sounded almost German when he was drunk. He skippered the boat, though he rarely went out before noon these days, and nobody ever called him Cap'm John.

She – the Candy half of John/Candy – was one of those painfully thin, ratty-haired blondes, with sunken, vacant eyes, though it did come with a gentle smile. They moored *Tor Helga* back behind The Horny Toad, an open-air seafood restaurant. Like most owners, they lived aboard their boat. Not only did that cut down on living expenses, but it provided a built-in security system, better than a dog, though John/Candy would easily have slept through the shadow boys pillaging the cabin.

She waitressed at the Toad and got paid in tips and free drinks. In exchange, Mr. Robert, a Dominican-born businessman, let them moor the *Tor Helga* at his dock behind the restaurant for free. Electric and water hook-up was extra, so they usually used the toilets on shore and had electric only when they ran the engines for a charter.

Charter captains counted on repeat business, year after year, from satisfied customers. John/Candy almost never had repeat business. Having a screw-up like Chicago Mike on board really didn't make any difference. They were one very dysfunctional family.

Chicago Mike moved John/Candy's finger from in front of his face and said, "Let me buy you a drink, Skipper." John/Candy stared for a moment, assessing the offer. Then he shrugged, nodded, and sat down. Even drunk and even knowing that Chicago Mike was a first-class screw up, John/Candy knew Chicago was the only one who would work for him. So, this ritual took place at least once a month.

Chicago turned to Patti and, with feigned casualness, asked, "Do you have any money, Dear?"

Patti shook her head, and we could almost see the body heat rise from annoyed to flat-out furious. Finally, she stood, took a vicious, pudgy-arm swing at him and missed, and stormed out of the bar, pushing two *touristas* out of her way as she went. "Works every time," Mike mumbled as we all watched her roll from side to side out onto the beach. We all turned back to Mike and nodded our approval. An evening with Patti the Beast was never a pleasant treat.

"Uh oh," Kid announced, "Beast comin' in at two o'clock," as Patti suddenly changed course and circled back. Mike cursed under his breath as Patti plunked her huge body back down in her chair, breathing heavily, like a steam locomotive idling noisily at the station.

"Jolly," Mike asked, almost pleasantly, ignoring Patti, "can you spot me a twenty? I'm good for it."

"I can spot you a one," I said, laughing as I raised my middle finger in front of his face.

"Man, everybody has his fingers in my face tonight," Chicago whined.

"That's because you're an idiot," Patti offered.

"Here!" John/Candy said, tossing a few bills on the table. "Here's some money. Now buy me a drink ... and fast. Buy Candy one, too."

As the laughter let up, I felt Bonita's hand on my thigh. First I thought she was feeling frisky. She liked that sometimes. Sex on the beach in midday, without caring who was around, or yanking the crank under the table while everyone else drank and the guys asked if they were next. She wasn't very subtle, and my eyes rolled back in my head.

But then her hand was gone. I patted my pocket and felt something inside. Her day's tips.

I sat back and hoisted my drink. Good booze. Good friends. A good woman. A tropical island. Not bad. It usually came between two and four drinks in; that was when everything made perfect, beautiful sense.

Then Chicago Mike began to whine. He did that around drink five for him. "Ya know, I use ta carry a bankroll a hundre dolla bills in my pocket, a wad big nuff ta choke a horse."

"Really?" Asked Blah Blah Brenda, probably thinking of some country club stable where she used to ride back in White Folks Bay, USA. She probably wore jodhpurs that made her hips look big, black boots that made her look like a Nazi dominatrix, and a sexless riding helmet that made her look ... well, that made her look stupid. I bet she also carried a riding crop and marched around the place like she owned it. Heil!

"A small horse," suggested French Tony.

"A little, bitty teeny horse," added Kid, giggling as he petted the imaginary horse in the palm of his hand.

"No, really," said Chicago, looking around as if he were back at the head of the table in the executive boardroom. "And I use ta have fi'teen suits in the closet, drive a Mercedes ... an a Jag-Jag-u-ar."

I chimed in in a high-toned voice: "I would have brought my Jag tonight, friends...." I paused and looked down the road, where my ten-year-old, dented, dirty white compact Kia was parked. The others, except Chicago, looked, too.

"But it's still in the *showroom!*" I delivered loudly, giggling, delighted with my own humor.

French Tony laughed and made a note on his napkin. I'd see something on one of his T-shirts next week: "I'd have driven my Jaguar, but it's still in the showroom."

"A good one," he said, as he put his pen in his pocket.

Kid stared blankly around the table. Blah Blah was confused and kept looking down the road for my Jaguar. John/Candy both shrugged. Calabash just looked down and quietly snorted his raspy laugh and repeated "Jolly, Jolly," as a commentary on my humor or lack thereof. Bonita smiled, not sure if she got the joke ... and not too worried about whether she did or not.

All the ex-pats on the island drove pretty much the same cars, depending on who was offering the best deals when the car rental companies on the island decided to upgrade their fleets. Most were small, had four doors, and were white, because it helped deflect and reflect the sun and heat. They were pitted with sand and salt, and their suspensions were rusted, loud and loose, thanks to the periodic speed bumps that no one slowed down for and the pot holes that no one repaired. And they all had small holes where trunk locks had been, which explained the sign that was still glued to the glove box of my car: Do Not Leave Valuables in Your Vehicle. Even the Trunk.

When I first came on island, I thought I'd gotten a good deal on an eight-year old POS – that's short for Piece of Shit, as Calabash explained – with just under 23,000 miles. Well, on a 36-square mile island, you don't cover a lot of miles in a year, but the ones you do are hard, hard miles. It didn't matter. Cars here were throw-away items. You bought one for less than three grand, drove it five years, and when it finally quit, left it on the side of the road for the shadow boys to pick clean. Insurance? Like registration, it was legally required but, like the green flash, a myth.

So, those 23,000 miles on my car were hard miles. The vehicle was about ready for the shadow boys. Nonetheless, somebody stole it. I was pretty upset when I saw the empty spot where it had been parked. Feeling helpless and uncertain, I asked a woman walking her dog who I should call to report it. I was new on the island back then.

"Listen, Jimbo," she had said, "did you read in the paper the other day about the cop car that was stolen out of the police compound?"

I nodded dully, and then the light bulb came on. "Ah," was all I said. "Good point." The cops couldn't even keep their own cars from being stolen; they really weren't going to care a whole lot when mine got driven off.

"Besides," the woman added, "they'll want to see registration, insurance, title-tax receipt. You'll probably end up in jail. Be smart. Don't report it. Let it go."

A week later, I saw my car parked on the street on the French side of the island. I recognized it by the distinct crack running across the windshield. I still had the key in my pocket, so I looked around and opened the door, scrutinizing the people sitting at the tables at the nearby street café. One guy, chatting with a beautiful brunette, looked up. His eyes widened and locked on mine. I held up my key, just so there was no misunderstanding who was stealing back the car. He gave the slightest shrug and went back to his conversation with the brunette. C'est la vie.

***

Chicago Mike was still whining and bragging about the life he had left behind. "I yousta vacation down here at four-star zorts … rye on this very islan. Rye, Honey Baby?"

Kid glanced at Patti, all swollen, 300 pounds of her, and then at me. "Honey Baby?" he mouthed and gave a fake, wide-eyed shudder.

Enough whiskey and anybody can become Honey Baby, I thought to myself.

"An loozers like youse youstta fetch me ma drinks."

I watched Mike as he slouched lower and lower toward the table, leaning heavily into Patti's shoulder. He was grumpy and sour and disliked pretty much everybody, mostly himself. He seemed to work hard at being miserable, and ran from the possibility of happiness faster than a hog from a butcher.

I knew a lot of guys like him back in the States. They were talented, too smart for their own good. They had lists of things that they wanted to achieve, and they equated the achievement of those lists with something bordering on happiness, or at least success. And before I get to sounding too arrogant, that was pretty much how I was back then. Still, these guys, and a few women, too, I guess, they were the super achievers. Some ran marathons. Others built multi-million-dollar businesses and multi-million-dollar homes. They climbed and climbed some self-designed ladders to the top. And it was never enough. No matter how far they ran, no matter how high they climbed, they could never get away from themselves. Never. And, at least it seemed to me, the more arrogant they acted, the more scared to death they were.

That's why some of them looked for strong, mean women, the kind who could cradle their heads at three in the morning. They wanted their very own Patti the Beast.

I once ran into a guy who barked and snarled and swaggered like a Jack Russell Terrier on steroids. He made me look shy and retiring by comparison. He was a little guy, barely five-foot-three. He was a got-it-all-and-did-it-my-way businessman who could – and would – bore people to death with endless tales about his exploits. He was always the best, always the hero of every story he told. He knew everything, and he'd tell you as much. The thing is that he was good. He had skill and talent. He was a respected member of the community, a certified sailor who would deliver boats to the islands on his vacations, a gun aficionado who was not only a crack shot, but also assembled his own ammunition. But being a boring asshole pretty much wiped out any of the good stuff. People hated him.

What scared me the most, looking at walking suicides like Chicago Mike, was that I had once been way, way too much like him for comfort. I guess I should thank Connie someday for walking out on me when she did. She short-circuited my whole climb-and-swan-dive, self-destruct pattern before it really got off the ground. Geez. No wonder she left me.

***

I was starting to feel a little drunk and surly myself. Okay, I thought, it was time for Chicago Mike's whine-skip-the-cheese show to end.

"Hey, Mike, shut up," I snapped, and he fell silent instantly. So did everybody else, which made me feel bad. I was ruining the party. Typical family gathering.

In an effort to get things back on track, I hoisted my drink. "To cheap women and sexy whiskey!"

Everyone cheered. Calabash said "Hear! Hear!" and John/Candy gave each other a quick kiss. I suspect that might well have been part of their wedding vows.

Bonita snuggled close. The taste of the whiskey had just about overpowered the smell of fish. It always did. Without looking at her, I wrapped an arm around her shoulder, gave her a thanks-Babe squeeze and rested my hand across that God-awful bluish green lizard tattoo on her arm.

I felt her head turn to me. I rubbed the back of her neck, delayed, and then finally looked into her eyes. Then for that exact, small moment, I was in love. I caught the glint, the barest reflection of the innocent young girl, perhaps even a once-upon-a-time, blushing bride full of hope and optimism, the devoted mother, the eager wife. I saw a flicker of shy belief, if only for a moment. God, she must have once been one helluva wife. I looked away, wanting to cry for the first time – at least when I wasn't asleep and battling memory dreams – since Jamie, my son, had told me he didn't want me in his life and hung up on me.

I reminded myself that I had the tendency to be a sloppy, maudlin drunk. That was one of my great talents – the ability to know what kind of a lousy drunk I could be. Some talent, eh?

"Come on, Hon," I said tenderly and almost told her I loved her. "Let's go for a swim." I took Bonita's hand and led her out of the Sunset.

***

We walked side by side along the edge of the road the several hundred feet back to the car. There were no sidewalks on the island. It was dark. There also weren't many streetlights, at least on this side of the mountain.

Suddenly, Bonita stiffened and squeezed my hand as something moved in the shadows behind one of the cars.

"Got one at two o'clock, Jolly," she said loudly, deliberately so, as she stared in the direction of the shadow.

I shook her hand off mine and automatically touched my knife hilt. I scanned the shadows and did an island pirouette to cover all 360 degrees. Whether on the beach or in town, it was just smart to do a periodic spin while walking. The islands were fun, but they were so much more dangerous than the *touristas* had any idea, partially because crimes, even when reported, were rarely published in the papers. No unnatural deaths were, either. That was one part of the great island mystique and myth: No one ever seemed to die down here. Even when the last hurricane blew through and sank dozens of boats in the lagoon, there was never a death count. Bad for tourism.

"Ah, got the other one at ten o'clock, Babe." We both stared hard at our respective targets.

It was common for muggers and pickpockets to travel in pairs. It was also known that, once you located them and locked in on them with full eye contact, they tended to fade back into the shadows. Glare; never smile. Look mean, hostile, cold, dangerous.

We reached the car, got in and headed back to the boat. Just another night in paradise.

***

One of the things I loved about relationships on the island, at least among the ex-pats, was that there were no standards, no weed-free front lawns to envy, no white picket fences, no sex-on-wheels cars to signal that you'd made it across some mythical goal line in your life.

That was kind of why I kind of, more or less, liked Chicago Mike. More or less. He made you realize it just wasn't worth it to keep score. I don't think Chicago Mike cared about any one or any thing anymore, well, except the right to whine about everything now and then. He said once that he'd come down one winter because he'd gotten tired of his wife after 27 years. He'd also left behind a multi-million dollar metal-coating business that was already heading south fast. From what I could tell, he had been one smart guy, and had done everything right. Then one day, something changed. Businesses don't fail for economic reasons, and marriages don't fail for no reason at all. Something goes wrong, mostly, I suspect, because something went wrong in someone's head. Sounded familiar.

I think I am the only one who liked Mike, and even then I didn't like him a whole lot. Still, caught in a jam, I'd hired him for a day mate before Kid had stumbled aboard. The problem with Chicago Mike – well, one of many – was that not only did he have no island skills, but he knew no boundaries, especially when it came to the women. He may have been smart – just ask him – but he had no sense. He also had Patti the Beast.

One of the *tourista* wives, her name was just Brenda back then, had had too much to drink on our half-day snorkeling excursion on *The Do Over*. "Too much to drink" is really being polite. In fact, she'd really pounded down the rum punches with zeal and gusto. While her husband had been trying to find a pair of fins that fit his size-15 feet, Brenda had decided that Chicago Mike was the sexiest thing on two legs. That's how drunk she was. Well, she and he were down in the starboard cabin, my cabin. I was trying to steer the boat, trying to get them out of my cabin, trying to make sure nobody fell overboard, and trying to keep one eye on Brenda's husband, who, having found his gear, was coming on to a giggly secretary from Leawood, Kansas, stuffed into a too-tight bikini that still had the Wal-Mart tag on it. Meanwhile, with the starboard cabin door banging open and closed as the boat sailed across the wind, Brenda, all nervous and anxious, was grunting and tugging on Chicago's shorts like they were a stuck set of dresser drawers, and dropping to her knees. A few eyes short as I finally tried to kick the cabin door closed all the way, I nearly collided with the *Bon Jour*, another day tripper out of the French side.

After the excursion, after the husband had stuffed the tip jar and was strolling with the Leawood secretary back to the parking lot, Brenda took Chicago aside and told him that she had decided to leave her husband. He gave her his usual sucking-on-a-lemon scowl and invited her to become his bunkie. That simple. That was it.

Only one problem: Patti the Beast. He wasn't living on board *The Do Over*, mostly because I wouldn't let Patti the Beast on the boat. He and Patti had moved out of their luxury townhouse with a sweeping view of the harbor when Chicago's money had run out. They had moved into a run-down apartment facing the dumpsters down in the low lands beside the desalinization station. Not exactly a swanky neighborhood.

I don't think Chicago gave his invitation to Brenda another thought. She did. A week later, Brenda, all giggly smiles and bouncing on her toes like she was about to pee her pants, showed up on the dock asking for Michael. "Michael?" I'd asked and then said, "Oh, you mean Chicago Mike."

By that time, I'd already fired him. He had a gift for doing absolutely nothing right, from throwing the anchor overboard without a line tied to it, to letching after a fourteen-year-old girl until her father had nearly punched him out, and, most of all, for showing up every day with a list of ways I could improve my business. I finally told him, "Look, Mike, I don't need another wife telling me what to do. I can screw up my own life just fine. Oh, and you're fired, so please get the fuck off my boat."

So, when she asked where he was, I just shook my head. Brenda's smile crumbled, then turned instantly into a penetrating, accusatory frown.

"Well, what am I supposed to do?" she demanded as if she was the lady of the manor and I was the not-too-bright assistant gardener. One of the things I'd learned over the years – and it was wisdom that I tended to apply way too infrequently – was that sometimes the best answer was no answer at all. Keeping my expression blank, I coiled lines, sorted gear and watched her out of the corner of my eye.

After a few minutes, her accusatory glare/stare crumbled just as quickly as the smile, and she started crying loudly, more like blubbering. For the second time in my life, I wished I had a gun. This was one high-maintenance woman. Gloria poked her head out of the marina supply shed and stared curiously from Brenda to me. Finally, apparently deciding that it had to be my fault, Gloria settled on a "What's wrong with you!" frown before shaking her head and ducking back into the supply shed.

I kept coiling lines and thinking that this Brenda just might be a perfect match for Mike.

Meanwhile, Brenda was working up her story, one I was going to hear at least once a week for the next year. Amid loud, Mary Tyler Moore (Oh, Rob!) sobs, she told me and the rest of the marina how she had walked away from her cold, uncaring husband, away from her unhappy, suburban home, complete with twice-a-week cleaning lady, away from her two unappreciative kids, to come down and become Chicago Mike's bunkie. (She must have liked the word bunkie, because she said it at least a dozen times.)

I just wanted to get away from her, so I suggested she might find him at The Sunset. "Ask for Jason. He'll know." Then I turned my back and went below.

Two hours later, I went to the bar for our standing Monday evening rendezvous with the rest of the ex-pats. I bumped into Chicago Mike on the way in and didn't think anything of it.

Mike saw the situation first. Brenda was there, perky, clean, and smiling, as if she were ready for a tennis match at the country club. Patti the Beast was there, too.

Chicago pulled up short so fast when he saw Brenda that I almost tripped over him. When Brenda saw Chicago Mike, she gave him a big, happy, cute-as-a-bug perky smile, called, "Hi!" waved like a six-year-old, and raced over to throw her arms around him.

I should be ashamed to admit it, but my first thought was, "This is gonna be good."

Patti the Beast at first just watched. Then slowly rising, she set out in the direction of Mike and Brenda. She moved, slow and determined, like that steam locomotive building up speed. I knew I wouldn't see the green flash this afternoon, but I had a strong suspicion I just might see some blood.

Patti the Beast wasn't known as Patti the Beast because she was a sweetheart. Hell, I was afraid of her, all 300 pounds of her. With glaringly platinum blonde hair (Lea called her "peroxide head"), a too-tight black tank top, and wrinkled mid-thigh shorts, a round, triple-chin, balloon-clown legs, and a corpse-white complexion set off by bright red lipstick and thick, black mascara, she had an attitude that made puppies pee just by looking at them. Even Black Mike steered clear of Patti the Beast.

Chicago and Patti the Beast were a perfect couple. She ordered him around, bullied him, and threatened him, while he, for the most part, ignored her as best he could, and had mastered the art of ducking fast when necessary. Thank God Patti was fat and slow. Speed was Mike's best defense, his only defense.

French Tony had once said, "Could you imagine their sex life?"

I couldn't, and didn't want to. "Picture having sex with an ugly rhinoceros," I suggested.

"An ugly rhinoceros?" Tony asked. "I don't think I've ever seen a pretty one."

"Yes," was all I said.

Once, when Patti was out of earshot, Chicago had said that Patti had to be the stupidest thing on two legs. Then he had paused and thought about it before adding, "Correction, let's include four-legged critters, too." That was the day I realized he loved it. He was having a ball, and this sicko relationship with Patti was mother's milk to Mike.

"If they were going to name a Chinese condiment after Mike and Patti," Squint had once said, "they'd call it Mean 'n Sour sauce." One glance at Patti, and there was no doubt which was the mean one.

So, when Blah Blah Brenda, as she got to be known after that night, saw Chicago come in, she ran to him and put her arms around him. Mike watched Patti out of the corner of his eye, and he was starting to panic. Acutely aware of the danger, he clawed at Brenda's arms as if he were being enveloped by an octopus or a hangman's noose. So, all eyes went to Patti, watching as she got out of her chair with an immense effort and slowly wide-stepped over to where they were standing, her fat arms flailing side to side as she walked.

I snugged up on a barstool out of blood-spatter range and took my drink from Jason without ever taking my eyes off Patti.

"Ten bucks on the Beast," Jason whispered.

"No takers," I said out of the side of my mouth. "This is gonna be gruesome."

Well, Patti the Beast straightened Brenda out and fast. That night, it was dinner and a show. Not much can beat a girl fight on a beer-soaked barroom floor. Well, maybe it's an acquired taste, but no one could say it wasn't interesting.

Patti got up close into Brenda's face and just stood there, breathing through her nose, glaring at Brenda.

"Can I help you?" Brenda asked, using that arch tone that only women ordering a wedge salad in an upscale restaurant can master, and looking at Patti with contempt. Brenda apparently thought that the basic rules of civil behavior applied down here, and one of those rules was that women didn't knock other women's teeth out.

Patti didn't say a word at first. Without warning, she grabbed Brenda by the throat and slowly squeezed. Patti's eyes glowed with fury. Brenda's bulged with fear.

Jason made a slow move for his billy club. I turned and shook my head. "Nah, she only kills when she's hungry, and she already ate today," I said.

Jason smiled and straightened up, but still kept close to the club.

Patti, nose to nose, stared into Brenda's eyes. Tears were starting to run down Brenda's face.

"Please. Let me go," Brenda managed to get out in a pleading, terrified tone.

Patti growled, "Stay away from Mike. He's not much, but he's mine. Understand?"

Wincing, Brenda nodded.

"Good."

Then, still slowly (hell, Patti only had one speed: slow), she pressed Brenda down onto the sandy floor in what seemed like the prelude to an interesting sexual act. Jason and I looked at each other, eyebrows raised, and shrugged like this is going to get even more interesting than we had imagined.

Brenda, both hands on Patti's huge arm, staggered slowly to her knees, looking like she was praying for mercy. I think she was.

"Do ... you ... understand?" Patti repeated, shaking Brenda's head back and forth with each word.

"I think she just wet her pants," French Tony whispered, but loud enough for everyone to hear. Everyone except Chicago eyed Brenda up and down to see if it was true.

Chicago, always a deep thinker, who prided himself on being one step ahead of the village folks with torches, was looking unnerved and probably wondering when Patti would finish with Brenda and get around to skinning and deboning him. He began easing toward the hedge where Tom and Jerry lived. Tom and Jerry were the bar's three-foot iguanas, ugly things that spent their days waiting for table scraps from *touristas* sitting at tables along the hedge. Most smart people steer clear of iguanas. They have razor-sharp teeth like a serrated steak knife. Fortunately, Tom and Jerry were considered to be domesticated. In other words, they knew where their steak scraps were grilled, so they were generally pleasant.

Apparently smarter than the average iguana, however, they took an instant dislike to Patti the Beast the first time they saw her. So, when she had gotten within a few feet of their hedge, they had lit out after her with a vengeance, chasing her down the street. "Hmmm. Didn't know she could run that fast," was all that Chicago Mike had said. Oh, that and, "Give me another scotch. Patti will settle up when she gets back."

So, Mike was smart to take up a position near the iguana hedge.

My eyes were roaming the bar, until I noticed French Tony. While most of us were laughing, or at least smiling, he was staring at Patti and Brenda with what appeared to be a full range of emotions – from anger to sadness to fascination. As I watched him, he apparently came to a decision. Setting his jaw with resolve, he loudly flat-handed the table. Shooting up out of his seat like a pistol shot, he marched toward Patti.

"That's enough!" He ordered. "Knock it off!" Though Patti had him by at least 130 pounds, Tony nailed her with a glare that offered no compromise. *Touristas* in the restaurant were staring, fascinated. Others – lawyers and preachers and weekend transvestites, who preferred that their names not appear in police reports – were herding their families and assorted companions to the parking lot, skirting the drama scene. Though Jason never took his eyes off Patti and Tony, his right shoulder dipped again as he gripped his billy club. I nodded. "I agree. This could get dicey."

Patti the Beast, still leaning over Brenda, looked at Tony for a long moment before hesitating and then releasing Brenda and preparing to confront Tony.

"Thank you. That's enough, okay?" Tony said evenly, like a mediator in a hostage situation. He nodded slightly, softening his face into the hint of a smile.

Patti just stared, and we could hear her breathing, the bull getting ready to attack.

Tony, still eyeing Patti, reached out a hand to the sniffling Brenda kneeling on the floor. Patti looked down and then slowly turned away from Brenda.

Brenda gratefully took Tony's hand and just about sprang to her feet to stand shoulder to shoulder with him. A you-can't-get-me-now smile crossed her face as Tony backed them both out of Patti range.

Patti just stared, pulled her knife out of her waistband and held it up for Brenda to see. "Someday, sweetheart," she said, with a dark smile before looking around for Chicago Mike.

Tony led Brenda to a small plastic table and two chairs out on the sand.

Patti spotted Mike. "Come here, Mister," she said. Still edging along the iguana hedge, he froze and, after a moment's hesitation looking around for Tom and Jerry, who were missing, meekly obeyed. We all settled in for round two, but Patti just grabbed his hand and took him outside and out of earshot into the parking lot.

"Someone's gonna get a spanking tonight," Kid announced.

And that was it. Crisis averted. Go on home, folks; nothing to see here. Everybody moved on to other island gossip. About half an hour later, Chicago Mike, looking slightly disheveled, and Patti the Beast joined the table like nothing had ever happened.

This kind of stuff reminded me that island life was like living in a small town back in the States. Everybody knew everybody else and everybody else's business. You could get into a knock-down-drag-out fight with your neighbor on Tuesday over his dog pooping on your yard, and then buy him a drink at the tavern on Friday night. We just couldn't afford grudges. We didn't have to like each other, but we did have to get along.

**

I worked hard to treat the excursion business like a business. I'd pick up my cargo of 16 cruise line passengers at the excursion dock at 8:15 in the morning, ferry them out of the lagoon, then unfurl the sails, billowing and then snapping full. Then we'd sail to the reef off Random Cay, giving them ninety minutes of carefully planned snorkeling adventure before pulling up anchor, pouring rum punches, and getting them back to the dock by 12:30 so they wouldn't miss their all-included lunch aboard the ship. On the good days in the high season, I'd then pick up my next batch of sun and sea adventure seekers for the afternoon excursion.

It was just business. That's why I prefer these days to stay away from the women and talk mostly to the guys. Besides, Bonita was good enough, a pleasant companion; more and more, I was less and less hungry for sights unseen. The men usually wanted to jawbone about the financial logistics of island life, from how I got down here (*Oh, I just headed out one day and never looked back*) to whether it was true that there was no crime on the island (*Absolutely none; still, it was always good to be careful. Oh, and keep your valuables in the safe in your room*) to how to make a living down here (*Well, you don't get rich in the islands, but the lifestyle is fabulous. Or you could buy a boat. That's what I did*). They'd ask, "Was it expensive to live down here?" (*It can be, but not if you have nothing and need nothing. Life is simpler down here*.) "Based on what we paid for this excursion, you must clear about $800 a day." (*Some days, but it's still gross, not net*.) "Do you have insurance?" (*Of course*, referring to Arnold, the fileting knife on my hip and the bogus certificate the cruise line representatives required in order to work with them.) "Could you trust the help?" (*Absolutely; the islanders have a natural sense of integrity ... and you have nothing to steal*.) "What if I bought a place and just used it in winter?" (*Sure, a lot of folks do just that, or they go with a timeshare. If you're interested, I know a guy you might want to talk to*.) "Or turned it into rental property? Or used it as a tax deduction?" Etc. Etc. Etc.

The key – again, I'm talking tips here – was to both titillate and stay at a bit of a distance from the wives. Cat Neil, from whom I bought *The Do Over* when she was known as *Sun 'n Fun*, once got tossed overboard by a snarling, irate husband, a burly, retired marine. Lesson learned: Think twice before accepting the invitation to put sun screen on the hottie wife's back ... or any wife's back, for that matter.

The truly best, most enjoyable excursion guests were the older couples. The guys had no fear and no ego challenges, and the wives giggled and played along when we rubbed up against them. "Hey, Baby, I'm looking for a new First Mate. Dump your hubby and come live with me. We'll have cold beer and hot sex every night."

The husbands would laugh and put their arms around some girl 30 years younger. "Go for it, Maude, I'll get by somehow."

And everyone would laugh and drink, and have fun. *Ka-ching*.

But back to the wives. They were on vacation from their routine lives, too, and I suspect we were part of the vacation package. It was the lean, rebuilt ones, usually in their 50s, with grown kids and the freedom of menopause, who loved the ersatz danger of toying with us. These were the same ones, some of us ex-pats fantasized, who fantasized about being kidnapped and forced to do it both ways by tattooed bikers, and then serve breakfast too. Still, the wives wanted to be noticed, and they noticed when we noticed. Some would settle down in the sun on the bow, quietly shake out of their bikini tops, lie back, and sun their breasts as if it were something they did every day in the backyard of their suburban homes. They were purposeful, though we never quite were sure what their purpose was. These also were the ones who'd flirt and chat and sometimes ask deliberately dumb, girlish questions about the boat, half teasing, half hoping we'd give them … give them what? Something to dream about before they'd roll over and doze off after a pretend-fun ride from their doughboy, sunburned, super-successful attorney hubbies? I no longer tried to figure it out. I just tried to steer clear.

I was in it for the tips, not the tits.

I did notice that most of them seemed to long for attention, as long as CPA hubby was within shouting distance. Because they were also a little afraid that we might be for real, not phony Hemingway wannabes. They wanted safe, little pony rides masquerading as adventure. That's what we gave them – half-day snorkeling excursions, timed just right to get them back to their cruise ships for the open-seating noon meal or ice sculpting lessons on the pool deck.

Still, with some, a quick wink or a touch of the arm while we were showing them how to put on their snorkel gear, and you could almost hear that deep, low moan-groan. And all I'm thinking is *Ka-ching*! Another tenner in the tip can.

The key was to know when to let up, because the big tips came from the men – ask any waitress in a restaurant, as he flips a large bill on the table, versus the gaggle of women who pull out calculators and divvy up the check, tipping ten percent tops for good service – as long as they weren't pissed or felt threatened by these tanned island guys with no shirts and hide-the-stares sunglasses.

THE STATES
The Divorce Chronicles

I really did not miss my life back in the States. Still, I had clung to it for a long time as if it mattered, like when I was a kid and couldn't bring myself to bury my dead parakeet for three days. I guess that's my own kind of Rock Fever. That was back when I thought things were important, that things had significance, that history mattered, that staying up to midnight on New Year's Eve was something we had to do. There was something about investing 25 years in something that was supposed to give it gravitas. Or so I thought. I was wrong. But I didn't know it then. Another freakin' myth.

When Natty was seven, she'd fallen face first off her bike into the driveway. I was the first one to her and almost, but not quite, got there in time. My gut rolled when I saw her scraped face, grated nose, one tooth hanging on her bloody lip. I was scared to death. Let me repeat that: I was scared to death. But Connie, right on my heels and all confused, all she saw was anger as I scooped up Natty and brushed past her to the car in a furious rush to get to the hospital. I wasn't angry, not mad at somebody angry. I was scared to death. That was fifteen years before the Great Divide, fifteen years before I told a shocked, surprised Connie that I was as miserable and unhappy as she was, that she wasn't the only one in this self-absorbed drama.

I think that, in spite of what some women say, men do love deeply, perhaps more deeply than women do. But we also hide it more deeply. That's why our wives think we're cold or just don't care as much. Usually, we carry our pain around more quietly. We run a mile, chop a cord of wood, fix the screen door, take the dog for a walk, smoke too many cigarettes, stare at a television, take the dog for another walk, or drink. Or we get angry. That's the best way to keep from feeling pain. It blocks out how scared we are. Connie never understood that.

Last Call

W hen Scott heard about what happened with me and Connie, he got real quiet, and I could see he went inside himself. He was thinking about Jo. This bit of news didn't fit into his known world. Mine either. The four of us had been kiss-the-other-guy's-wife close. Nothing kinky or anything, though Scott and I had sometimes good naturedly poked around at the idea, usually between the second and fourth drink. I think we would have done it, too. Who knows? But we knew the girls wouldn't. So, we were safe to talk all we wanted, as long as it wasn't in front of the wives.

Connie and I had been separated for two months, and Scott was the first person I'd told. I'm not even sure why I brought it up. Maybe it was because, for the last twenty years, we'd had one thing in common. We were both crazy nuts in love with our wives. Not that it showed to anybody else. We knew it. Jo knew it about Scott. And I thought Connie knew it about me. That's one reason – yes, there are others – why guys like Scott and I worked endless hours, and that's why we came home every night, sometimes late. Wasn't that enough? I guess not.

I had always thought the idea was to build safe walls to protect them from all the dangerous things we knew were out there. I guess Connie got to see those walls as a prison trying to keep her in. That's what I mean about men and women. They have a hard time seeing the same thing in the same way.

The bartender, a hot-and-tarty looking blonde barely old enough to drink herself, let alone pour drinks for us, put the next round in front of us and lingered just long enough to look deeply into Scott's eyes. I'd seen that look dozens of times before, and it cracked me up. I'm one of those guys who is average when it comes to looks. That's it. Average. But Scott, he has that electric something that causes people to make a sudden turn to the left or right. They notice him and either veer away or move in close.

And I always got a kick watching how people reacted when they'd first meet him. He looked dangerous, the kind of dangerous that makes women turn their heads with a gaze like they'd give up anything for one hour under his command. But in all the years I've known him, I never once saw him look back. Men who didn't know him stepped out of his way when he strolled into a room. Or they moved a little closer to their wives. Then they'd hear his affable laugh and their glares softened. He was an innocent, though he looked more like an outlaw biker than Mr. Middle Class who spent weekends trying to figure out how to get chinch bugs out of his lawn.

One time, just the two of us, after a few beers, he started giggling and said, "Ya know, Joth, I just don't understand what all this fuss is about battered women. I've been eating mine plain for years." Then he giggled some more, and it was the most innocent sound you'd ever heard. The idea that some couples took swings at each other, or that somebody might have been offended by the joke, just never occurred to him. And that was Scott. He could tell a joke like that and nobody, not even the women in the room, took offense.

My point is that he looked rough, and he talked rough. But he adored Jo, adored as in worshipped. Just as he knew I adored Connie, at least back then.

So, when I told him about Connie and me, he got quiet. Then he screwed up his face and looked me hard in the eye for a second just to make sure I wasn't pulling his leg or that he was sitting next to the right guy. When I lowered my head, he followed my gaze, let out a loud breath, and stared while I peeled the layers off my coaster.

THE ISLAND
Blah Blah Brenda

That night at the Sunset, like a beaten dog hoping to be adopted by a good owner, Brenda forgot about Chicago Mike and fell madly in love with French Tony. I figured it had something to do with him being her hero. But Jason later said it was because he bought her a few drinks and listened for the rest of the night while she unloaded her life story on him, nonstop.

And she really did go on and on and on. A couple of us – actually, all of us – took the long way to the restrooms, veering out onto the sand and past Tony and Brenda's table. From what we could tell, Tony did all the listening, while Brenda did all the talking. I could see his expression go from delighted, to interested, to listening, to barely listening, to trying to stay awake, to pure boredom.

Later, when by some unspoken signal everybody got up to leave, Tony and Brenda were still sitting at the table in the sand. Patti the Beast and Chicago Mike led the pack. As they looped past Brenda and Tony on their way to their car, Patti paused.

Jason, cleaning up, shook his head at Patti, as if saying, Please, no more trouble. Patti ignored him.

Brenda, talking about how hard it was living in a gated community in a Kansas City suburb, was so absorbed in her own story that, at first, she never saw Patti. Tony did, and he kept a wary eye on her.

Noticing someone out of the corner of her eye and thinking it was the waitress waiting for her next order, Brenda ignored Patti for a few moments.

"So, I patiently explained to the salesman, again," she was telling Tony, "that I had ordered both remote starter *and* separate, driver and passenger, heated seats. Not just the remote starter. I asked him, 'Are you new around here?' As anybody knows, you cannot survive a Kansas winter without heated seats. Do you believe it? They'll hire anybody."

Tony was already learning that no response was necessary. He was also realizing that there were two Brendas. One was the snotty suburban bitch. The other was the sniveling, crying child. And she could go from bitch to child and back again in two seconds flat. "Holy crap! No wonder her husband never came down to try to bring her back home," Tony told me several months later. "He sure as hell got the better end of the deal."

Finally, still without looking up, Brenda picked up her glass and dangled it to show it was empty. "Another margarita, double salt," she said dismissively. When the shadow beside her that she thought was the waitress didn't move, Brenda finally looked up, ready to straighten out the hired help. Patti was standing so close that Brenda could see into her flaring nostrils. Brenda froze in terror. Tony just leaned back and watched this time, not sure that, after hours of suffering through Brenda's life story, he wanted to get into it with Patti again. He later told me that most of us could condense our life stories into three minutes max. Brenda, three hours into hers, showed no sign of wrapping up. Worse, it had not been an all-that-interesting life.

Patti just stared for a good thirty seconds, and I began to think that Brenda just might wet her pants again. Finally, Patti snorted and heaved her shoulders upward, which made Brenda jump. Then shaking her head as if to say that this bug wasn't worth squashing, Patti turned to Tony and loudly said, "Blah. Blah. Blah. Does she ever shut up? Blah. Blah. Blah."

Patti then clumsily marched across the sand toward the parking lot, first giving Mike a glance to show that he was expected to follow.

"Heel, boy," Kid whispered. "Good boy."

Without giving it a thought, the rest of us all marched out, single file, past Tony and Brenda's table in the sand.

"Good night, Blah Blah. Good night, Tony," we said one after the other, leaving the two new love birds to walk alone together on the beach and later watch the sunrise … or whatever it was that new love birds did.

Actually, word had it that Brenda wasn't done yet. Tony ended up listening for hours. I figure Brenda unloaded decades of nobody listening to a word she'd said. There was good reason. She had nothing whatsoever worth listening to. After that night, Tony stopped listening to her too, but it didn't matter. She latched onto him and never let go. Actually, she became a major asset in working with the customers in Tony's *Risqué Island* X-rated T-shirt shop. She knew how to sell and convince them to buy.

Still, it wasn't long before, outside the shop, he was treating her like shit, but she tagged along like a mindless puppy. I guess that's because being Blah Blah Brenda on the islands was still better than being Blah Blah Brenda, even without the official title, back in the burbs … along with all the other Blah Blah neighbors.

The next day, I put up the sign, Even A Lousy Day in Paradise is Better than a Great Day Back Home, over the tip bucket on the boat. *Ka-ching*.

Runaways & Castaways

A s I said, I admired Jason. He was steady and level-headed, with a friendly, all-American look and a billy club never more than two steps from his right hand below the bar. He was a truly professional bartender. According to Calabash, he was the only mixologist on the island who knew how to make a decent straight-up Manhattan.

True to the bartender's code, Jason could talk philosophy or sex. But he never got into politics, and rarely discussed himself or his own life. "My job is to listen, not talk," he'd told me after we got to be friends.

Other than that, he had no history. Still, after one quiet evening of trading shots, he had once mentioned that he was from St. Louis. When I asked how he ended up on the island, he'd smiled broadly and said, "I came down for three weeks. That was, let's see, four years ago."

***

It was almost sundown, so I perched myself in a wobbly plastic chair, lit a cigarette, and looked to the western sky, really not expecting to see the green flash, but looking nonetheless. I think that's called hope. Mostly, it was the white sand, the blue Caribbean, and the clean, clear sky that I just enjoyed looking at. Sam would have loved this, I thought. Then I smiled and shook my head. It had been 27 years, since high school. So, why did I still and always think of Samantha when I watched a sunset on a beach? She had not been a mythical ideal, just a beautiful, loving woman-girl. Maybe that had all been my imagination. Just one more myth. But I didn't think so.

Maybe it was because she had not loved me for who I could be, was supposed to be, or just simply wasn't. I don't think she loved me because I was dangerous or sweet or part of the in-crowd. I guess she loved me for who I was, as I was. The funny thing is that she knew who I was, even though I sure as hell didn't back then ... or even now, I guess. As for that kind of pure caring, is it even possible outside of high school? I doubted it. Like the green flash, it was a myth.

Most of all, she had never posed the question, the question all females, it seems, get around to asking eventually, or at least asking me. Some say it out loud. Some just give a look and think it. But it's the most painful question a guy ever hears: "What's wrong with you?" What makes it so painful is that it means the woman he almost desperately needs to believe in him does not. It means she does not see him as the steely-eyed noble knight on the hoof-stomping steed. It means she sees him as just a guy, and guys hate that. Not a hero or great and powerful protector. Just a guy. Or maybe less than a guy.

Some women snarl or spit it out with icy, unbelieving contempt: "What's *wrong* with you?" Others just shake their heads, purse their lips and seem puzzled, like we're some kind of odd looking bug. Most of all, we're not what they had expected or hoped we'd be. That's why some women say it slowly, almost confused, maybe pityingly gentle: "What's wrong with you?" And it destroys us, if only because it strips away the myth of who we wish to be, want to be, desperately delude ourselves into believing we are or can be.

One exception was my mother, who, though she used to say it to me, used to laugh lovingly when she did, often comparing me, quite unfavorably, I might add, to the family dog: "What's wrong with you, Jimmy?" she'd say and laugh. "I swear, son, sometimes I think Penelope has more sense than you do."

The other exception was Sam, who seemed to like me just the way I was, like I was perfect and without any need of being fixed or changed. As for Bonita, still with me for now, well, maybe she just didn't know me well enough yet or still hadn't found the words or the look.

***

The sun disappeared. No green flash. Nothing. Just instant darkness. On the islands, there was no dusk. One minute it was day, the next night. Poof. I shrugged and ambled back to the bar, ending up standing next to the three topless girls.

"Well?" Jason asked, anticipating my order and placing my next drink loudly on the bar beside one of the girls.

I stood at the bar, my bare feet sifting through the light covering of sand on the floor tiles, and my bare skin just brushing the arm of the blonde on the end. "I tell ya, man, it's a myth. It does not exist." The girl, she was one of Black Mike's latest arrivals from the States, turned and gave me her best beauty-pageant, whore-on-the-clock smile, making me forget for a second that she and her friends worked for Black Mike, and the bigger the smile, the bigger the tips. *Ka-ching …*

"What's a myth?" she asked.

"Exactly," I agreed and focused on my drink, but wondering what Blondie sitting next to me was running away from.

***

We all dream of running away. Some women used to talk about a room of their own, something I had never understood. Connie had pretty much owned the whole house. I was grateful for the garage, my man cave, and the pre-fab, green and tan molded plastic shed beside the compost pile. Plus, there was the lawnmower, whose loud sound helped me tune out distractions and just let my own thoughts rattle around in peace. A lot of men hid inside that noise. I pity the men who have convinced themselves – or been convinced by their wives – that they should hire the neighbor kid to cut the lawn. Lawn mowing is therapy.

Of course, maybe it had something to do with the fact that most men, just being ourselves, had the gift of being able to drive women crazy … and, no, not in a good way. When I was a kid, we had neighbors, Marlene and Joe. They seemed to be happily married, as happily married as most folks. But every now and then, Marlene would slam a kitchen towel down on the counter and say, "Joe, why don't you go to a movie tonight?"

I guess that's because men can be notorious re-arrangers, fixers, problem-solvers. We're wonderfully helpful, especially with things nobody asked us to help them with. We move things without notice, bring home surprise puppies, upgrade things without being asked, even if they don't need upgrading. So, I guess I do understand about women wanting a room of their own. We drive them crazy. I wonder if they truly know how mutual it is.

So, some women need space. Then there are some who, like men, need an escape, a complete break, a do over. These are the ones who, when they're really being honest, maybe like topless Blondie here, fantasize about chucking the Sunday school straight life and coming down to the islands. And speaking of Black Mike's topless blondes, one of the things I learned was that Black Mike didn't need to manipulate, coerce or seduce his girls with drugs, threats or even money. Mike only had one condition: His girls had to dye their hair a ferocious platinum blonde. So, they came to him, sought him out, stayed as long as they wanted, and then went home … sometimes. These were the white girls from the States. They came down to escape a dull life. Then most of them went home, married a middle manager, and explained that they'd been bartenders down on some island that they never expressed an interest in visiting again.

All that crap about poor little victims being seduced into a life of prostitution. Sorry, but everything I saw indicated that that was a snow job, another myth, like the idea of people getting eaten by sharks on a daily basis. Maybe that happened in other places – in fact, I'm sure it did – but not here.

Maybe it was a way of justifying their choices, an excuse that made it possible for them to go home again when they were ready. I used to hear about women who fantasized about being kidnapped by a biker gang and forced to be their sex slaves. I'm not sure how true that is – it does sound more like a fantasy made up by teenage boys. Still, I've seen rough-looking biker babes clinging to the back of some dude's Harley and proudly sporting those tattoos that read *Property of West Des Moines Biker Club*.

Sure, guys can be such dogs, but it's also good to see that some women – either out of courage or total disillusionment, or both – get to do the fun, kinky stuff, too. And then they get to say that they had no choice, that they were victims, or that they had just tended bar somewhere in Fresno or St. Kitts or Juneau.

That's another reason I liked Bonita. Like Henry Ford (or maybe it was Benjamin Disraeli), she never saw the need to explain or to complain. She never seemed to give a rat's ass what anyone else thought.

So, when it came to Black Mike's topless blondes or other by-the-hour ladies, it turned out that many had left behind carefully laid-out career paths, pantyhose and black heels, manicured lawns, well-behaved husbands, late-model cars, scheduled, romantic date nights, and January diets to drop those pesky ten pounds before bikini season.

The less adventurous, more timid ones, they stayed home and quietly drank or relied on pain killer prescriptions, traveling in dreams if not reality. Or they dedicated themselves to community service and a periodic, discreet affair that no one ever, ever heard about.

Some, like Patti the Beast, a hideous example of a human being, had even left behind children, or so it was rumored. It was also rumored that Black Mike wouldn't take Patti. Can't blame him. Besides being fat, mean and ugly … well, she was fat, mean and ugly. She scared most of us.

But those were the white girls from the States who headed south, often quietly desperate to escape sheer boredom.

Then there were the girls from the brothel on the road to Dawn Beach. Some of them eventually ended up at Yvonne's Place. These were the brown and black girls who came north from other islands or from South America. They came to escape a truly awful and dangerous life, trading up for one that was just hard and unpleasant. Yvonne, who it is rumored came out of the brothel herself, helped them pay off their debts and buy their freedom.

So, I guess some women fantasize about the freedom of getting into a brothel; others dream about the freedom of getting out of one.

Men? I think we're pretty simple. And shallow. As simple, shallow, and instinctive as dogs. Most of the guys I know fantasize about nothing more kinky than a weekend in Las Vegas with a leggy showgirl wrapped all over them ... maybe two showgirls after a really bad week at the office. I even knew one guy, a sawed-off little ego-maniac doctor who acted like he knew everything about everything, whose wife had once had way too much to drink and showed me the pacifier she kept in her purse. When I'd looked confused, she said, "You oughta see his pink diapers."

Weird fantasies aside, some men come to the islands to pretend it's real, to find themselves, to reinvent themselves, or just to lose themselves. Most of the ones who stay just have no place else to go, and they end up as rummies like John/Candy.

Then there was Dave. He's a police chief from a small town in Northern Wisconsin. He comes down by himself for two weeks twice a year. He'd arrive as Dave, a clear-eyed, straight-arrow, big chested peace officer, with close cropped hair. Once on the island, he'd step into his room and, two hours later, come out as sweet, long-haired, doe-eyed Daisy. Then, after two weeks, he'd pack up, switch out the lace panties and make-up for striped boxers and an NSA T-shirt, go back home and be Chief Dave again. Lea, one of the lesbian girls, said Daisy had a wife and kids back home. The wife knew about his *need*, as Lea described it. Daisy had become friends with Penny and Lea. She enjoyed sipping white wine with them, wearing flowing gowns, perfume and make-up, talking about fashion, and painting at their gallery in whimsical pastels. Now and then, she'd sing a duet with Joel, the transvestite owner of L'escargot. Apparently, there was nothing sexual about it.

Though none of the women seemed to care, some of the guys on the island were uncomfortable about Daisy/Dave. A few even made a pass at him, and were quickly straightened out.

I had no opinion at first. Finally, I came to the conclusion that very few people got to do what Daisy/Dave got to do – just be. And for that, I admired her … or him … or … doesn't really matter, I guess.

MANGROVE COVE
Better'n Sex

The hurricane was coming and coming fast. The forecast was for it to run right over the island. You could feel it. The air was thick and blustery, snotty is the word sailors use when they want to impress landlubbers. And while the rest of the island was battening down, I was heading out.

I turned and faced the bow, both hands on the wheel. And then my mind just stopped. Hurricanes and debts and ex-wives all sat down, strapped in, and shut up. This was my favorite part of the day, any day, even better than sex. At the wheel. My heart raced in pure joy as I motored across the lagoon. I was exactly where I was supposed to be, and doing exactly what I wanted to do.

The wind was picking up, starting to gust hard. I looked up. I always looked up, not so much to check the rigging or the wind rag, but because I loved the sight of the lines and guy wires and, today, the unfriendly, heavy clouds. The wind was singing through the rigging.

I gunned the engine and spun the wheel, whipped it around as hard and fast as it could go. Just for grins, I did a 360 degree turn for the folks who were watching from the dock and wondering what this madman was doing setting out from the safety of the almost completely enclosed lagoon, out into the Caribbean Sea. *The Do Over*, as always, responded quickly. There was nothing sluggish about her. Even though she was a tad flat-footed because she was a cat and the cabin was slung wide between her two coffin-like pontoon hulls, she never pounded or plowed through the waves, but slid and slipped gracefully through them, as if she were as joyful as I was about heading out to sea. She was that topless newly-wed who trusted me enough not to screw it up or ask her to do more than she was comfortable doing.

I grinned at the crowd at the dock. Everybody was moving tables and chairs inside and taping up windows and hanging up plywood in prep for the big blow. As I headed through the drawbridge and out into the open water, a wondrous calm came over me. The thought of being afraid never occurred to me. If I were to die, this was how I would want to do it, at the helm of *The Do Over*, out on the sea. But I had no intention of dying.

Hurricane Olive

I was three hours out of harbor and probing the edges of Mangrove Cove looking for that channel, when I heard Kid behind me say, "It's left about a hundred yards."

I nearly jumped out of my skin and swore a blue streak about the sexual virtue of his mother. Then we both just grinned at each other. Someday I had to learn his full name, or even his first name. But fair was fair – he probably had no idea who I was either. Just Cap'm Jolly.

"You weren't supposed to come, you idiot!"

"Uh huh." He smiled, lifted the cooler top, and pulled out two beers, which was strictly against the rules while under way.

Anticipating my rebuke, he shrugged and said, "We're both gonna die, anyway, Cap'm. I wanna die drunk."

The wind was gusting hard, and the rain was starting to sting in big splats.

"How'd you get on board?"

"Bonita covered for me. While she was doing her foot-stomping whining, I slipped back on."

Well, that explained it. Honestly, I was glad he'd stowed away. I took a beer and pretended to be pissed, but I couldn't pull it off.

"You know we're gonna die, right?" I asked.

He shrugged. "Eventually, yes. I'd rather die doing this out here than riding out the storm sitting on a cot in some concrete bunker waiting for my lunch of SPAM-on-stale sandwich."

"You didn't stow your latest bunkie along, too, did you?" I asked, scanning the boat for signs of female life.

"Nah," he said, swinging topside, hanging onto the mast, and pointing to the channel opening. "She decided to get off the island before the hurricane hit, go back to Bubba in Jacksonville."

"Disappointed?"

"Nah, not really. Cap'm, we're getting shallow. Want I should pull the skegs?" As I wheeled around, a gust hit him hard and almost knocked him off his feet. He braced himself and we exchanged surprised, slightly nervous glances. This was going to be one helluva blow. I wondered for a moment whether I maybe should have just abandoned *The Do Over* and headed for high ground with Bonita.

But I knew I couldn't have done that. "Yeah, good idea." I was heading out more to save the boat than to protect myself. I couldn't have imagined leaving her tied to the dock, or even mooring her out in the middle of the lagoon and leaving her. Loyalty? Didn't know for sure. Didn't care, for sure. Unlike most novels I've read, life doesn't have a logical plot. It has lots of loose ends and unanswered questions.

Kid swung below deck to crank up the two stabilizer skegs, a fancy word for retractable keels.

While he scampered around, I eased into the cove and thought about my boat. *The Do Over* is mine, bought and paid for with cash on the binnacle. She's my 38-foot sailing catamaran, with two tall hulls. The rest of the cabin, with galley, head, and common quarters, straddles each hull, sitting about three feet out of the water. The open bow is rigged with strong webbing slung between the hulls, with enough room for up to sixteen people, which was the maximum number I took on half-day snorkeling excursions around the reef or on beach barbecues over on Bird's Nest Cay.

Our personal cabins were in the two hulls. As I mentioned earlier, the starboard side was mine. Kid lived on the port side. I kind of thought of each hull as a long, narrow coffin.

She's wide enough that she sails flat-footed, and I almost never ask her to heel over onto one hull and do tricks. She's not that kind of lady.

The wind was starting to whip. When Kid came back on deck, I tossed him a life vest. He hated to wear them. So did I.

"Put it on!" I ordered, sounding like a skipper.

"Only if you wear the bike helmet," he grinned, referring to past conversations we'd had about safety gear.

"Put it on."

Standing with his feet planted topside, he grinned, then shrugged into his vest and snapped it closed. Holding onto the helm, which was starting to fight me, I did the same.

"Why are we doing this again?" he shouted over the rising wind.

"I have no idea," I shouted with a grin, knowing it was the only and best thing to do.

Kid grinned back at me. "Quick question."

I grunted.

"I know the captain goes down with his ship. How about the first mate?"

"I'll check the rule book," I shouted. "But I'm pretty sure the first mate and captain go down together, wrapped in a love embrace."

"Can you just set me adrift in a lifeboat?" Kid offered. "Or feed me to the sharks?"

"I vote sharks. Better entertainment value."

Kid nodded at the wisdom of that. "Okay. Thanks. Just wanted to clarify that."

This beat some thumb-thumping video game or a three-on-three pickup game of hoops at the local high school gym. Or golf. This wasn't pretend. We might not get another do over if we screwed it up. And that was what I think really charged us up. We both paused and looked at each other, grinning like idiots.

Then we settled down to work. I swung the boat around inside the channel and held her steady while Kid set two anchors, one off the bow and the other off the stern. We had eight more lines to go before the storm hit. And it looked like it was going to hit hard.

THE STATES
Crossing the Street Without Permission

When I was five, back in the Ozone Park section of Queens, New York, I had packed up Jocko, my stuffed monkey and best friend, headed down the red-brick back steps, down the driveway, down the block, and announced to the neighbors that I was moving in. I even crossed the street without permission. Gutsy! Mom came and got me ten minutes later. I was disappointed. It wasn't even that I liked the neighbors especially or that Mrs. Lynch was a good cook. She wasn't.

It was a feeling that infected me, consumed me, instantly and completely took over my soul. This good and warm feeling stayed with me, has never left me, that feeling of taking charge, of getting away, of crossing the street without permission, of turning my back on bad endings and heading away, of heading anywhere, anywhere, toward new beginnings. From that day, that feeling has always been inside me. I'd see a road and wonder how far it ran, a river and try to imagine where it ended, a plane in the sky and just wonder. That feeling never left me ... ever. Though I suppressed it – and did so without complaint – it tugged at me even during my long and mostly placid domestic years with Connie.

Maybe it was that same kind of overwhelming desire that drove Chief Dave to slip down to the islands twice a year and become Miss Daisy.

I still remember that Ozone Park feeling 40 years later. As a teenager, I'd dreamed of captaining a sailboat around the world. Salt-crusted skin tanned to leather, sporting severe, dark sunglasses, and wearing frayed cut-offs, I saw myself hoisting sails or, feet planted squarely, swinging the helm onto a course for some exotic isle named after a saint.

I guess that's why I ran away to the islands not too long after Connie left me. Finally. I'd lost interest in the business and the kids were avoiding me like liver and onions. So why not? Or as my brother had once said with a shrug, "If not now, when? Go for it, Bro." I should thank Connie someday for leaving me.

Why had I come down here? For some reason, I thought of Chief Dave. It took me 40 years to decide to follow this dream. How long had it taken Chief Dave to decide he was going to become sweet, buxom Daisy when on vacation? Or how long had it taken each of Black Mike's topless blondes to decide they were whores ... and that it was okay, that being known as a whore was no different, really, than being known as a manager, a chef, a housewife, an entrepreneur, or a sailboat captain?

Dead Ends

I n the bar, as Scott watched me work on the coaster on that blustery winter night, it sank in, at least for him. He sighed slowly and whispered a curse as he exhaled. Then he looked around like he needed to take a whiz and wasn't sure where the men's room was. He didn't want to be there. I can't blame him; I didn't want to be there either. Friends – at least guy friends – let their friends bleed in private. So, he looked up and off, as far away as possible, embarrassed for me and not wanting to embarrass me any more than I had already embarrassed myself. And I knew it would have been better just to shut up.

When he finally turned back, he laughed, trying to redraw the lines. "Well, that explains why you guys have been avoiding us. I called a couple of times. Connie said you were out of town. Half the time, nobody answered."

"I'm kind of living at the office." My words trailed off.

"Hell, I was gonna say how great you looked. Lost a few pounds there, eh?"

I chuckled. "I call it the New Age Divorce Diet. Painful, but effective."

"Divorce, huh?" There, the word was out. It hit hard, like a final blow, a no-going-back line was now crossed. Worse than saying fuck in Church. Scott studied his beer like he'd never seen one before. I knew he was thinking about his Jo.

"Man," he said slowly, "I don't know what I would do if Jo ever left me." He glanced over to make sure it was okay to keep talking about it.

I shrugged, just as amazed as he was that we were having this not-possible, impossible, no-way possible conversation. Then we both wrapped our hands around the security of our beers and stared at the rows of liquor bottles across the bar. For about two minutes, just sitting there, that was the best I'd felt in more than two months.

The funny thing was that there was really absolutely nothing to say. We all knew friends who had gone through this. "Sorry, man. That really sucks. Anything I can do? Let me know."

And then we'd ignore it, absolutely and totally, believing it could never ever happen to us. John and Martha. Susie and Bruce. Judy and Dwayne. Some good friends. Some acquaintances. Couples. Families. Until suddenly they weren't. They weren't just not couples. Suddenly, they just weren't there. They just weren't. Gone.

And the thing that never dawned on me back then was that there could be life after divorce, something waiting for those with the unraveled dreams. We had made our stand, made our commitment. There was nothing else. Once we locked in and decided on marriage, kids, house, work, mix-breed dog, Sundays, and more – once we'd decided that this was not just it, but that it was all there was, and it was enough – we pushed everything else out of our minds. We had to. That was how it worked. Total focus. We didn't let ourselves dream about cruising the islands or taking a mental health day off in midweek. Eventually, our minds got narrower and narrower, and we developed a kind of dreamlike tunnel vision to the point that we wouldn't think of taking the 7:23 train to the city in the morning rather than our customary 6:57. That would border on anarchy. We were committed. And it wasn't a bad life. It really wasn't. No, it wasn't what we had thought it would be starting out. It was a life of sacrifice, a sacrifice we had made for our wives and our children. No, that sounds too high-ground moral. We did it because that was what we did. We sacrificed, though we would never have used that word: sacrifice. As men, we gave it our all for our wives and children. Period.

Still, we all lived in such tightly wrapped, narrow points of view. But that was also by choice. Sure, we fantasized about Marcy the Hot Blonde down the street, occasionally whacked off to the Victoria's Secret catalog, but that was it. If we were dumb enough to have an affair, we hoped that, if we ever got caught, the wife would know that it was just about sex, oh, yeah, and the danger. Love? I love you, Babe. Don't you know that?

So, when divorce hit – others, not us – the players in the game would all do all the same things in a bold attempt to assert their independence and individuality and to hold onto their sanity. Because, in truth, the leaver and the leavee didn't really want to leave (or get leaved by).

She'd spin out, get full of energy, go back to school, cut her hair, start going by a different name – Martha became Matty, Susie became Suzaaanne (with a very long, soft "a"), Judy became Glickstein, just Glickstein – give up church, find a church, take up new hobbies by the handful, from knitting to running marathons to drumming, and tell harsh jokes that compared men, quite unfavorably, to phallic-looking fruit and vegetables. She'd begin most conversations by calmly explaining that she had just gotten out of an abusive relationship – if not physical, verbal, if not verbal, emotional, always. As she talked, she'd move around a lot, sitting on arms of chairs or maybe bending into a lotus position on the couch, as if physically reveling in the expression of her new-found freedom. Meanwhile, her eyes would dart nervously around the room as if making sure *he* wasn't there. Most of all, it wasn't her fault. She had been a victim, but now vowed to be a victim no more. It wasn't her fault!

He'd get cool, calm, cavalier, tone up, buy a sports car, complain about the judge and child support, and boast too loudly and too often about being free and enjoying the good life, trying to make the rest of us envious. He would never speak her name. It was always her, she, or The Bitch. And he talked about The Bitch all the time. It was for the best. He was better off without her. And it was obvious to everyone how much he hated being alone. Most of all, it wasn't his fault. He had been a victim, had let himself be taken advantage of, but no more. He had things to catch up on. So, he would date, and it would be loud and it would be showy. And in the kitchen, on the sly, nodding in the direction of some woman with no idea why he had brought her along, he'd always ask, "So, hey, what do you think? Not bad, eh?"

They would become crazy, he and she. They would put out tremendous effort to look calm and in control. And inside, they were raging, crazy, frantic, frenetic. Total lunatics trying desperately to look and act like normal people. But they weren't. They were exhausting; that's the kindest thing we could say about them. And then they'd try to give us advice, tell us how great it was where they were, organizing the First Wives' Club or putting together an all-guys fishing trip or poker weekend, complete with a stop at a titty bar. But you could never get over the sense that they had their noses pushed up against the window wishing they could get back in again. But they couldn't. And we couldn't help them. Even if we tried; and usually, after a few weeks, we got tired of trying.

To the rest of us, all of us steady-as-rock couples, all of us veterans of the straight, good and joyous life, these walking wounded, these bleeding corpses were the last things we needed in our lives. They stunk up the place, upset the balance we all worked so hard to maintain. They brought different light and different air into the group. And it didn't work.

We, the happy couples, would go home at night and shake our heads, agreeing it was a pity, then lie awake, alone together into the night, wondering ... just wondering. Was it really good? Was it really better? Maybe they were better off. Had it really happened again to yet another couple? Curiosity, anxiety, desire and wishful thinking all drifted and swirled through the night. "Could it ever happen to us?" one of us, usually her, would whisper, broaching the unspeakable subject. Damn! "Let's try to get some sleep. We can talk about it in the morning. Glad we're different. They had problems. Not like us."

Then in the morning, we'd repeat our convictions, re-pledge our vows. "Do me a favor; if you ever think maybe...." "No, no, it'd never happen." "Have a good day." "Don't forget your gloves. See you at dinner, usual time." "Love you." "Love you, too."

And so we'd slowly, gradually close ranks. They weren't like us anymore. In a very real way, they were a threat to us. We didn't really think it, but we sensed it. Deep down inside we feared that it was contagious. If it could happen to Susie and Bruce ....

Scott and I sat in silence, each thinking about the couples who had broken up.

He suddenly sat up straight. "Hey, you remember Sam?"

I tensed. "Sam who?" I asked cautiously.

"You know. Samantha. Hell, man, you were engaged to her once."

I chuckled and hid my face in my glass of beer. "That was a long time ago, Buddy Boy. What about her?"

"Well, you know that guy she married after you two broke up?"

"What, did they break up, too?"

"No, Man. He died. My cousin Chrissy works at the same hospital as Sam."

"Yeah? Your point?"

"Well, her husband, he just keeled over with a heart attack a few months back."

"Hmm. How about that. Why you tellin' me?"

Scott just frowned, and we sat for a few more minutes in stupid silence. Then I guess he felt obligated to return to the topic of the day, or at least to talk about something, anything.

"Sorry, man, anything I can do?" he offered.

I wanted to talk, needed to talk, but I was now one of ... one of what? Them? One thing was for sure. I was not who I had been two months earlier. Everything that had defined me was slipping away, just about gone. Scott wanted to understand, but he couldn't. That made me a curiosity. I figured I'd better head off the tough questions.

"I still don't believe it," I started, then realized I still had nothing to say. Keep it light. "Hey, the good news is that diet. Thirty pounds in two months. I feel great."

Scott wasn't going to play. "Yeah, right. So, what'd you do to piss her off so much?"

"I don't know. Mid-life crisis or something. I think her hormones are going nuts."

"So, there's hope, right?"

"Oh, yeah," I said casually, not all that convincingly.

"Is she ... seeing anyone?"

The silence closed around us. It's like asking, "Hey, did you jerk off last night?" My gut wrenched like someone had put anger, fear and hopelessness in a small cage to fight it out.

"Yeah," I confessed in a whisper.

For some reason, I had to get it said: "She said no at first. But, you know, it's funny. I heard somewhere that if you think your wife is having an affair, it's a ninety-nine percent shot she is."

Scott thought about that one for a moment. I knew he was thinking about Jo again. All men had suspicions, unless they're married to dogs.

"Well, how did you? You know? How did you know?"

"Changes."

"Changes?"

"Real subtle. Okay." I sat up, warming to an impersonal explanation. Anything was better than more details.

"You know Jo. I assume there's a certain way she does things. Routines."

"Routines? Yeah, I guess," Scott said slowly, not really knowing. "Okay, yeah, so what kind of changes?"

"Too long at the store. Too many trips to the store. A missing twenty minutes here, an hour there. Nothing, really, until you begin to add it up ... and it just adds up. I passed Connie in my car one day and she was coming from the wrong direction."

"Wrong direction?"

I struggled to explain. "Yeah. I expected her to be one place, but she was returning from a different direction. Later, when I asked about it, she said she was just out for a drive. A drive? Scott, when the hell was the last time you just went out for a drive?"

Scott shrugged. He was trying to wrap his mind around what I was saying.

For some reason, it was important that he did understand.

"Okay," I continued. "Little stuff. I found some music CDs in the car. Groups I'd never heard of before. Forget that crap about coming home and finding them in bed together. It's like rabbits."

"Rabbits?"

"When I was a kid, we had rabbits. A male and a female. We always kept them separate. Mom didn't want any baby bunnies. So, I said, no problem. We kept them in separate cages. I would let them out together, but only when I was there. Mom said don't do it. But who listens? Sure enough, somehow, we ended up with a litter of bunnies. I don't know how. But it happened. So, when your wife has an affair, you'll be the last to know."

Scott stiffened. "My wife won't have an affair!"

I stopped. That pissed me off. "Yeah, mine either," I said, challenging him. I wanted to argue, to warn him against being so smug, thinking it couldn't happen to him. But I also knew that it would sound stupid.

Scott and I were now officially different. He was safe inside the walls of the castle talking down to me from the parapet. I was outside looking up. As the sun set, he would turn and go into the great hall, with a fire burning and his wife and kids around. I would wrap my cape around myself and slink off into the night, alone. We were no longer alike.

It wasn't Scott's fault, but I felt like I'd been knifed through the heart by my best friend. Or maybe that had been Connie. It was getting harder and harder to keep track.

THE ISLAND
Black Mike's Girls

Topless Blondie caught my smile, swiveled her barstool, and leaned in closer, brushing a tanned breast against my arm. "What's a myth?" she repeated. I kept smiling, caught in the moment, not knowing how not to flirt.

Before I could say anything, though, Jason marched over and too loudly asked, "You ladies need another?" But he was looking at me, giving me a furrow-browed frown and an almost imperceptible head shake.

I froze and felt for my knife. Where was the danger likely to come from? Then glancing a few barstools away, I saw Black Mike watching me. When our eyes met, he grinned, half greeting, half warning. I never could read the meaning behind a black man's smile.

Black Mike was big – muscle, fat, and tall – and black – island black, midnight dark – with a few rasta locks for the tourists. He had a head like a bull and spoke like an islander: "Yo, Mon, I got sometin make you member yo a man. How yo member?"

Sometimes, though, when we were drinking together and really enjoying each other's company, he'd slip into the cleanest, clearest Queen Mother's English. "I say, Old Chap, you must remember to steer a clear course around my beautiful doves. They are quite lovely, don't you think? But when you come around and hover, you discourage paying customers from approaching. You must respect my business. Ignore that and there is a mighty likelihood of evisceration."

Watching Black Mike watching me now, I raised my hands in an Oops gesture. Still grinning, but also glancing at my knife hand, he shook his rasta locks as if to say, "What am I gonna do with you?" and patted the barstool beside him. I took my hand off the hilt of the knife and joined him.

As I sat, he grabbed my face, as he often did, turned my head sideways, and looked at the knife scar on my neck. Then he'd let go and our conversation of the day would begin. I never knew what that topic might be, but Mike was always interesting.

"Jolly, how Bonita doin?" he asked, casually. He looked over the menu, as he did most evenings. Then he'd always order the same thing: a double platter of jerk pork, oozing fat and grease, smothered in island hot sauce … a slow, delicious death wish.

I once asked him, "Do you want me to give you CPR when you have your heart attack?"

He frowned at me. "Yo keep yo mout away from my mout," he'd warned, his eyes big. "When I die, I don't want yo ugly white puss ta be the las ting I see. Besides," he added almost wistfully, "when I goes, I goes. Dat mean da Lor want to take me home."

"So, how Bonita?" he asked again, still scanning the menu.

"Damn, is she on the menu again?" I said, leaning over and grabbing Black Mike's out of his hands.

"Dat white chic ripe," he said, shaking his head. "How you sleep wit her, Mon?"

"Given enough time, liquor and loneliness, you can get used to just about anything, my friend." That ended the conversation.

Somebody had told me once that Bonita's name used to be Cathy. However, many things, including names, change on the islands. A few days after she became my bunkie, I started calling her Bonita. Why? I don't know. Bonita means "beautiful" in Spanish, and she wasn't Spanish, so that made sense, though there was a hint of delicious beauty about her. Also, her pungent aroma reminded me of three-day-old fish on a hot day. So, I started calling her Bonita, as in tuna. She didn't seem to care either way.

When I had shared her new name with Chicago Mike, he had rolled his eyes and corrected me. "That's bonito, Jolly, with an O, which is a species of mackerel."

"Oh." I thought about it for a second before saying, "Well, actually, you can spell it with an A also. Besides, I'm not gonna start calling her Mac. Besides besides, she likes Bonita. I like Bonita. So, she's Bonita."

Chicago Mike scowled, so I asked him, "Hey, do you know what I like about you, Mike?"

He grunted and said, "No, what?"

"So, you can't think of anything either, huh?"

As for Bonita, the name stuck. An unsubtle, sometimes overpowering whiff of fish odor aside, I liked her, mostly for her easy-going, get-along personality. She had no expectations, made no demands. Somebody else probably, long before me, had broken her heart, stomped on it, shredded it, let her down, and disappointed her. Am I repeating myself? Oh, well, my point is that by the time we met, she had lowered the flag of her expectations to just about zero. As a result, she was one of the happiest, most pleasant people I had ever met. Mostly, she never gave me that What's-wrong-with-you? look, at least yet. So, she was perfect in her own way.

Oh, and one more thing. When she took off her top, it was just because she enjoyed being topless. No agenda. Nothing. She blew Jason's three-types-of-women-who-go-topless theory out of the water. Another myth shattered. Kaboom!

Once, as she sauntered into The Sunset, French Tony watched her coming and said, "In the words of Oscar Wilde, 'Blessed is he who expects nothing, for he shall not be disappointed.'"

"No, that was Ben Franklin," I'd corrected him, smiling at Bonita in response to her usual broad grin and greeting, "Permission to come aboard, Cap'm?" as she approached and then, leaning over me, gave me that long, lingering, wrap-around kiss. That's how she always greeted me. I know. I'm repeating myself, but people do that, except in novels. We repeat ourselves endlessly. Besides, I'm bragging. When Bonita wrapped her arms (and sometimes her legs) around me, for just that brief moment, I was a good man, a great man, a perfect man, oh, and a very, very, very sexually aroused man. Woof. Yes, it felt that good.

Woof.

"Actually," added Chicago Mike, bursting into my real life sexual fantasy, "that was Alexander Pope."

"Who?" had asked Blah Blah Brenda, totally confused and looking around for some guy called Alexander ... or maybe she was looking for the pope.

"Alexander Pope," Mike snapped, "in a letter to John Gay. He was a writer," he added, with a look that said he doubted Blah Blah had ever read anything other than an Abercrombie & Fitch fashion catalog. Brenda still looked lost. I think he was right.

"You know, books?" Mike added. "The things you read in the crapper, or, in your case, Blah Blah, when you're having sex with Tony."

Mike glanced at Tony, who just smiled and mouthed, "Comic books. Archie."

"Makes you almost appreciate Patti the Beast, doesn't it?" I said to Mike, and we both looked around to make sure Patti wasn't present. She didn't like being called The Beast. Hell, she didn't like anything.

Blah Blah just kept looking around. She wasn't dumb. She just knew absolutely nothing and had no desire to learn anything. I guess that made her willfully stupid, like a lot of folks in this world, people who didn't like being troubled by facts. These are the ones who say, "I don't know anything about the science/research/history/facts of it, but I know how I feel, and this feels right."

***

So, Black Mike and I, sitting at the bar, our menus on the side, we were done talking. As he dug into his jerk-pork dinner, I glanced at my wrist, though I hadn't worn a watch in more than a year, slipped off the barstool and headed back to what we called the family table. Monday nights, those who could make it gathered at Sunset for dinner. It was a loose collection of expatriate odds and ends.

Kid, a few drinks in already, was playfully lecturing Patti the Beast and Chicago Mike. Kid was the young pup. He'd come down maybe a year ago from Ohio, right out of high school. "Hey, I love you guys," Kid said with a laugh. "But I look 'round at you old farts and I ask myself, Do I wanna be like you bums in 20 years?"

"You're already like us bums," Chicago snapped. "You're just 20 years ahead of schedule."

"May be right," Kid agreed, pondering. "What do you think, Beast?"

The whole table froze. No one called Patti the Beast the Beast to her face. Well, except for Kid. He once told me he could outrun her like a gazelle outruns a rhino.

"Yeah, but if she ever catches you …"

"She'll pound you flat. You'll be a Patti patty," added Squint, giggling at his own great humor. "Or maybe a Beasty burger."

This time, though, Patti ignored the insult. Kid looked disappointed.

Then there was Chicago Mike, who was mirthless. His eyes were dark and blank and cold like a shark's. Actually, he made a shark look like a warm, fuzzy puppy. He had salt 'n pepper hair and a mustache that accentuated his Polish/Slavic background. Mike was the smartest man in the bar, maybe even on the island. We all knew it was true because he told us so at least once a week.

"They asked me to join MENSA, the high IQ society," he'd say, "but I told them to shove it. I'm too smart for those goons."

I had my doubts. When he and Patti the Beast had first arrived on the island, they'd rented a small retail space at one of the glitzy tourist malls. It was actually an arched alcove in what had been an old brick warehouse along the harbor that, about two hundred years ago, had housed barrels of rum and sugar. Their store was one of more than a dozen little shops that sold souvenirs, mostly junk, to the visitors. They had a unique, though stupid, angle.

Patti, who imagined herself to be a gifted photographer, took pictures of the memorable spots on the island. Then Chicago enlarged them and mounted them in wooden, full-size, six-paned window frames that weighed about fifty pounds each. That way, Chicago explained, people could buy the frame with the photo, have it shipped home, and pretend to look out the window at their favorite island place.

Though I tried hard to see the brilliance of the idea, I couldn't. I thought the idea was stupid. So did the tourists. For one thing, it cost a small fortune to ship the frames to the island. Plus, Mike and Patti wouldn't listen when we tried to explain that people wanted small souvenirs, the kind they could carry home with them, not the kind that had to be shipped – again for a small fortune – back to the States.

"What you really should do," Kid had offered, "is open a kiss sock ..."

"A what?" growled Mike.

"A key sock," Kid continued.

"It's called a kiosk, you moron."

"Yeah, that's it. A kiosk." The whole table paused and waited for Kid's idea.

"Set up a kiosk on the edge of the bitch ... the beach at sundown, and sell glow-in-the-dark condoms."

"Huh?" Mike said, scowling.

"No, wait. Better wait till around 'leven o'clock, after ever'body's stewed. Then have sexy babes ..."

"Topless?" suggested Bonita.

"Good idea. Topless," Kid continued. "Walk through the bars an 'long the beach selling 'em on trays. They'd sell like ha'cakes at a church fun raiser." He paused and looked around. "The bes part? Huh? The bes part. Imagine lookin' down da bitch half an hour later. All lit up, like dozens a light switches switchin' on an' switchin' off."

Kid looked around and waited. We all just stared at him. So he added, "And the backseats of the cars, too."

Bonita started giggling. "And behind the bushes. And under the tables in the corners of the bar."

"What about the goddam' kiosk?" demanded Chicago Mike.

"Fo'get the goddam' kiosk."

Bonita was lost in thought and deep in giggles. "Like lightning bugs blinking all over the beach."

Kid's face lit up. "Ya see. Brilliant, huh? Come on, Bonita, les do this. We'll make a fortune."

"Where's the kiosk?" Mike asked one last time, as the rest of the expatriates at the family table slowly started to giggle.

***

Okay, back to Chicago Mike's dumbass business idea. Smart business owners would have cut their losses and shut down within two months, but Chicago and the Beast held on for almost a year. I think Mike wanted to get out sooner, but Patti just knew it was a brilliant idea ... brilliant until the last of Mike's money ran out.

That was when Patti had approached Black Mike about becoming one of his girls. The only reason he had not said No immediately was because Patti the Beast was intimidating. He had said, "I'll get back to you." He never did.

***

I moved over and sat down next to Kid, who gently bumped my shoulder by way of greeting. I liked Kid. When I'd first met him, he had seemed nervous and fearful, like one of the skulking, stray island dogs, wondering whether you were going to throw him a rib bone or just kick him in the ribs. No one ever cared enough to ask his real name. From the first morning Calabash had found him sleeping on the beach, hung over and hungry, using his backpack for a pillow, his pockets turned out by the shadow boys, he was Kid. We knew he had a mother, and was from Columbus. That's it. That was enough. We liked him … well, all except for Chicago Mike, who, as I said, didn't like anybody.

He came down for the fun, he said. The rest of us – the old farts, like me heading fast toward age 50, up to wheezy Calabash, with his gap-toothed smile, shaggy hair, and nicotine-stained mustache, who had been kicking around the islands for more than 40 years – we all came down for … well, who knows what for or why we came down.

What amazed me about Kid was how he'd changed, I mean, almost overnight. Within weeks, he had become confident and playful. The funny thing was how he had developed a special fondness for Patti. He teased her, tormented her, and played jokes on her, but he also sometimes just talked to her. She often threatened to break his neck, but he was the only person she ever smiled at.

Plus, Kid had that Midwest work ethic. So, after I'd fired Chicago Mike as first mate, I offered the job to Kid. He had more playful fun in him than Kevin Costner in the western movie *Silverado*, and the *touristas* loved him. Plus, he was just easy to get along with. I paid him next to nothing, but gave him a bunk on the cat. We each got a hundred square feet – four feet wide, 25 feet long, and four portholes.

I sort of expected that he'd get Rock Fever and head back to Columbus to help out his mother and go to college. He'd mentioned leaving once, and I'd told him to go home. The others told him to have another drink to clear his head. He did. And he's still here ... for now.

That's the thing about Rock Fever. It makes some people claustrophobic. It drives them off the island. They're afraid that if they stay it would latch onto them and never let them get away, keeping them until they're old and dead. Others it holds onto and makes them afraid to leave, like the guy who has a so-so job back in the States, but with could-be-worse benefits, so he hangs on, not really hating it and never truly loving it, until 40 years go by. These are the guys who live for their hobbies. Almost makes sense. Almost.

No, not really.

Kid, all foolishness and nonsense, he made sense.

***

Whenever Black Mike's dinner would arrive – that steaming, double platter of jerk pork – he'd look at it with something akin to lust. I was always tempted to reach over and grab a piece, but, friends or not, I suspected I might lose a finger. Mike was as protective of his food as he was of his girls, maybe more so.

"Well, speaking of dinner," I'd say, and he would glance at me like a feral dog guarding his bowl, and watch me as I pushed away from the bar. And then I'd think of Gloria – sweet, black, spooky Gloria.

***

I hadn't been the master of *The Do Over* long when Gloria asked me if I liked the spicy, rich, jerk island food. When I said, "You bet," she lit up. Gloria is Jamaican, so I was told to be wary of her. Tall, deep black, with a beautiful smile that melted my heart and inflamed my fantasies, she was the head housekeeper at Skipper Bud's marina where I moor my boat.

Cat Neil, who was Dutch and who sold me *The Do Over*, warned me to stay away from the Jamaicans, both the men and the women, but especially the women.

"The men are bad, and you know it. You can see it in their eyes," he'd said. "Violent. Jamaica is a rough island. You gotta stare 'em down. The women, though, they're pure passion. On one hand, they're the happiest folks I've ever met. And in bed they'll let you take 'em any way you want 'em. In return, they'll take you places you never knew existed. But be careful. They're just as hard and violent as the men if you get on their bad side. They won't argue, pout or cry. They'll punch you, stab you, or just grab you by the balls and squeeze. Steer clear. Their favorite way to deal with a cheating husband or boyfriend is to wait until he's asleep, take out a knife and … ."

My eyes grew big. I got the message, but Neil wasn't done. "I knew one, her name was Isabella. She had buck teeth, hard hair, all sticking out in different directions, and a wild look in her eyes. Rumor was that she kept her husband's balls in a Crown Royal bag. Called it her mojo. Mean. Meaner than Patti the Beast. Mark my words. Steer clear."

I had kept that in mind, and was standoffish with Gloria for the first months I knew her. She was the same with me, always kept a wary eye on me. She wore a Christian cross, but I also once heard her offer a whispered curse against evil spirits when a three-foot iguana had planted itself squarely in her path on the dock and had tried to stare her down. She hesitated just a split second. Then, brandishing a knife that had come from God knows where, she marched up to the lizard, grabbed it by the snout, flipped it over onto its back and cut its throat. Within two minutes, she'd gutted and cleaned it, hosed off the dock, and dropped the carcass in a bucket that she later carried home.

As she walked past *The Do Over*, she snapped on her warm smile and asked, "Like 'guana?"

I shrugged. "Never tasted it."

"Tase like cheeken," she said and laughed that broad, lusty Jamaican laugh.

I smiled, but I was thinking about Neil's advice, and how Gloria wielded that knife.

The best advice, Neil had explained to me, giving me a lesson in island race relations, is to always always keep it strictly business. "Here's what whites don't ever think about and blacks never forget," he'd said. "When things go wrong down here on the island, the blacks, they go to jail, get beat up or shot. The whites get left alone or they're asked to please leave the island. So, the blacks prefer to settle their differences personally. Watch out. They have their own kind of justice."

Still, Gloria's smile was as radiant as the iridescent green nail polish on her fingers and toes. Kind of reminded me of Kid's idea for glow-in-the dark condoms. Eventually, Gloria and I went from business terms to friendly terms. Then, one day, I touched her arm, just a friendly gesture, as I said, "How are you today, Gloria?"

She pulled back like I'd jabbed her with a lit cigarette, and her eyes turned hot and dangerous. Confused, I gestured no offense, but she kept glaring.

What? I gestured again, remembering Neil's words and wondering where she kept that damn knife. I'd crossed some line, but I had no idea what it was.

"Cap'm Jolly, Sir," she said, "you got da evil eye." She pointed to my face and backed away.

I was puzzled. "Evil eye? Me?"

Then I realized that she had noticed my lazy eye. I'd had it since I was a kid. My left eye looks straight ahead, but my right eye tends to drift off to the side, especially when I've had too little sleep or too much whiskey. My kids used to call me lizard man. Most people got over it quickly, but I realized that Gloria, like many of the islanders, was superstitious.

Suddenly, the dark skin, the fear and danger in her eyes, and her artless smile, when she smiled – suddenly, I understood how some women – many women, actually – were drawn to dangerous, charming guys, the ones who, guaranteed, were going to do them terrible wrong. It was the danger that made me want her, and it was the danger that made me want to steer clear of her, like Cat Neil had warned.

MANGROVE COVE
On Solid Ground

The wind was blowing harder overhead, singing in a high-pitched scream through the rigging, but the quarter mile of entwined, hardwood mangroves was doing its job so far, blocking the wind and waves down low, by the waterline. I watched Kid swim out to a large mangrove root I'd pointed to off the left bow. For a kid from Columbus, Ohio, he had learned fast and knew his stuff. He was a natural first mate and maneuvered around the boat like a mountain goat on a steep slope. We worked well together. With a nod, point, or word from me, he knew what to do and how to do it.

Still, he was struggling. Because of his life vest, he was bobbing like a cork. He had a line in his hand and was trying to tie it to the root, but he was too high in the water to get it around.

We were running out of time. If the boat wasn't secured properly before the full force of the storm hit, *The Do Over* could end up piled on top of the mangroves, and Kid and I would look like Jocko, soggy like rats and all the stuffing knocked out of us.

I cut the engine, peeled off my vest and dove in. I pulled up beside Kid, and we tied off the line together. Then he swam back to the boat for the second line while I headed across the channel to a root off the right bow. Before diving in, he slid out of his vest, too.

We had talked about vests one evening while steaks sizzled on the charcoal grill over on the stern of *The Do Over*. I had explained how the cruise line insisted on them for insurance purposes. Finally, Kid had said, as he slipped a hand between the thighs of Gay, his latest bunkie, "Look, Cap'm, I think they're stupid, like bicycle helmets."

"I agree," Gay chimed in, eager to agree.

Kid got up to flip the steaks and poke the potatoes. "They're for people who think that a life with absolutely no risk is the absolutely best life in the world," he said, and I suspected he was thinking about life back in Ohio. I was right.

"That's my brother," he said, "a cubicle-dwelling wage slave who works for the university. He knows to the day the day he will retire. And, yes, he makes sure his sanitized wife and three perfect children wear dorky helmets when they go out for Saturday bike rides on the Olentangy River trail. Nothing wrong with safe. Just not for me, Cap'n."

I didn't say a word for a few minutes. Finally, "Well, what if that leggy Gestapo cruise director said she'd give you the best blow job of your life IF you are wearing a life vest when she does it?"

Silence filled the darkening sky. Gay looked at him anxiously, like Kid's answer was going to define the course of the rest of her life, like she expected him to say, "Oh, no, she could never be as good as Gay." The only sound was the sizzling steaks, the only light was the glow from the grill coals. Finally, Kid answered, "Only if *she* wears a bike helmet."

Gay was gone before we'd finished our steaks. God, how I hated all that boy-girl drama shit. The steaks were perfect, though.

* * *

Meanwhile, back in Mangrove Cove, we were done. We had a total of eight come-along, adjustable lines going off the boat, pretty much leaving her hog-tied and splayed across the channel. What felt good was that we knew what we were doing, swimming back and forth across the mangrove channel, securing the lines, and attaching the come-along winches so we could let out and bring in line as the sea rose and fell. As we worked, we saw a few sharks dart by. One even paused to bump and sniff Kid, who snout punched him and told him to move on. We were all busy trying to survive. No time to play.

Finally, back on board, I squatted in front of the mast and mentally surveyed the coming storm, the boat, and the lines. I'd seen hurricanes before, and I'd seen boats pulled under because they were tied too tightly to a dock when the water rose. So, the come-alongs would allow us to pay out or take in line as needed. It would rise. I just wasn't sure how much. So, we'd have to keep a close eye on the lines. As long as we paid attention, and as long as the cleats held, this should work, at least in theory... maybe. Or at least that's what I kept telling myself.

Kid popped two beers, plopped into the mate's chair, threw his bare feet onto the long dash, and grinned. *Well done*, I indicated with a nod, taking my beer and clinking bottles. I peeled open a package of high-protein trail mix, took a handful and tossed the rest to Kid. The wind was starting to blow hard. It felt good. Kid threw the trail mix back to me and got up to go find some Ho Hos.

I thought about the day Calabash had found Kid on the beach. Dirty and hung over, he had looked scared, uncertain, and dumber than a stump. Actually, his expression reminded me of the look I'd seen on the commuters heading into work on the train each morning back in the States. Probably fewer than ten in a hundred had any idea what they were doing or why. They just did it. But Kid had learned fast and well. Today, he knew what he was doing, and he knew that the why didn't matter.

"Don't get too comfortable," I told him as I finished my beer.

The wind was continuing to build, and the boat was beginning to pull and fight her moorings, like an animal at the vet's resisting being held down. I checked my gauges. The wind was gusting at 75 miles per hour. And I knew the worst of it was still two or three hours away. Shit! Hurricane Olive was going to be a very nasty storm. Watching the lines snap and pull, and listening to the creaking seams of the boat as it bucked, I wondered if this had been such a good idea. I had been in bad storms before, but I was not so sure I had ever been in one this big. Then I figured, well, I had no Plan B worth thinking about, so we'd better stick with Plan A.

Meanwhile, Kid, grinning from ear to ear, was having a ball, just watching the sheer magnitude and fury of the building storm. I tended to feel the same way about storms. There was something stimulating, thrilling, exciting, and sensuous as hell about the big ones, the ones that were furious, intent on destroying everything in their path. I loved them. I was tempted to sit back and just watch. "Damn!" I said with a start.

I jumped up. We had things to do.

"Let's drop that mast, Kid."

"Aye, aye, Cap'm," he yelled cheerfully.

Water Parks

I never understood hobbies. I never collected stamps. I never wanted to become the world's best skateboarder or ride every monster rollercoaster in the country. I'd tried and had been disappointed by jumping off a bridge with a bungee cord hooked around my ankles, even though I'd puked my guts out on the fourth bounce. Even golf puzzled me as a hobby. I understood it as a means to closing a business deal, certainly, but for fun? It just never made any sense to me. (Connie's father had been an avid golfer, and I thought he was crazy about the sport. Then the day he retired, he put his clubs in the closet and never played again. That was how much he loved the sport.)

No risk. No excitement. That's what I thought every time I watched the day's crop of cruise ships steam up to the liner piers and saw the people crowd off to wander through the everything-the-same tourist shops, take carriage rides, and, yes, even book a half-day snorkeling excursion on cat boats like *The Do Over*. It was all just pony rides.

That's why being out here in Mangrove Cove trying to save my boat ahead of Hurricane Olive made sense.

As Kid and I finished lowering the mast and lashed it to the boom, I could feel the boat buck and kick in the wind, which seemed like it might be gusting at a hundred miles an hour.

"Having Fun yet?" I roared into his ear.

He grinned and said something that I missed.

"Whaaat?"

"I'd rather be hung for a goat than a sheep," he bellowed.

I just smiled back. We'd had this conversation before, too. The conclusion: Everyone ends up hung and ends up dead in the end. Might as well enjoy life the best you can before it happens. Playing it safe made no sense.

I looked at him and we both belted out the line from the Jimmy Buffet song, "Growing Older But Not Up" – "I'd rather die while I'm living than live when I'm dead."

I patted Kid on the back and went below. Though relatively dry, the cabin was screaming as the wind hit it and water came through every seam in the windows. I checked the bilges in the pontoon hulls and debated putting on the pump. Not yet. Instead, I double checked the lashings on the large hand pump secured to the gunwale. If we lost our batteries, this would be crucial. I also clicked the radio, but realized that no one would be available, even if we needed help. Miles from anywhere, we were on our own.

"Yeee haaa!" Kid yelled as he stumbled into the cabin, water pouring in after him. We were both soaking wet. I was watching the long front windshields bow and buckle in the wind. This was getting serious. I didn't mind if the boat swamped and sank. We were only in about six feet of water. But if she broke loose – and she just might, even with two set anchors and eight lines lashing her to the mangrove roots on both sides of the channel – we'd be a smashed up mess in seconds. Right now *The Do Over* was fighting the lines and the wind. I figured if two broke loose, they'd all go, and she'd get torn to pieces, along with me and Kid.

I toweled my head off and lit two cigarettes, handing one to Kid. For the next five minutes, we both sat in the cabin smoking, staring at our feet, and listening to the boat. I didn't like what I was hearing.

I snuffed out the stub of my cigarette and threw Kid's life vest at him.

"Oh, this is really gonna help!" he yelled and laughed.

"That's so they can find your body!" I yelled back and didn't laugh. He shrugged and put the vest back on. I put mine back on, too.

I heard a ripping, creaking sound, sort of like the lid being peeled back off a can of dog food. Kid heard it, too, and looked at me. I could see him mouth the words, "Dot not goood," and shaking his head before he reached into the pocket of his cut-off jeans and popped a red foam clown ball onto his nose.

I had to smile. The idiot was still having fun.

Though I couldn't see the bow for all the rain, I knew that the portside cleat was tearing open the hull, probably peeling back the fiberglass skin. I ducked down to take a look inside Kid's cabin and saw water pouring in. If one pontoon filled, the boat could topple over from a good wave, and the whole boat would tumble and crumble. Or worse, she could split in half.

I came back up midship. Plan B finally came to mind. "We have to scuttle her," I yelled to Kid.

"What?"

I didn't have the lungs or the desire to explain. I checked the gauges. They were all dead, but I suspected the wind was pushing 120 miles per hour. Waves were starting to break over the outer mangroves and lifting the boat, with the mooring lines then crashing it back down again. *The Do Over* was getting beat to a pulp.

I felt guilty. I'd taken this beautiful boat to a dangerous place, and she could be destroyed. My fault. I guess it's always my fault. A stomach-turning feeling washed over me. It was the same feeling as when the judge had banged her gavel and declared my marriage to Connie officially over. It had been my fault. I could have done something. Tried one more time to talk Connie out of it. Spent less time on the road or at the office. Said, "I understand how you feel," rather than, "What bug crawled up your ass this time?"

If *The Do Over* was destroyed, it was my fault.

Do something. But what?

Like I said, Plan B came along just in time. The idea flashed through my head, and it made total sense. Okay, I sink her. It was a calculated risk. I knew, or at least hoped, she'd do better settled on the bottom of the channel, out of the wind and waves. Besides, I'd be damned if I was going to just sit there and wait to see what happened. Better to be hung for a goat than a sheep? Maybe.

I cupped my hand over Kid's ear. "We-need-to-let-out-three-feet-on-the-front-four lines," I roared. "Sink-her-bow-first."

He shrugged a combination of *you're-the-boss* and *you're-an-idiot*. Then he signed me three fingers and pointed to the front four lines to confirm. I nodded.

Okay, he nodded.

THE ISLAND
Pirates

Not sure exactly why, but I decided to buy an eye patch to cool off Gloria after she got upset over my lazy eye, calling it the evil eye.

Having a dash of Italian blood in me, I understood the evil eye. I know that it scared Gloria and, I wanted to believe, turned her on at the same time. Still, that wasn't the real reason I decided I wanted an eye patch. I'd always wanted one. Every guy does.

It's the same reason we brag about our scars instead of trying to cover them up like women do. They mean we've been somewhere, done something, been in the battle.

So, the next day I went to Yousef's *Buccaneers* in town. Yousef is a Palestinian who owns a goddamn goldmine of a shop that caters to the *touristas* interested in the pirate history of the islands, or at least the Johnny Depp and Errol Flynn version.

"Yo ho, Cap'm Jolly," he said when I came in, and he smiled a broad shopkeeper's smile. "Welcome!" he announced loudly, removing his trademark, tri-corner pirate's hat, and sweeping it extravagantly across his chest. He dressed the part, including a lace kerchief at his neck, too-heavy, red, broadcloth coat, with tails, black boots, and a black, not-plastic sword in his wide, black belt. I figured he was gay, but also married to a nondescript, invisible wife.

I smiled broadly back. Back then, though I'd only owned *The Do Over* for a few months, word spread fast through what that Jimmy Buffett song refers to as the coconut telegraph. Besides, it's a small island. I was already Cap'm Jolly. I admit, I liked the name. This whole island was becoming my *Cheers* bar, where everyone knows your name.

Meanwhile, half a dozen visitors from one of the cruise ships in harbor until 2:15 looked up from fingering the goods. They wanted to see a real island captain up close. I guess I fit the image well – ragged cut-off jean shorts, two days' worth of stubble on my face, unbuttoned island shirt, shaggy hair tied back in a short ponytail, and sun glasses that I could put on, take off, spin in my hand, stuff in my shirt pocket.

In other words, I wore the not-so-imaginative ex-pat uniform, sort of an island version of the suits the beasts of burden back home wore while stuck in their bumper-to-bumper traffic jam on the drive to work every morning.

I had only one hard and fast rule: I avoided the dopey, stereotype skippers' cap, *à la* Gilligan's Island. Instead, I wore a practical, long-brimmed, faded-out baseball cap. That was mostly because, as a spoiled teen on the South Shore of Long Island, I remember seeing men with more money than sense buy huge cabin cruisers, even though they didn't know port from starboard. Usually, after a few misadventures embarrassing themselves playing bumper boat banging into the well-padded piers at dockside restaurants in front of amused patrons, they'd rarely take the boat away from the dock again. Embarrassing themselves didn't fit their carefully crafted success images. It seemed that most were scared to death of looking foolish. Instead, they'd default to overseeing cocktails for weekend friends on deck … always wearing that stupid, blue skipper's cap, with a shiny visor and a gold anchor embroidered on the front. My heart broke for the boats that never left dock. You could buy one ten years old, and, though it had gone through two refrigerators and three air conditioners, it may have less than a hundred hours on the engine.

So, no captain's cap for me. That was for the wanna-be's.

Though it was only about ten o'clock in the morning, Yousef produced a bottle of watered down spiced rum from behind the counter and set out half a dozen shot glasses.

"The usual, Cap'm?" he asked, and without waiting for my response, filled each glass.

The usual? I'd thought. Since Yousef and I had never done this before, I figured it was for the *touristas*, a term almost no islander ever used in front of the hundreds of thousands of men and women and families who came ashore for vacations each year. The preferred term, according to the Chamber of Commerce, was "visitors" or "guests," rarely tourists and never, never, ever *touristas*.

Yousef's theatrics had struck the right chord. The visitors were watching us carefully, enjoying the free-wheeling and outrageous idea of drinking before noon.

"And you, friends, will you join us?" Yousef offered with another elaborate gesture, picking up shot glasses of cheap rum and passing them around.

With nervous smiles, pleased at being invited to join in this slice of island life, most took the glasses. One young woman shook her head, and one couple walked stiffly out. Baptists!

The last thing I needed was a drink before noon, especially with an afternoon snorkeling excursion scheduled, but business was business, and if it helped out Yousef, he might be inclined to recommend *The Do Over* for a private excursion or romantic evening harbor cruise. Besides, I was enjoying watching him work the crowd.

The guests waited, glasses in hand, making sure they did not break some island protocol by drinking too soon. Yousef raised his glass for a toast and then looked at me.

"It is customary for the skipper to make the toast," he said, deferentially.

I smiled, mostly at his brazen theatrics, and wanted to kick him in the ass so hard his teeth flew out. Still, I raised my glass, looked around the store to make sure everyone felt included, and said: "Remember, even a lousy day in paradise is still better than a good day back home. Cheers!"

The guests responded with grins and shouts of "Cheers!" or "Hear! Hear!"

Then we all downed our rum shots, except for Yousef, who wasn't drinking. He did, however, quickly refill everyone else's glasses. Like all island merchants, he knew that slightly inebriated customers were always likely to spend more, so free booze flowed freely at every store, from jewelers to hair salons. On *The Do Over*, we usually went through a gallon or two of rum punch on the return trip to harbor after an excursion. We'd crank up some Jimmy Buffet or Bob Marley tunes on the speakers and begin pouring. It was great for tips.

At *Buccaneers*, I held my glass in my hand and asked about a patch for my right eye. Yousef looked me in the left eye, grunted, nodded knowingly (men don't generally look in each other's eyes; I could not tell you the color of Scott's eyes), and then pulled one out of a bin containing several dozen and gave it to me.

"For you, my friend. A gift."

"Are you really a captain?" a 40-ish woman with fifteen extra pounds asked. She was with an older couple, probably her parents, who were helping her get over an ugly divorce ... probably.

I smiled and jokingly put on the patch with a *what-do-you-think?* gesture.

"Aye, pretty lady, that I be," I said with a leer. "Skipper of the bonny sailing vessel, *The Do Over*."

She giggled and said she liked the name.

"Aye, we all need at least one do over in our lives, me beauty, don't you think?"

"Amen," she said, and then corrected herself. "Aye!" And then under her breath, she added, "Maybe more than one."

"Amen," I said in a whisper, leaning in, flirting, and hoping it was true.

The older couple nodded approvingly. Amazing how parents of older, unhappy daughters hope they get laid. Meanwhile, other visitors from one of the cruise ships in port stopped, looked through the open doorway and wandered in through a frigid wall of air conditioning to see what was going on. Even though electricity was expensive on the island, produced by burning diesel oil, Yousef and the other shopkeepers knew that open doors brought in tourists, and air conditioning helped them stay longer and buy more. *Ka-ching*! It was a massive business expense, but worth the cost.

"An' remember, Lass," I added encouragingly, quoting from one of Yousef's T-shirts, "good girls don't make history."

Enjoying the attention, she raised her eyebrows and smiled. Then I pulled off the eye patch and shook myself all over to get out of the Long John Silver character. Extending a hand, I said, "Good morning, folks. Yes, I'm Captain Jolly, skipper of the cruising catamaran *The Do Over*. Do you like to snorkel? Or barbecue on a remote beach?"

"Love it," the 40-year-old woman gushed.

"Then come on by for the afternoon sail. I think you will enjoy it." I gave her my card.

As several of us shook hands and did introductions, I invited them all on the day's snorkeling excursion.

"Cap'm Jolly is the best skipper on the island," Yousef tossed in gratuitously, though he had no idea how good a captain I was.

Nice to meet you, they all agreed and apologized because they had to be back on board their cruise ship by 11:45 for lunch, included in the price of the cruise.

"Ah," I said, acting disappointed, though I knew their ship schedule better than they did. "Well, then, just don't let this old pirate, Yousef, pick your pocket."

"Seriously," I added, putting my arm around Yousef's shoulder, "Yousef here, a truly honest man, has the best goods on the island, at the best prices. Yousef," I said, turning to the shopkeeper, "take especially good care of our new friends. Give them the island discount."

As I went out the door, I could see items piling up on the counter. *Ka-ching*.

***

Later, after I'd bought my eye patch and was hosing off *The Do Over* following the four-hour afternoon excursion, I was watching for Gloria to wrap up her chores and head down the dock to the parking lot. As she approached, I could see that she had started to veer to the other side of the dock to avoid me and my evil eye. I turned away, slipped on my patch, and then turned back. Intercepting her and jumping on the dock, I opened my arms and dramatically announced, "Ta da!"

She froze in her tracks and stared at me, her expression blank. For a long moment, I thought, oh crap, I had made a big mistake. Hard bodied, tough, with a knife that I knew she knew how to use, why was I flirting with disaster? She could gut me, I suspected, faster than she'd done in the iguana who, by the way, also made the mistake of blocking her path along the dock.

Slowly, after studying me and my patch for a good thirty seconds, her blank expression gradually, slowly broke into that beautiful, heart-melting smile of hers. "You a funny mon, Cap'm Jolly." Then she reached out and touched my arm to let me know she was over the evil-eye stuff.

I thought about inviting her onboard and offering her a drink, but that just wouldn't work, if only because Big Bud, who owned the marina, would have a fit.

Then out of nowhere, she asked, "You like jerk?"

"Jerk?" For a second, I wasn't sure what she was talking about. Then she made a hand-to-mouth eating gesture. "Ah, jerk! Pork? Chicken? Hot and spicy?"

"Goat, too. Very hot an' very spicy."

" Love it. You make jerk?"

She beamed anew. "Bes jerk place on da islan call Da Jerk."

"Da Jerk?" I asked and then corrected myself. "The Jerk?"

She nodded. "It owned by a Jamaican. Beef. Spicy goat. Pork. Cheeken my favorite. You like feet and pig snout?" She added with a laugh, already suspecting the answer.

"Feet? Snout?" I shrugged, hesitating.

"How 'bout pig ears?"

I made an icky-poo face, and she laughed.

"Only kiddin." She paused and made the same face. "We feed da pig ears to da dogs. So, doan worry. Da Jerk got lots of white man parts, too."

I hoped she meant parts that white men ate, not white men's parts.

She read my mind and laughed. "It good," she said, cutting through five centuries of anything but good race relations. "Les go now? Hungry?"

It had been a long day, and I was tired and hungry, the best kind of tired and hungry, with salt spray caked on my body from a hot Caribbean sun. "Absolutely," I said. I held up a finger before jumping back on board *The Do Over* to hose the salt from my hair and body, remembering that fresh water, created by the diesel plant via reverse osmosis, was as precious as gold on the island. Then I threw on a T-shirt, grabbed my wallet and left the boat.

"My treat," I said, knowing that she worked long hours for poverty wages. Islands really didn't have borders and men and women from poorer islands flooded those where a living – albeit a substandard one – could be earned. And there was no minimum wage. So, that iguana Gloria had killed and gutted had probably been dinner for the whole family.

Gloria held back and eyed me, cautious again. A big-boned, attractive woman, she knew that a lot of white men traded in soft currency with the island girls. She was weighing the true price, and I knew it.

I decided to be direct. "Just food and your company. Maybe a kiss." I looked at her cross and, recalling my Roman Catholic upbringing, made the sign of the cross.

"Jus food and company. No kiss." We smiled at each other. I suspected she was processing our relationship. How many white men had she trusted? A lot of the young island girls did, I had been told, and it rarely worked out well for the girls. But she was no teenager.

She made the sign of the cross, and nodded.

"Deal. So, let's go," I said and almost touched her arm. She sprang back, but I think mostly because I'd surprised her. Islanders ran at about a third the speed of folks from the States.

It was late afternoon, though there was no rush hour on the island. This alone made me want to call Connie and say thank you for divorcing me.

We took my car. I loved driving on the island, mostly because there were no rules, or at least none that anybody obeyed. Yes, the speed limit was 35, everywhere, but nobody seemed to notice. You set your own speed. Directional blinkers? Sometimes. Accidents? All the time, but nobody ever asked for your insurance card, probably because nobody had any insurance. Most cars were inexpensive, white, recycled from the rental car lots when they upgraded every year or so. When they broke, the owners just walked away and let the shadow boys do their strip jobs. But I already said this, didn't I?

The system was very efficient in its own way. Last year I needed a new radiator hose, so I talked to the Boys in the Trees. (More on them later.) The next morning, the hose was on the gunwale of my boat, along with a ganga joint. I tracked the boys down later that day and sent $20 up the tree in the parking lot that was their office. "We good?" I called up into the tree. "We good, Cap'm" came the reply. Everything worked in its own way on the island.

Driving the two-lane roads, I zigged and zagged over potholes and around washed out shoulders. At one point, we came to a complete stop. Ahead, two old friends had apparently met, stopped, got out of their cars and caught up on a year or so of happenings. Nobody honked; nobody seemed to mind. Island time had its own set of rules. Actually, island time had no rules. Nobody, except the *touristas* from the States, was in a hurry to get anywhere. It could drive people crazy.

When I was on island less than a month, I'd invited some new friends to dinner. "Four o'clock," I'd instructed, still thinking that time actually mattered. They'd showed up at 6:30, all smiles.

But I learned, adapted. The first time I needed a generator repair on my boat, I was told, "Ah'll be dere at two, Cap'm Jolly." At 7:15, this big black man in bib overalls came sauntering down the dock, all smiles. He wasn't late by island time. Back in my big-bucks business days, that would have driven me nuts. Somebody would have gotten fired. These days, I just shrug. I just have to make sure I'm dead-on on time for the cruise ships, though. They don't run on island time. They run on clean white-panty time, as Kid calls it.

As Gloria and I drove across the island, she pointed to a side street and then another side street, as we slowly climbed up the mountain. The one-story clapboard and corrugated steel houses, mostly faded out shacks painted faded green or just rust, got smaller and rougher looking the more we drove. The road was pitted and narrow, making slow going. The dogs, chickens, and pigs scavenging the streets didn't help either. This was not tourist town. I was grateful Gloria was with me, and I hoped I could trust her. With each turn, as we climbed the mountain, the road and the shacks got worse.

"Is it okay for me to be here?" I asked in a low voice. Unlike in the States, islanders didn't pretend to be colorblind. On one hand, everyone got along, mostly, but blacks and whites also mostly kept their distance. I think that's why they got along. Mostly.

Gloria didn't say anything. She knew what I meant.

She did, however, become more alert as we hit a curbless intersection. She pointed to a spot, and I pulled off the road and parked in the dirt lot in front of an old, wood-frame, open-front building. The white paint was chipping off the beams. The sign, which indicated this was The Jerk, was battered and faded. This place probably didn't have a website. You either knew where it was or you didn't.

When we got out, some grimy looking young men loitering around the front looked up with inquiring expressions. One of them was wearing one of French Tony's T-shirts: "If it smells good, eat it." I won't describe the graphic.

Their eyes were dark and cold. One put a pointer finger to the side of his nose. Gloria shook her head, making it clear we were here for food, not drugs.

I wasn't afraid of the shadow boys. They were mostly interested in tourists. With my dusty shirt and greasy cut-off shorts, I looked nothing like the well-scrubbed visitors off the cruise ships or staying at the hotels. Still, I glanced at their feet. I had put on a pair of treaded boat shoes. They were ideal for traction on board and speed on land. Funny how you think on the island.

They had on flip flops. I knew I could outrun them, even the younger guys, who I knew had me beat by 25 years and 25 pounds.

After a critical glance at me, they ignored us. We had passed muster. Even the young ones knew the rules. Number one: Don't scare or hurt the tourists; they were everyone's bread and butter. Number two: If you do rob a white man, don't hurt him, ever. Number three: No matter what a white man does, including murder, the worst he'll get is escorted off the island. These kids knew the rules. Also, I was with a black girl, one who was sending out all-clear vibes.

Most of the locals preferred to be ignored. They didn't really mind the horny white guys with cash who came up the mountain in search of girls. I got the impression that what they hated the most were the do-gooder tourists who hit the island with money to burn and a foolish need to show the natives that they were all alike, brothers and sisters under the skin. This generally included getting a picture with their new, nervously smiling island friends in housekeeping to show the folks back home. It made the do-gooders feel wonderful about themselves, and the locals knew it was good for tips. *Ka-ching.*

Live and let live worked for most of the islanders, and it worked for me, mostly because I didn't care about black, white, brown, gay or straight. I had no causes. If a white man threatened me, I either walked away or flattened him; same for a black man.

Though I was not in my part of town today, I had Gloria with me. Kind of like having a guest pass. Still, I had my doubts. What if Gloria had a coked-up husband or jealous boyfriend or black militant brothers?

Stepping into the shade of the old, wood-frame building, I caught the spicy aroma of pork ribs, chicken and goat dishes. The customers' plates were heaped with mounds of beans and rice, chicken feet, pigs' knuckles, and other animal body parts I could not recognize. I also noted the pungent odor of body sweat from the all-black clientèle. Some were laborers, relaxing after a long day's work; some hadn't labored even a short day in their lives. The black-sweat odor contrasted starkly with the intoxicating aroma of the food.

It was a soul-food, Spanish Caribbean mix, not the kind of stuff the *touristas* would ever put in their mouths, if only because the price was about a third what they'd pay down the mountain in tourist town. The black girls behind the counter smiled shyly and pretended to shoo the flies off the food. As I strolled confidently in, all eyes followed us. Outnumbered twenty to one, I felt relaxed and comfortable. Most natives still deferred to a white man, as racist as that may sound.

But for me, it was more than that. It flashed through my mind that this felt more comfortable than walking into the nineteenth-hole bar at the Northbrooke Country Club. There I would be surrounded and backslapped by a bunch of business people trying to act like they were my best friends. They also didn't mind missing a few easy putts in exchange for an opportunity to screw me out of a few thousand dollars on a too-hot-to-pass-on business deal. Backslapped and back-stabbed. I couldn't recall any of these well-scrubbed country club friends picking up the phone to talk after hearing that Connie had left me and my business was heading into the crapper. No, these folks at The Jerk were tame by comparison.

Actually, as I said, I liked these folks better, if only because they didn't glad-hand me or pretend to be friends. I even liked the shadow boys better, especially the ones who would swoop in close with a glare and glance off my shoulder just to let me know they weren't afraid of me. They were honest about wanting to pick my pocket.

And if any of them in the future would pull a knife on me, they'd look me in the eye when they did it. In truth, I liked them. Unlike most people I knew, they acknowledged they were thugs. The relationship worked because all the players knew their roles.

It made me think about The Boys in the Trees, a rag-tag bunch of island teens who sat in the branches of a big tree in the middle of the dirt and sand parking lot at Rouge Beach. I'd park my car and, even before they could start chattering at me, hold up a five dollar bill. As they snatched it up into the tree, I'd wag a finger up into the leaves. "You watch my car good, boys. Got that?"

"Do terrific for ten."

"You'll do fine for five."

"No problem, mista," they'd yell, laughing and grinning warmly from ear to ear, and I'd shake my finger at them one more time for good luck. "I'm not mista, boys, I'm Cap'm Jolly. Got it?"

They'd laugh and hoot and make fun of me, but they'd leave me alone. My car was never disturbed. In return, I'd tell tourists around me that this was insurance. The island way. "Think of it as valet parking without the parking." Otherwise, there was a very good chance that the car would be picked clean or at least broken into before they got back. Also, if they wanted some happy weed, these boys could provide the best quality for the best price. It all worked out. *Ka-ching.*

So, I felt pretty comfortable at The Jerk. While one young fellow with slow, uncertain movements and glassy eyes bummed a cigarette from me, Gloria chatted and laughed with one of the girls behind the counter. These folks here weren't going to invite me over for dinner, and that was fine. They'd probably try to serve me pigs' ears. Some would bum a cigarette off me; others might even mug me if I was in their neighborhood after dark. Know the rules. Know the roles. Know how to get along.

THE STATES
Somebody Do Something!

Sitting in the bar that winter night back in the States with Scott, I continued, more interested in talking than in being listened to. I didn't care.

"Know how I found out?"

Scott looked at me, but didn't say anything. I caught him glancing at his watch.

"The kids told me on Father's Day," I said, recalling how Connie had gone into the drug store before we all went out for a pretend-we're-a-happy-family brunch.

Scott still didn't say anything, so I shut up.

Connie and I had already separated, but it was all vague. So, I was feeling hopeful. I even told Natty that maybe things were getting better. "Mom seemed in a good mood," I'd told her while we waited in the car. "Maybe we could work it out." Natty shook her head and stared at me like I was a dope. "Dad," she'd said, "Mom's getting calls when you're not around." She glanced around to make sure her mother wasn't coming out of the store. "She's seeing someone. When you were gone last week, she went out. I heard her come in. Then she called him again, to let him know she was home safe.

"Mom and I had a fight about it," she had continued. "She told me to mind my own business. She told me I didn't understand. She said she was doing it for us, too, that we'd be better off not living in a home with tension and sadness."

"Doing it for you, huh?" I had asked, frowning. "How fucking noble," I added, this time to myself.

Natty had looked at me from the backseat of the car. Her face was all teary. She pleaded, "Dad, do something!"

Dad, do something! Those were the words that kept ringing in my ears. Do something! Do what? I had been the fixer, the guy in charge, the control freak. So I tried to do something. I tried to talk to Connie. She'd just smiled sadly and recited a brief talk she must have been preparing for weeks. "Joth," she'd said, "I do love you. I'm just not in love with you."

I remember just staring at her. Hard to argue with what you don't understand.

THE ISLAND
Rummies

A nother day in paradise – blue sky, blue sea, fluffy white clouds, a just-right gentle breeze. We motored *The Do Over* through the lagoon and around to the supply dock for a few essentials we couldn't pick up at the marina store, mostly a case of cheap rum, some artificial punch, and a better price on ice for the cooler. We'd meet our sixteen guests at the cruise line's excursion dock in an hour. As always, I studied the names on the roster, not sure what I was looking for, but reading them over nonetheless. Then I handed the clipboard to Kid, who had finished stowing the supplies. I fired up the engine, jerked the motor into gear, loving the sound of the low growl as the gears meshed noisily. Spinning the wheel, I maneuvered away from the dock. I studied the sky, looked up at the mast, winked at Jocko II, and tried to put John/Candy out of mind. We wouldn't unfurl the sail until we were through the drawbridge and clear of the lagoon.

My thoughts were all jumbled.

John/Candy wouldn't go away. They kept jumping all over my mind like three monkeys wrestling over one banana. I really shouldn't care. They were just a couple of rummies around the bar most nights. Still….

Time and place and space jumped around like those monkeys.

I found it easy to imagine what they could have been like years ago, when they had first arrived. I suspected that, like so many of us, they had come – and stayed – for some vaguely defined idea of freedom and escape, even if that meant the freedom to drink themselves to death and the desire to escape reality.

I had always sort of suspected that one day they would both just disappear – murdered, drowned, or just gone, hopped a tramp steamer off the island. Or they would turn up under some seaweed in the rocks off to the side of one of the beaches. She must have once been pretty – whimsical, wispy-blonde pretty, with doe eyes, a dark tan, and a shy smile. But by the time I'd met her, she was too beat up and used up even for the brothel on the other side of the island, even though white women had a special appeal to the mostly black patrons.

She wouldn't fit in with Black Mike's all-white girls, either. I'd seen Black Mike give her a few bucks, but he never took her on. That's why I could never think of Black Mike as a pimp. No, he was more of a manager, a businessman, not a thug. Still, though he could be a dangerous enemy, he was also a loyal friend, I'd learned.

The two of them, John and Candy, had come down to the island as young adventure seekers, bought the *Tor Helga*, and planned to run fishing charters to pay for their food, booze, and cigarettes. It was a simple plan, and it should have worked. Calabash told me that everybody liked them, and they had been hard working at first. That was when they had become known as John/Candy, even if only one of them walked in the door.

Eventually, as happens so often on the islands, more and more money went for booze. They became rummies. The playful dream gradually became a tired nightmare. After John had disappeared, and we all assumed suicide, a long swim on an outgoing tide, Candy became ... well, she had very little left to lose and even less to offer. She often hung out with the scrounging island dogs, who slept with her on the beach and gave her some degree of warning before the shadow boys stumbled on her.

The few mornings when I found her sleeping on board *The Do Over* had been the only times I'd ever seen her sober, though with haunted, bloodshot eyes. Shame. She was bright and articulate, even with a hangover.

Pony Rides

As for the day's roster, most were couples, I noticed, but you couldn't always tell.

Kid was alone again, no bunkie since that tall, tight-cheeked Aussie girl took off with Hans, an affable German with tattoos, several dozen piercings and big, big muscles. Kid didn't seem to mind. When he ran into Hans a week later at Iggie's, he bought him a beer and offered a tip on how to find her sweet spot.

Me? Well, the cash box was running a bit low, thanks to rainy day cancellations. So, I guess I'd powder my nose and turn on the charm. I know that being personable and friendly did increase tips; that and making the rum punch stronger than usual. And how did that make me different from Black Mike's topless blonde girls?

So, I started thinking about the names on the roster for today's excursion. I'd sometimes try to guess what they were like by their names, but I rarely got it right. I imagined that someday I'd run across an old friend, maybe even Sam. Ya never know.

So I just watched. Some of my day trippers would get on board, strip down to their bathing suits, tilt back their heads, and pose themselves atop the rope webbing at the bow between the two hulls, as if they did this every day. Some, with studied casualness, even went topless. Older couples, or true landlubbers of any age, would stumble and lurch around for a while, looking for a good spot to drop their beach bags and claim as their territory for the duration of the cruise. Others, usually the guys, would become curious about the boat, and ask engineer-type questions about displacement, engine size, or insurance costs.

The women all had one thing in common. They loved it when Kid and I paid attention to them. (I was amazed when I first realized how many people were starving for attention.) And, yes, I admit that, on the way back, after the drinks were flowing freely, I used to sometimes do the classic arms-around-and-hold-the-wheel and pretend to let them steer. They loved it, even the married ones – steering the boat in the arms of who they wanted to think was an exotic island captain – as long as we all knew damn well that hubby was watching. It was all part of the show. If I played it right, even hubby got off on it. Seeing his wife being chased by some island beach bum was a turn-on for some guys. Great for tips. But if I played it wrong, the hubby would get pouty and sulky (which was okay) or downright pissed off (which was not). Bad for tips. Just so that he didn't tattle to the cruise director.

I guess that meant my role, ultimately, was to be the imaginary face on the guy who screwed her that night. She could pretend she was being taken by a pirate, and he could pretend she was a biker slave, or something like that. Weirdly, I noticed that, after I bought that stupid eye patch, trip tips went up twenty-five percent. Look dangerous … but don't be. A touch of danger … but not too much. They all mostly wanted safe pony rides, not open-water, endless-sea adventures. The women who wanted true adventure went to work for Black Mike or came down to the island for a two-week vacation and were still here four years later. Even Kid's bunkies, they mostly wanted a toe-dip taste of the exotic island life and a good screwing, which usually lost its appeal when the clean panties, shampoo, and toothpaste ran out.

Most even moaned the same – long, loud, and luscious – when they supposedly had orgasms. I noticed this when I'd hear Kid's bunkie-of-the-week let loose. They all sounded like Meg Ryan in the movie *When Harry Met Sally*.

As for the real adventure seekers or drone-on life escapees, Black Mike once told me that he was approached by women at least once a week.

"Are they desperate?" I had asked, thinking of Candy.

"Nah. Dey jus want someting mo dan de safe, predictable life dey had back home. Dat life kills mos folks. It kilt me."

At that last comment, I had looked up and into Mike's eyes. He stared back, and I couldn't tell if it was a challenge, a dare, or an invitation I saw in his eyes. "Hmph" had been my only response.

No, most of these women on *The Do Over*, most of them – and their husbands, too – they just wanted pony rides, slow, plodding, one-foot-in-front-of-the-other turns around the ring, with some old cowboy guiding the reins and steadying the saddle. I wasn't always sure if I was the cowboy or the pony. Yee haa! Honey, you look wonderful! They'd take pictures and talk about their island adventures to the cookie bakers at PTA meetings for months. And they'd come back to the exact same island, stay in the exact same hotel, eat in the exact same restaurants, and take the exact same excursions year after year in this wonderful, safe, exotic paradise.

Down here three years, I was starting to get repeat customers. They'd greet me loudly, like we were old buddies, even though our entire relationship consisted of four hours together on a boat with 15 other touristas twelve months ago.

"Hey, Captain Jolly!" they'd call out. "Remember me?" And I'd always bellow back, "Hey, matey, good to see you. How long's it been?" They loved the myth of the exotic, romantic island life. But it was just a myth.

What we didn't tell the *touristas* was how most of us lived with bars on the windows and a fileting knife under our pillows, and how even that didn't keep out the shadow boys. The moneyed folks lived in gated communities, walled off from the riff raff.

Nobody owned guns. That was because, as it had been explained to me, the island police didn't care if you stuck someone, but they got all worked up over shootings. "Hurt 'em a little, Jolly, but doan kill 'em," Ahmani, the harbor master, had told me as I laid cash across his palm to keep my boat from being impounded.

Most of the islanders were good with a knife. Black Mike, for example, could snap out a shiny blade now and then, and I even saw him once put it to a guy's throat. Oh, yeah, that guy was me. And then there was Gloria, who I'd seen kill and gut that iguana in two minutes.

My knife was an eight-inch, wooden-handled fileting knife with a stainless steel blade and a sharp tip. It slid easily into a leather sheath that I had to scrape hard once a week to keep from mildewing and strung warningly on my canvas belt. A couple of times I'd had to put my hand on it and, steely eyes on the other guy, unsnap the strap. Back home it took a Lexus and a silk tie that cost more than the car payment to get respect; down here, a knife worked just fine. Nobody bothered me, but that was mostly because I didn't bother anybody. Still, I'd never pulled the knife on an excursion customer (that would have gotten my contract cancelled by sunset), and almost never on a *tourista* in one of the bars or on the street. Just bad for business. We had a happy-island, no-problems image to maintain.

What really kept the natives off *The Do Over* after hours or when I was at The Sunset was a simple strategy I learned from Calabash: Have nothing to steal and nobody will steal it. That was why I'd never keep more than a bottle of rum on board, storing the cases for the rum punches in my marina locker.

Even so, I caught a guy one day coming on deck from my cabin with my shampoo, a stupid bottle of shampoo. We glared at each other on the dock for a long moment before he slowly walked away. So I gave up shampoo.

THE STATES
Do Something, Anything

I must have been staring off into space at the liquor bottles behind the bar.

"Hey, Man, you okay?" Scott had asked, almost affectionately, but maybe with more pity than affection in his tone. I had a sense that our clock was running down.

I slowly turned and looked at him. Forcing a smile, I said, "You can imagine how much fun that Father's Day brunch was. Know what Connie said when I told her I knew? She said, 'Joth, I think you'd better get on with your life.'"

"She said that? She said you should get on with your life?"

"Yeah. Sweet as can be, as if she was urging me to wear my scarf on a chilly day. That was her way of ending twenty years of marriage. Two kids, a home, all that we'd been through. 'I think you'd better get on with your life.' Of course, that's not what she said at first. She said he was just a friend, and I shouldn't be jealous. I was being unreasonable."

Scott went back to studying the bottles. Then he said, slowly, snarling, "I'd kick the bastard's ass from here to Timbuktu."

Then he glared at me, as if challenging my manhood.

"I did," I said almost under my breath, trying not to sound like I was bragging. Now speaking louder and breathing out heavily: "I went to his house, grabbed him by the shirt, threw him through the storm window of the front door." I couldn't help but laugh when I said it. God, that felt good.

"Good for you."

"Yep. Then he called Connie, who called the cops. When they arrived and asked if I'd beaten him up, I said, 'Nope, I threw the fucker through the door.'"

Still chuckling, I turned to Scott and added, "I spent four days in the county jail, charged with assault."

"Oh," was all Scott said, shaking his head, but chuckling, too.

"I think it was worth it," I said with a shrug.

Still, the good feeling didn't last. "All I managed to do was drive Connie further from me ... and to him. It provided more evidence that she was a sweet little victim, and I was the big bad wolf. She took out a peace bond on me."

Scott looked at me. "What?"

"A restraining order. I can't be within a hundred feet of her or him. The worst part – I gave her exactly what she wanted. Justification. She can now officially play the victim. Triumphantly, she's telling anyone who'll listen that I'm an animal. She was in an abusive relationship, married to a man with a terrible temper, and she's lucky to get out with her life. She's afraid."

"Afraid? Of you?" Scott stared at me as he processed how the break-up game is played. Then he laughed. "You beast. Maybe you're better off without her."

"That's what I keep telling myself. Do I sound convincing yet?"

"Keep workin' on it."

We slipped back into silence. I was starting to think that maybe, just maybe, I should give up. Whatever I was trying to do, it wasn't working. Sitting there in that bar beside Scott on a weekday night, the frustration – that battle between fear, anger and hopelessness, all wrestling around like three pissed-off cats tied in a bag together – rose fast and unexpectedly inside me again, tearing at me.

I exploded in disbelief. "Twenty years!" I hissed. A dark hole loomed in front of me, the frustration of being impotent to do anything about my life. Natty's words from Father's Day lived in my head: "Dad, do something!" Do what?

Stupidly, I looked at Scott as if he could help. My voice sounding too thin and too small this time, I said again, "Twenty years." In my head, I thought, Scott, do something. Somebody do something, please. Anybody?

When I realized that Scott didn't know what to say and that even this, my relationship with my oldest friend, was going to slip away from me, the strangest feeling came over me. I wanted to go home. Not just home, but all the way home. I wanted desperately to see my parents, to go back to the home I'd grown up in. I was forty-five years old and hadn't really lived at home since I was eighteen. But I wanted to run home and just bury my head in my mother's arms. I hated being a grownup. Mom, do something.

Sam, do something.

THE ISLAND
John/Candy

I steered *The Do Over* out of the lagoon, my cargo of sixteen giggling *touristas* excited about the prospect of their half-day snorkeling adventure.

Me? I looked up at the sail and smiled. It was not complicated. Not at all. I think that was because I guess I was just getting tired of women. More accurately, tired of trying to maintain relationships. Tired of the drama. Too much work. That was why I liked Bonita so much. No future. No plans. No expectations. Was she my pony ride? Safe and unadventurous? Maybe. I didn't know. I didn't really care.

I radioed in my request to raise the drawbridge and checked the weather channel. There was a series of tropical storms lining up out in the Atlantic, and they were making their way to the islands. Nothing unusual about that. We normally get around a dozen tropical storms, and about half of them turn into hurricanes. I've been told that one hits the island about once every twenty-five years. Still, good to keep an eye out.

I snapped the radio back into its cradle and cut through the open drawbridge. As soon as we were beyond the short channel and out into open water, Kid glanced at me, and I nodded. He jumped up to let out the sails, and in less than two minutes we were running under full canvas. Then he jumped down into the cockpit cabin and nodded at me. I killed the engine. As always, the quiet sound of *The Do Over* gently slapping through the light sea and the wind filling the sail made me pause and take a deep breath. That's a feeling I never got in church.

I stood at the helm. She handled easy in the relatively calm sea. While Kid prepped the gear, I let my mind drift back to Bonita. I think from the start that was why I liked her and wanted to have her around. She was uncomplicated. And if there were deep-down complications somewhere inside her, she kept them to herself. I liked her. It was as simple as that.

So the first night she'd stayed over on *The Do Over,* after I'd overcome her tuna aroma, I'd laid it out for her: "Don't try to change me. Don't tell me what to do. And don't mock me. Ever. Other than that, I don't care what you do."

When I was finished, she'd looked sleepily around, as if to see if there was anyone else in bed with us I might have been talking to. Slowly, her eyes returned to mine, and she stared blankly at me for a moment in the dim light of the cabin. Finally, she'd said, "Okay," yawned, and rolled over, spooning her butt into my crotch, and fell asleep.

It isn't even as though she moved in. She was just there, with a toothbrush, a backup pair of shorts and top; no underwear, no bra, no discussion, always cheerful, but not annoyingly giggly cheerful. I didn't try to tell her what to do; she didn't try to tell me what to do. When the past caught up with me now and then and I got melancholy and felt the need to talk, she'd listen, just listen, never asking questions, which was fine with me. If she ever felt the need to talk, I never knew about it.

I knew people back home, mostly women, who would have loved to dissect and pick apart Bonita and find out what she was hiding or repressing. Me, I loved it that she did her thing, and I did mine.

***

Though I'd never really given it much thought before, I was surprised to learn that it was the women who were in control, who were doing the seducing. This is something that would never occur to most guys. We love to think we're the hunters, the chasers. The girls? Hell, weren't they the prey trying to protect their ever-precious gift, holding out for the right man? That's what comes of a traditional Catholic school education. It never dawns on most guys that at least some of them want us as much as we want them. Revelatory? For some of us, yes. Girls were supposed to be sweet, smell nice, and put up an honest fight to keep us out. Myths.

I'm 45 years old and, in truth, I never would have figured it out by myself. One morning, after John of John/Candy had finally disappeared, and I'd found her on board *The Do Over* curled up under a tarp half under the gunnel, she'd said, "Jolly, for a grown man, you still don't get the grown-up facts of life."

"Good morning, Candy," I'd said, gently trying to move her off the boat. I felt good about myself around her, beneficent, kind of how a self-satisfied person feels patting a needy dog on the head. "Come on. I have to get ready for an excursion, so it's time to wake up and head out."

Then I stopped being business-like and smiled slyly. "Or," and I dropped my voice, "we can just say, screw it, and you and I head around the point and spend the day balling each other's brains out."

"Sorry," she said with the hint of a smile, pretending to be offended, "I have standards." Ladylike, she unfolded herself from the tarp, exposing arms and legs that looked like thin sticks. Her eyes remained dull. She was a burnout, no longer susceptible to flattery or flirting. She was a skeleton, like one of the mummy movie babes. No meat. No joy. Nothing.

She had long since forgotten about sex, though I suspect she got rolled over, raped by the shadow boys, and left to the dogs for company more than she even remembered, and it didn't matter to her. For her, life was rum, beer, a mooched cigarette, and a few scraps of food now and then. If there was sex involved, it had to do with obtaining a shot of rum, beer, a mooched cigarette, and a few scraps of food now and then. Life for Candy could not have been simpler. I think that was true even before John had taken what we all decided had been a long swim on an outgoing tide. In a deep, deep down way, I almost envied her. Almost. She had become the ultimate minimalist. Give me a few more years.

As she sat up, Candy was even less in the mood for mirth today. That's when she said, "Jolly, for a grown man, you still don't get the grown-up facts of life."

"Yes, darling," I shrugged, really not in the mood for a lecture from a burnout this morning. I had a long day ahead of being charming Captain Jolly for the excursion *touristas*. Still, I teased, "But as long as there are girls who will giggle, there will always be boys who will make fools of themselves."

Bonita, still sleepy and hair scruffy, had come out of the cabin and snapped on the switch to start the coffee, which was now ready on the catamaran's 18-foot wide dashboard. She poured several mugs and snapped off a piece of stale baguette for Candy.

Candy took her mug and smiled faintly at Bonita.

"So, tell me, Candy," I said.

Anger flared in her eyes. "No, Jolly. We're John/Candy!" she corrected me sharply.

As quickly as her anger flared, it collapsed. "Leave me that," she said softly, but with a defiant flare in her bloodshot eyes.

"Yes," I said in a low voice, taking my mug of coffee that Bonita offered. "So, tell me, John/Candy, how are you this morning?"

I waited as she took a sip of coffee. Then with a grimace, she gnawed a disinterested bite off the small chunk of the two-day-old crust of bread. I suspected her yellow-black teeth hurt.

The coffee cleared her head, and she began the lesson, ignoring my question. "You, men, you flatter a woman, compliment her smile, her breasts, hair, legs, butt."

She talked with her mouth full, indifferent to the food, waving the piece of baguette at me.

I looked her body over, focusing on where her no-longer breasts should have been.

"Hey, Dim Bulb," she said, with the hint of a smile. "My eyes are up here."

"Yeah," I responded with a playful smile. We both knew the routine. "But your tits are down there."

She shook her head, smiled and muttered, "Men are such dogs."

I grinned. It was good to see her smile. She was hard not to like. "Thank you. I've been promoted. Most women call me a pig."

Returning to her point, she continued: "And when she giggles and smiles, you think you're on seduction highway. You think you're in control. Her giggles and smile make you feel good. But she's the one seducing you."

She slurped her coffee, dribbling some on her dirty T-shirt, and wiped her mouth with her hand. "I mean, we're not that stupid, Jolly. We know that when a guy's being nice, it has nothing to do with being nice."

I quit fooling around. Squatting down in front of her, I sipped my coffee and listened. Behind me, Kid was starting to stir, popping open a soda before getting right to checking the gear for the day's snorkel excursion. Bonita looked out over the harbor, half listening to John/Candy's sermon and looking for signs of life on *Outrageous* across the lagoon. She was mating for Captain Ronnie on *Outrageous* today and wanted to make sure she was ready when the boat swung by to pick her up. Timing was crucial. She stood on the side of the boat and steadied herself on a stay wire. That was the signal that she was ready to jump across to *Outrageous* when Ronnie motored over, then came about hard, and without ever slowing down, put his boat so close to mine that all Bonita had to do was step across.

I ignored all the activity. I wasn't being patient. I liked Candy. Besides, I've gotten better wisdom from drunks than from scholars over the years. Plus, I knew, this was her way of paying for her bed and breakfast. It was all she had left, the barest shred of tattered dignity.

"But women," she continued, "unless they have been beaten down, are never susceptible to flattery. Never. Oh, we smile and giggle, but that's all part of the game to make *you* feel special. Right, Bonita?"

Bonita nodded without turning her head. She was also watching for Ahmani, the harbormaster, who could cost us our day's wages, and he would if he could.

I jumped in. "So, when I tell you how beautiful you are ..."

"It's either true or a lie. And we know it. We don't need to hear it from you. We have mirrors. Sure, you make us feel good, but it's really us who make *you* feel special. That's how we get free drinks, limo rides, even" – she waved the scrap of bread in my face and smiled – "free breakfast."

"My pleasure," I said, smiling back, and knowing she was dead on right.

"Remember, no matter how much we play along, we're not as stupid as you guys think we are.

"Now, men, on the other hand," she continued, "are always susceptible to flattery. Always."

"Oh?" I nodded, a little offended, but searching my memories.

"For example, Jolly, I have to admit that you are handsome, in pretty good shape, and you have a winning smile. That's why women like you."

I grinned, filling up with my own sense of sensuality.

Then she opened her hands, made a bad-tooth frown, and said, "See what I mean? Even a burn-out drunk bitch like me can make you giggle like a pimple-pussed teenager."

Bonita came down off her perch. She reached over my shoulder with an empty Styrofoam cup and handed it to Candy. "Yes, but he's my pimple-pussed teenager," she said with a smile, "and Ahmani just fired up across the lagoon and has us in his sights."

"Cap'm, we have to shove off," Kid warned, seeing the same thing. He cranked up the engine and checked the gauges. "Ahmani, that fat fuck asshole, is on the move, and he's heading our way."

We all looked up to see a small tender visiting the boats along the docks. On board were three serious looking islanders in ill-fitting, off-the-rack uniforms. It was always better to be able to hold up and flash your paperwork, fake or real, so they might just keep going. Give them an opportunity to come on board and they'd take their time rummaging about, finding any excuse to slap a nuisance fine on you, payable in cash … on the spot. They also knew where and when you had to be, so delaying you meant money in their greasy palms.

I once ran into Ahmani in Luana's restaurant. A few drinks into the night, I came over to his table and suggested, "Why don't I just buy your dinner tonight, and we can skip the morning inspection?"

He turned to his girlfriend, smiled, nodded, and called the waitress over. "'Scuse me, Angelica," he said slowly, all teeth and doing a half-way decent imitation of being personable, "please be sure to give my tab to Captain Jolly here. And please give us two grilled lobsters and a nice bottle of wine, one of your finest."

Then he grinned at me like a python about to eat his catch.

"Stupid," I said to myself about myself as I skulked away. "Stupid."

Candy was well aware of the need for speed. They had owned *Tor Helga*, and for a brief period, had worked with the cruise lines. The lines ran on precise time, like clockwork, not island time. That was why John/Candy had lost the contract within a month. They showed up late. They showed up at the wrong dock. They never showed up at all.

She also knew Ahmani and hated him. A black man, Ahmani loved lording it over whites, especially white women.

Suddenly alert, John/Candy took the Styrofoam cup, thanked Bonita, tried to transfer her coffee from mug to cup, spilling most of it on herself, and leapt nimbly onto the dock. Bonita watched as *Outrageous* pulled out of its berth, cutting off the harbormaster's boat, and headed fast and straight at *The Do Over*. Almost on top of us, Captain Ronnie spun the wheel hard and, never slowing down, came right up alongside us. Bonita stepped aboard and was handed gently down by two men, who grinned. She turned, flashed me a warm, child-like smile, and blew me a kiss. "Have a glorious day, Cap'm." The skipper of *Outrageous* nodded, gave me a casual salute and gunned his boat.

I saluted back, took the helm from Kid, and watched Candy, old again, walk slowly up to the chain link gate leading to the parking lot. Spinning the wheel, I nodded at Kid, and headed off to work like any commuter getting ready to merge from the onramp onto the beltway.

Kid dropped the lines and pushed our nose out into the harbor as I ground the engine into forward gear and then adjusted the speed controls. The boat eased forward. Just a hundred feet behind us, Ahmani honked his horn and shouted at us to stop. Fortunately, even though the idiots on his crew had weapons, they knew it was bad for business to shoot the boat owners, at least in broad daylight. The slow and clumsy harbor boat had lights and sirens, but we also all knew that Ahmani had strict instructions to never use them. Again, bad for business. Kid ambled over and stood by my shoulder. Studiously refusing to look back or in any way acknowledge the horn and shouts from Ahmani's boat, we knew we just had to stay ahead of him for a few seconds as he called and tried to cut us off before we got out into the main channel of the lagoon. We knew we'd be okay once we neared the excursion dock. No one was allowed to be in a bad mood around the *touristas* – all grins and smiles – and even a dim-witted, greasy-palmed civil servant like Ahmani knew that. Business.

Other boat owners, mostly the ex-pats from the States, were watching this routine comedy routine and cheering us on. I sometimes felt like I was a teenager back in church on Sunday mornings trying to slip past the burly ushers and make my escape after communion.

Kid nodded approvingly as I wheeled *The Do Over* across Ahmani's bow, missing him by a few feet. This scenario played out at least once a month, sometimes more often, my Road Runner to Ahmani's Wile E. Coyote. "Beep! Beep!" I laughed out loud. "This is gonna be a magnificent day!" I announced to Jocko II, as I made a bee line across all the other boat traffic and headed to the excursion dock, which was kind of like home base in a game of olly olly oxenfree hide-and-seek. Kid looked back at Ahmani and waved. "Good morning, Harbor Master!" he yelled cheerily and under his breath, said, "You fat fuck."

When he turned back, he asked, "You ever gonna let me take the helm?" He asked the same question every morning.

"Maybe tomorrow," I answered, giving him the same answer I gave him every morning.

Better than any bottle of whiskey or the three seconds of an explosive orgasm with a hard-bodied woman, this moment was my greatest joy. No, besting Ahmani was a bonus. I meant being at the helm of *The Do Over*. I looked over at Jocko II, strapped to the mast, a little stuffing sticking out, and nodded. This was all we had ever asked for, ever. This made Connie's leaving me, losing my business and my money, even having to surrender my key to the locker room at the country club worth it … in spades. Some people drove a boat. Some steered it. Me? Well, *The Do Over* and I, we did it together. I knew the feel of her, whether under motor or sail. I knew when we had too much sail out before it even thought about snapping in the wind. I knew when the tide was running and how to head through it, cutting the water smoothly, gently, swiftly.

I could steer this beautiful 38-foot catamaran in my sleep, with my eyes closed, in the moonless dead of night. Unlike most people I know, this boat was easy to love. *The Do Over* never argued, never tried to change me, never fought me. She was even better than Bonita. And I, in turn, understood when she needed me to let her go and run with the wind, to turn her into the tide or just let her swing at anchor.

No, as Cap'm Jolly, I would never give up the wheel. Over the years, I had lost all my money, most of my family, and the vast majority of arguments. On board, there was no drama, no agendas, no debates about where to go and how to get there. That was why, when I picked up the day's *touristas*, I did so with mixed feelings. Part of me wanted to keep them off my boat. But, oh yeah, there was that per-head payment that kept me and *The Do Over* afloat.

With that shiny, oversized, stainless steel boat wheel in my hands, I had to wonder sometimes whether, like John/Candy, I would ever leave this island. Some people saw dead John and drunken Candy as tragic. Not really. Not even close. My only question was whether I'd end up dead or a rummy. Neither end bothered me a whole lot. Just curious.

MANGROVE COVE
Scuttled

The hurricane was in full blow. I'd never been in a category 5 hurricane before, but I figured I was dead-on in one now. A cat-5 has winds higher than 155 miles per hour. Few houses could survive in one of those. The island, at least the older sections with homes and shops made out of wood, would be flattened. I hoped The Jerk would survive. The newer places, built of cinderblock covered with plaster and paint, most of them would make it, though they might lose their windows and roofs. The boats in the harbor? Even if I'd made a bad choice to head out to Mangrove Cove, I think the boat owners who opted to stay would never sail their boats again.

So, here we were, me and my beloved *Do Over*, my flat-footed cat, in the middle of nowhere. Worked for me. The mangrove cove would have been perfect up to a cat-3 blow, with maximum winds of 130 miles per hour. But we were way beyond that.

Kid and I were sitting in the midship common room. We were both watching the large tempered glass windshield. It was bulging and groaning and likely to give way any minute. When that happened, besides being at risk of being impaled by the shards, we'd likely get blown out the back of the cabin like a cannon. The only safe place, I had finally concluded, was underwater. The more I thought about the idea, the more it made sense.

We needed to sink her and sink her fast.

The wind was screaming at full pitch. I grabbed Kid by his life vest and yanked him outside. Then I unclipped the man-overboard line at the base of the mast and snapped it to his vest. I did the same to mine. The rain and wind were coming from everywhere.

I grabbed his face and pulled him close to mine. "Be careful!" I yelled, and he grinned back, giving me a thumbs-up and a kiss on the nose.

"Idiot!" I thought and then realized that I was grinning, too.

Automatically, without another word, he cut left and I went right and we clawed our way on all fours toward the bow. The wind was so strong I felt like my life vest was being torn off me. It kept pulling me off balance.

I had made it to my point on the starboard bow and was giving each come-along six pulls, letting out three feet of line. Kid was done, too, and I could feel the boat buck more wildly. Now we needed to pull the drain plugs and get her under water fast.

Kid stood up to give an arms raised, King Kong sign of triumph, ready to steady himself on the mast wires. He could find those wires in his sleep. But he must have forgotten that we'd just dropped the mast; the wires were lashed to the deck.

I smiled at his clowning as he stood there for a moment and then the next wave hit. It had to be five feet over our heads, and I heard the crash of the windshield. I was swept over the side.

My man-overboard line held, and I was swung violently back, banging against the hull. I assumed/hoped that Kid was on the portside. I climbed aboard. The boat was already half swamped as I ducked below and yanked the starboard plugs. Water poured in, and the boat settled quickly and clumsily to the bottom. I hoped that meant Kid had pulled his portside plugs. I could feel the hull scratching on the sand. I could also feel that she was no longer being battered about. This might actually work, I thought for a moment.

Now to find Kid. No, not yet. Now to survive and pray that Kid had, too. We were both on our own for now.

THE ISLAND
Rules and Roles

People don't think the same way in the islands as they do back in the States.

I remember one night, coming out of a restaurant with my brother, who was visiting the island. My car was partially blocked in by a small delivery truck. I decided to see if I could ease my car out. However, after back-and-forthing it for ten minutes, I was still two inches shy of being able to get past the truck's bumper. Two freaking inches. I was getting hotter and hotter, slamming the gear shift harder each time from reverse to drive to reverse to drive.

That was when this skinny, old black islander with yellow eyes came along. I'd seen him earlier as he roamed the parking lot looking for tips. This was his self-appointed domain. As we headed into the restaurant, he'd approached and asked me for a few bucks to watch my car, to make sure no one bothered it. Glaring at him, I'd told him no, but God help him if my car was damaged when I got back.

Well, here it was, after dinner, and I was trying to get my wedged-in car wedged out. The same black guy came up and stood beside the car window. He was timid, like a dog who'd been kicked too many times. When I looked at him, he said, "Pardon, Beeg Mon," and then he waited.

"What?" I'd snapped.

He broke into a big smile and said, "We leeeft it."

"What?"

"We leeeft it," he repeated, this time gesturing with his palms moving in an upward, raise-the-roof gesture.

I stared at him for a moment, puzzling over what he'd said.

Four of his friends were standing around behind the car, nervously watching, smiling.

I paused. Then I understood what he was suggesting and realizing that back in the States, nobody would even have thought of lifting a car by hand. ("Honey, call a tow truck.")

I looked at my brother. He shrugged.

"Okay, let's do it," I said, half curious how this was going to unfold.

I got out of the car, slammed the door and nodded to his friends. We all huddled around the rear of the car and leaned in, over the trunk. Then, on my count of three, we all lifted the car just enough to scoot it several inches to the side. I studied the space between the delivery truck bumper and my car's bumper, snorted, and then climbed in. Turning the wheel tight, I backed out into the parking lot, gliding past the truck with a quarter inch to spare.

This time it was my turn to look like a timid dog. Getting out of my car, I said, "Thank you, my friend. I owe you. What can I do for you?"

Without hesitating, he smiled and suggested, "You kin buy me and ma frens a beer?"

I looked around the group of black men, all dressed in dusty T-shirts and dirty black pants, with yellowed eyes and yellow-black teeth. They all grinned at me like I was their best friend.

"Deal." I nodded and smiled back and then gave him a small bill to split up.

"Oh, mon," he yipped, as his friends came closer. "Ga bless ya, Mon." I thought he was going to hug me, so I backed away. "We gots 'nuff fo tree beers each." He and his friends were deliriously happy.

I wasn't sure if I envied them or pitied them.

As we headed back across the island, my brother was grinning ear to ear. "I love this place, Jimmy. It's paradise."

"Yeah," I'd said dryly, trying to remember what it was that could make someone from the States get so thrilled over what had just happened.

Finally, I said a phrase that was becoming common to me: "Yeah, well, after a while, even paradise just gets to be home."

"And that's a problem why?" my brother had asked.

Good point, I thought, and grinned.

THE STATES
The Emperor's Clothes

As I mentioned, after Connie filed for divorce, I spent a lot of nights sleeping at the office. It sucked. I remember one night, padding down the hall to the men's room, I turned the corner and bumped smack into the janitor. Thrown back decades in a flash, I was five years old and just about pee-my-pants scared of monsters in the basement. I wonder if we ever really believe there are no creatures lurking in dark basements. Hell, even not-so-dark basements. Just basements. And nighttime office buildings. And other places.

Both of us startled, he and I each shouted/screamed an octave too high for men, grabbed our hearts, and then laughed nervously, exhaling hard to catch our breaths, all the while releasing a string of rapid-fire profanities. Oh, Jeez! Holy shit! God damn! Whooph! Scared the hell outa me!

That adrenalin dissolved into awkwardness. "Just working late," I felt the need to explain. "You can skip my office again."

My eyes followed his as he glanced down at my slippers. He nodded in agreement. Or in sympathy. Or understanding. He knew. I hated that.

You can tell when people know. Their "How are you?" takes a little dip. They drop a note or two on the *are*, cradle it gently. "How *are* you?" they ask a tad too kindly, or maybe too nosey. The hale and hearty "How are you?" we hurl at each other all day long becomes almost a whine. "How aaare you?"

The janitor knew. Though I always put the pillows and blankets and Dobb kit behind the couch each morning, my office looked like someone was living in it.

I'd known the janitor for a few years. He and his wife cleaned the building several nights a week, moving slowly from office to office. They were ghosts who inhabited the nighttime office. I remember being surprised when the insurance agent in the suite down the hall told me that they owned the building. "Nah," I'd said dismissively, though in the years I'd been a tenant here, I'd never actually met the landlord; I just sent my check each month to Mithun Properties Management Corporation. This guy didn't look like a Mr. Mithun. I had no idea what he looked like. Just the janitor, I guess.

His name was Henry or Harvey or Frank. Beats me. I really didn't care. He and his wife – at least, I assumed she was his wife – both had that old, dusty-gray, faded look about them, like they had a 40-ish divorced daughter and grandson living at home with them and they all ate dinner together in front of the television.

The janitor, he was in his usual, probably-brown sweater with buttons up the front, semi-blue work pants, brown scuffed shoes.

I never really noticed. I think I saw them a dozen or so times before I really noticed them at all. Even then, I didn't really see them. It was that slow-crawl motion that caught my eye. One night, back in my past life – back in the days when my business empire was expanding rather than struggling to survive – I'd been working late when she came in, towing a large gray plastic trashcan on wheels. "Oh, I'll come back later," she'd said deferentially, surprised to see me, and left at that same one-mile-an-hour pace, noiselessly closing the door behind her. My only thought was, why aren't you retired? What a lousy life, dumping wastebaskets and swabbing out urinals in the middle of the night, making sure the toilet paper rolls weren't empty. I was less sympathetic than perhaps I should have been. Actually, back then, I had no patience or time for such people. You should have worked harder when you were younger, I'd thought. And not spent every dime you'd made, probably to bail out the ex-husband of that divorced loser of a daughter of yours. If you had, then maybe you'd still be home tonight, sitting in your matching recliners in front of the television and sipping Ovaltine, not dumping trash cans. Idiots!

Once in a while, I'd hear them chuckling and talking quietly together in the maintenance closet, the door ajar, as they resupplied. Losers!

Still, they didn't look that swift, so I really shouldn't judge. They were probably doing the best they could with what they had. In fact, they could easily have been mistaken for homeless bums living under a bridge. I could imagine her creaking along, pushing a shopping cart while he checked trash barrels for aluminum cans. In truth, I never really gave them a thought. They were part of the building, came with the lease. Didn't know. Didn't care.

As we both regained our composure in the hall after our near collision, he hesitated just a click. His tired old eyes looked at me, and I could tell he knew and, worse, that he was about to say something. I wanted to cut him off, turn and run, stop him from acknowledging what I still couldn't. Besides, who was he to be offering me pity or advice? Loser!

"Boy, am I busy," I blurted. "Burning the old midnight oil."

He nodded, understanding, then began to move past me.

"Don't work too hard," he offered, not looking back. "It's not always worth it. Gotta take time to enjoy life."

"Thanks. Good night. You either." Yeah, and look what that philosophy got you, I thought. Loser!

He paused and looked back, and for a second I thought I had spoken that comment aloud. His eyes were gentle, sad, tired.

"God bless."

I nodded dumbly and kept nodding, like a bobble head.

Those two stupid words, like a battering ram, slammed into my emotional, tough-guy solar plexus like a fist. I have no idea why. For some reason, I wanted to double up and cry, to just let go and stop being strong and tough, just for a second.

Instead, I cleared my throat, gave him the circle-finger okay sign, thanking him for the good wishes, and answered evenly, "Yeah, you too."

THE ISLAND
Jus White

In The Jerk with Gloria, one old man, black as night, wearing a graying, once-white T-shirt and dirty, long, black pants, looked at me through yellow eyes and raised a beer to me in greeting. I nodded back vaguely and smiled, with a question on my face.

He laughed and said, "We leeeft it."

After another puzzled moment, my face burst into a full grin, as I recognized my savior from the parking lot that night. I leaned over the counter. "Gimme two beers."

I popped the tops off and brought one over to my best friend of the hour. We clinked bottles. "I'm still grateful," I said.

Taking his beer, he grinned and acted as if I'd given him the keys to a Jaguar. "I knows. You jus white. Doant tink like islan folks." He raised the beer in a salute. "Tank yo."

"Jus white," I thought, starting to realize that these islanders, many with almost nothing to show for their lives, felt sorry for us white folks. We all thought we were superior. Well, maybe we had another think coming. Hmmm.

I thought about one of the first lessons Jason the bartender had given me when I first hit the island. "Ya know that circle finger okay sign you might give someone?"

"Yeah," I said cautiously. "It means good. We're okay."

"To us. To an islander, it means zero. Make that sign, and you're calling that person a zero."

As I turned away from my yellow-eyed friend, I noticed that I was the only one in The Jerk wearing shorts. Even though the weather was almost always warm, the islanders almost always wore dark, sometimes ragged pants. Many, especially those working in businesses that brought them in contact with white visitors, generally also wore long-sleeve shirts. But I was a white guy, so it was okay. Jus white?

"What do you suggest?" I asked, walking over to Gloria.

"What do I suggest?" she repeated loudly, looking over the chalk board menu behind the counter. "Hmmm."

It was like a cue. The place erupted with joyful shouts. Everyone had recommendations and was eager to share. A big man came close up behind me and, pointing over my shoulder, said, "Yo wants pork, extra spicy. Put hair on yo chest." He had a voice like a barrel.

"Feet or ribs?" I asked stupidly, wanting neither.

"Oh, ends, mon. Ribs be good, but jerk pork ends best. An beans."

I turned and looked at him. I looked to Gloria. They both nodded openly, so I said, "Gimme the jerk pork ends, with some sweet potato fries and red beans and rice, extra spicy." I thought about buying meals for everyone, but realized that would be awfully white of me and awfully patronizing.

Everybody howled with delight. One of the girls behind the counter smiled at me invitingly and nodded her head coyly to the side. A moment later, I felt Gloria's rough, scratchy hand slip into mine. I quickly registered that maybe Gloria didn't want me, but I was still off limits to the other island girls. Again, I hoped Gloria didn't have a jealous husband.

I also had a passing thought that hanging around a white man gave her some kind of status. Or maybe it was just that women universally got jealous when there were two shes and only one he, and it had nothing to do with race. "The fact is," Calabash explained to me later, "it's simpler than that down here. Knowing a white man is good insurance for islanders when the cops come calling."

As our Styrofoam plates were being filled and we moved down the cafeteria-style counter, Gloria said, "I likes yo patch, Cap'm."

I nodded my appreciation, then asked, "Where's the owner?"

She nodded to the end of the counter. I looked, but I only saw a man with distinctly Asian features sitting on a stool behind the cash register. However, he had a proprietary look about him. As I paid for our dinner, I asked, "Are you the owner?"

"Yes, I am," he answered quietly, in formal English, with a touch of a British accent. I wondered if he knew Black Mike.

But mostly I was puzzled.

"This Mista Chin," Gloria said by way of explanation.

I was still confused.

Mister Chin nodded politely, first to me and then to Gloria.

"Mister Chin," I said, having difficulty hiding my confusion, "Gloria said that the owner was a Jamaican."

He smiled. "That is correct." He offered nothing more as he totaled up our bill.

Damn inscrutable Chinaman, I thought, but instead said, "Help me out."

There was nobody behind us in line, so he leaned forward, and I could see that he was about to tell a tale he had told before. Everyone else in The Jerk also paused, waited and listened. Apparently, they loved this story.

"If you know your history, Captain Jolly ..." he said familiarly, and waited.

I paused, not recalling that Gloria had introduced me by name. Then I shrugged. Small island. Inscrutable.

Picking up on his formal language, I said, "I admit that I do not know my history when it comes to Jamaica, Mr. Chin."

He did not look surprised. "Well, the British governed Jamaica after 1655," he began. "The island didn't become fully independent until 1962."

"Really?" I asked, not sure what else to say.

"Really. In the seventeenth century, hundreds of thousands of Negroes were imported from Africa to work the sugar cane fields. By imported, of course, I mean captured, stolen from their homes, and sold as slaves."

He looked around his restaurant, and I did likewise. The thought ran through my mind that Mr. Chin was attempting to incite a riot.

However, the other patrons, all watching with great interest, nodded and looked pleased, proud of their heritage.

"They were the great, great ancestors of these fine men and women," he said.

"In 1838, nearly 30 years before your Civil War freed the Negroes in the United States, my friend, England emancipated the slaves on Jamaica. The British, I've come to recognize, are almost as civilized as the Chinese. Almost."

"Almost," I echoed, enjoying his subtle playfulness. I groped for what I wanted to say. "Am I correct in assuming that you are Chinese?"

"You would not be correct in that assumption, Captain." He paused and took a sip of tea from a small porcelain cup beside the cash register. Nobody in the place moved or said a word. We all just waited. Mr. Chin would have made a great teacher.

As he put the teacup down with a gentle clink, he continued: "After the slaves were freed, many were unwilling to go back to work in the fields of the sugar plantations. It was hard, back-breaking labor, and the pay was not much better than slave wages." He paused, appreciating his own subtle joke. His customers nodded and mumbled their agreement.

Then he continued. "Many went up into the wild hills in Jamaica, preferring to survive by hunting and working small plots of land, and some banditry. They'd rather live a subsistence existence than deal with the plantation owners. Freedom. It is a funny thing, don't you agree, Cap'm? Worth more than gold to some people. Do you understand, Captain Jolly?"

I nodded, mesmerized. Oh, yes, I thought. "I'm starting to, Mr. Chin."

He took another sip of tea, and we all waited. "For people from the United States, you think of freedom as democracy, as some government system with voting in elections. That is not really true. It is not that complicated. The United States has democracy, but there is not much freedom there, or so I have heard. Down here, however, while there is no democracy, we," and he gestured around the restaurant, "enjoy freedom."

I frowned and listened, my food getting cold on the counter. I also wondered what any of this had to do with this oriental-looking man.

As if Mister Chin heard my thoughts, he began again. "A funny thing," he said almost under his breath, as he carefully placed the teacup down in its saucer again. "In China at that time, there was terrible political turmoil, warfare and famine. So, when my ancestors were invited to come to Jamaica in the 1850s, many seized the opportunity to move to that beautiful island. Still, the sugar cane fields were horrible places to work. So, many of us, like my great, great grandfather, eventually started businesses. We kept to ourselves, as is our nature. We also retained much of our culture from China. Still, we are not Chinese, not anymore."

He paused again, before adding, "So, I am ..."

"So, you are," I said, interrupting and hesitating as I put together the facts, "Chinese-Jamaican."

He grinned and nodded, not the least bit surprised by my ability to follow the story.

"Just as you, I assume, are ..."

I nodded also. "Italian-American, though I prefer to be known as an American of Italian descent."

"Very good. I understand. As I am a Jamaican of Chinese descent."

He gestured around The Jerk. "Just as our friends here are islanders of African descent."

The story was officially over, and the other customers turned back to their own conversations.

While Gloria and I ate our meals, I tried to adjust my stereotypes. I had, of course, expected to see a black Rastafarian, complete with dreadlocks and a big ganga stogie in his mouth. I was expecting Bob Marley.

***

Gloria and I became friends, not drinking buddy friends. We watched each other's backs at the docks. I helped make sure island hopping boaters, notorious for running up bills and slipping away in the middle of the night, didn't stiff her for her cleaning fees and provision bills. In return, she made sure the shadow boys steered clear of my boat. She was the best kind of friend.

However, in the island tradition, except for a few nights drinking rum together, along with one ending up as bunkies, and weekly, unkept promises that I'd join her at church next Sunday, we generally kept a deferential distance. That's how islanders survived. We left each other alone. Not like in the States, where blacks and whites feel they need to love each other and be buddies, if not bunkies.

The morning after Gloria and I had spent our one night together, I awoke and watched in stillness as she slipped into her faded jeans, purple bra, and tie-dyed T-shirt. The shirt had a glowing yellow cross in the middle. To me, watching a woman dress was almost as sexy as watching her undress.

Sensing my eyes on her, she turned and smiled at me. Her expression was sad and wistful. We were not just from different cultures and races, but from different worlds, maybe even different planets. She touched my cheek and said, "Yo a good mon, Cap'm Jolly. What eatin' you ain't gonna kill you. I know. We all got tings eatin' us."

I pulled her back into the bunk for a moment and hugged her long. She kissed my cheek as we separated.

We never again sat down to a meal together or sweated up the sheets in the starboard cabin. Still, as we went about our own business on the marina dock, we'd connect as we encountered each other on the dock, but only through a nod and a smile. And now and then, I'd drop by The Jerk and bring her some take-out, handing it to her and walking on.

MANGROVE COVE
Jocko II

There wasn't much left. Most of the gear I'd kept on *The Do Over* had been washed out the windows and door when we scuttled her. I thought about it as jettisoning, getting rid of unnecessary cargo. That worked. I was about the only thing left, and, necessary or not, I was damned if I was going to give up.

While Hurricane Olive tore at *The Do Over* and me, I spent the rest of the day and the night playing Superman. It was an idea Kid had had. Even though I was sure he was dead, his idea just might save my life.

"Don't fight the storm," he'd decided in Zen-like fashion. "Just relax and let it wash over you."

I had only half paid attention at the time. He had many ideas. Most were off the wall. Some had potential. Still, you had to pick through a lot of horse manure to find those few good kernels of ideas.

While the hurricane beat the stuffing out of me, I managed to wrap my man-overboard line around the base of the folded-down mast, and I clung to the cabin roof railings. A few feet in front of my nose, lashed permanently to the base of the mast, Jocko II stared back at me. He looked like a drowned rat.

I conserved my energy by going with the flow, not fighting the wind and pounding waves, just letting them slip over me. My two biggest problems were that I was shipping a lot of salt water through my mouth, and my throat was swollen and pained. I was also starting to chill. Even the warm tropical water can suck heat out of the human body to the point of death. I was in danger of dehydration and hypothermia.

I managed to position myself just behind the cabin roof, so most of the force of the surf passed over me. The daylight quit fast. Hurricanes in the Northern Hemisphere swirl counterclockwise. So, I knew how the storm was going by the direction of the wind and waves, and it was hard to adjust my position as the wind moved from head-on-dead-on to pounding me on the portside.

Every now and then something bumped into me – a dead bird, panicky fish, a mangrove root not strong enough to survive, a piece of Jocko's stuffing.

I wasn't afraid, just uncomfortable, pummeled by the wind, rain and waves. I also felt alone, but that was something I was used to. I think most men are alone, especially the ones who are vice president of the service club and make a point of surrounding themselves with dozens of friends and golfing buddies.

I had to admit that I missed Kid. At least I had Jocko.

My arms began to stiffen up and cramp from the cold and exertion of holding on.

Still, by pre-dawn, the wind was fading, down to perhaps 70 miles an hour, and I was still alive, though parched and shivering, with a real bad sore throat. I'd taken in a lot of sea water. Though I'd tried not to swallow any, my throat was seriously swollen.

The hurricane was easing, moving on. Only part of the monster storm swirl had actually hit the island. I would live. *The Do Over*? She might spend eternity in this unnamed channel in Mangrove Cove. Maybe I should name it Kid Channel, after my late first mate.

Sheer stubbornness made me hang on. I closed my eyes and drifted in the waves that were no longer pounding me, but gently washing over me. The wind was nearly pushing the stern now, so I figured the worst was way past, and Olive was heading into the Gulf of Mexico. I was close to surviving the night. Hell, I'd survived lots of nights worse than this one. It all depended on whether or not the sun came out in the morning. If so, that would warm me. If not, I could be in real trouble.

I found myself thinking of the night I had just about given up, having jettisoned everything, one of those nights I used to spend in the office in a past life.

THE STATES
Lists

I didn't sleep well in the office. So, I would get up a lot. One night I pounded the office couch and my pillow into submission and then got up and found the bottle of whiskey in my desk drawer. The whiskey helped make things murky and confused. It made pretending real, and the real like pretend. Welcome to marriage … and divorce.

Like the one memorable day that sends everything skittering across the room, the day it becomes a lie, a lie that nobody told and nobody believed … until that day when the tape measure snapped shut and she sees that he's not ever going to be a Prince Charming, and he sees that she never was a demure, beautiful Princess. Even that may be a lie, but it's a lie each has to stick with for as long as they can.

I slowly settled back on the couch, slapped my arm across my face, and took a hot gulp from the bottle.

This looping tape – the lie tape – wasn't going to stop playing in my head. Crap! Just let it play.

And that's what really pissed me off, I thought, as I capped the bottle, punched the lumpy pillow on the lumpy couch again, and rolled over. All of a sudden, Connie, who'd never asked anything more than "Would you like steak for dinner?" or "Are you sure we can afford to take the kids to Disney World?" suddenly must have taken a good long look at me and asked "Who is this guy?" Or worse, "Am I happy?" (The answer, by the way, is always "No!" If you think it, if you have to ask it, the answer is "No!")

After that, shit, everything went up for grabs, and we both started lists:

He doesn't always flush the toilet.

She hovers when I cook peppers and eggs or asks too many questions when I'm trying to figure out what's wrong with the leak in the pipe.

He got drunk and threw up on his own shoes at Don's birthday party. Ewe!

She never leaves anything where I put it. I think she hides my stuff.

He went off to play poker without asking if it worked for me to stay home and watch the kids.

She bought that new outfit that she knew we couldn't afford. Yeah, and she let the kids' Taekwondo instructor deep kiss her after the tournament.

It would be nice if he showered before he wanted sex. Yeah, and I found that porn site on his computer.

It would be nice if she wanted sex or actually moved during sex.

It's those goddamn lists that screw it up. They get trotted out like show horses, first to each other, then to friends, then to the idiot marriage counselor, and finally to the weaselly divorce lawyers. Suddenly, everything that makes us human makes us shits. Most of the time, we ignore it. That's what makes marriage work, ignoring the shit that drives us crazy. Ah, hell. Where's that bottle?

She'd called earlier. Sounded a bit guilty, which, I admit, felt good.

"I need to ask you a question, Joth."

This was it, I'd thought. She'd finally come to her senses. My bones relaxed. Aha. She wants me to come home. She wants to work it out. Her voice was quiet, hesitant. Oh, thank God.

"What is it?" I'd asked gently, almost romantically, encouraging her, as if she'd just stepped out of the bathroom wearing a soft and sexy negligée, her eyes smiling, head demurely down, offering and yet questioning, seeking approval, and I'd affirmed her offer.

"Joth, the realtor wants to drop the price on the house."

Fuck! Fuck! Fuck! Fuck!

Calmly. Cooly. "Oh, I don't know. What do you think?"

"He says we're asking too much for it. I say let's do it. Do you agree?"

"Yeah, sure. Makes sense," I'd answered steadily, quickly going all business, zipping my heart up fast. "I think it's a good idea. Let's get it sold and get it done. That house is a financial drain neither of us can afford." Fuck! Fuck! Fuck! Fuck!

"Okay, thanks. Talk to you soon."

There was a gap before she hung up the phone. This is where we would have said, "Love you," and the other would have said, "Love you, too."

But this time there was just a longish silence followed by a faint click.

Brooding, I could hear the janitor and his wife slowly walk past my door, then stop. Bottle in hand, I froze, listening. I heard them whisper to each other; then something softly brushed the door before they shuffled on.

A few minutes later, I heard the metal back door to the building click behind them. I got up and opened my office door and looked around for hall monsters. At my feet was a foil-covered plate, with a note. Back inside, I sat at my desk and unwrapped half a dozen brownies. I unfolded the note and read it in the twilight of my desk lamp: "Mr. Mithun and I thought you might enjoy these. Good luck. Betty."

I glanced out the window and saw a cream-white Lexus drive up the early-morning street.

MANGROVE COVE
Rock-a-bye

The boat was rocking gently, brushing the sandy bottom of the cove. It felt soothing. I don't think anybody ever gets over the pure, soothing comfort of being rocked as a baby. I was on my back, lying on the roof, one arm over my eyes. The sun had come out, and it felt good on my chest as I soaked up the heat.

My lips were cracked and my throat was raw from the seawater. My body felt so beat up and crusted in salt I could not open my eyes.

The Do Over, sunk beneath me in six feet of water, kept rocking impatiently, and it felt good. She was ready to come up. I was ready to bring her up. How?

"Good morning, Beautiful," I croaked, as *The Do Over* gently rocked me. "Did we make it? Sorry for the hurricane. I hope it was no inconvenience."

I heard a bird calling plaintively, probably crying in search of its lost mate or babies. The sound broke my heart, but I also knew it meant the storm was over, gone, done, off to the west. And the boat kept rocking, grinding gently on the sandy bottom of the channel in Mangrove Cove. It made me think of Sam.

Sam? I thought. Sam?

THE STATES
Sam

I s first love innocent or just naïve? Or are those just two words for the same thing? You trust. You believe. The word "forever" doesn't sound stupid, and you use it a lot. You identify with that one, special love song. You don't fuck; you make love. Even if it is awkward and fumbly – and it's always awkward and fumbly – it's also beautiful, romantic, mostly because you don't know any better. Every touch, kiss, lick, and brush of lips on a breast is a heart-speeding adventure, pure joy. Forever. You don't think of new and exotic and bizarre ways to satisfy each other, because just touching and kissing and discovering how boy parts fit warmly against, around, and inside girl parts is new and exotic enough.

That was Sam and me, right out of high school.

Imagine life without a setback, without a scar, without a regret. Dreams made sense. The world was nice, not dangerous or threatening. It was waiting for us, waiting to serve us. We'd curl up on her parents' couch in the den in the dark late at night, well into the early hours of the morning. We'd make out and make love, sometimes lip licking kissing was more than enough, with one ear listening for the sound of parental footsteps on the landing, one over-the-shoulder eye alert for a darkening shadow in the doorway. Mostly, though, we'd just talk and touch, and hold each other. We had no idea.

We didn't even drink all that much or smoke happy weed. We didn't need it. We were children in love. We talked of running away, yes, sailing away, together. Rocking gently on a boat.

MANGROVE COVE
Dead and Alive

I was listening, dreaming, eyes closed, lying on the roof of *The Do Over*, still rocking gently and scraping on the bottom of the channel. The storm had passed.

Had it been a good call to sink her as the hurricane hit? Would she ever sail again? Would I? I was rousing slowly from one of those deep, bone-weary, drug-like sleeps, the kind you rarely get as an adult. Now I had to move to get out of the sun and find some water, but my body felt leaden. It refused.

Was I dead? I almost began to worry about that and then thought, "Don't know, don't care," as I sank back into that coma-like sleep.

All I knew was that the rocking of the boat felt good, which made me think about Sam again and still.

Sam? Finally, a good tape to run through my mind. I smiled in my dozing sleep, and my sunburnt and salt-baked lips cracked painfully. "No," I said, refusing to allow this dream-like tape to be taken from me by wakefulness. I settled back into the gentle depth of my dream.

I could smell the warm, intimate scent of her young body, which I hadn't caressed in more than 25 years. I began to doubt that I was on *The Do Over* in the middle of the

Caribbean. Was I in the living room of her parents' house? Or maybe back on the couch in my long-abandoned office?

I liked option number one, so I dialed in. I could feel Sam's warmth. She was snuggled close, having wedged herself under my arm, feeling so protected and contented she nearly purred. I think girls like that. I was sitting tall and proud beside her, feeling like the king of the world. Guys like that.

I smiled again, and my lips cracked again, reminding me again that I was scuttled in a mangrove channel, with no reason to smile. No, that really wasn't true.

My body felt dead, but my mind was growing clear and more focused. Awake or asleep, it didn't matter. I found that I could probe and explore the Sam memory, which was stronger than the salt air and the rocking of the boat. I was there, crossing two decades and about two thousand miles. Time and space didn't exist.

Young, we were like one person, one heart, one mind. The rest of the world was of no importance, crowded out by a smaller, better one of our own making. We needed nothing beyond the intimacy we found in each other, and we believed that feeling would never change. We knew it would never change. We knew it. But it did.

My mind was in both places, both spaces. The best part about being young, I thought atop *The Do Over* in Mangrove Cove, was that we had had no idea what we didn't know. We had had no idea about the odds against us. We had had no idea that life was going to crush us. Ignorance was bliss … is bliss.

I slid back to the suburban house on Eastern Long Island, allowing myself to remember how we had had long, long talks and simple confessions about everything from our silliest hopes to our most ambitious dreams.

"Of course, there hadn't been much to confess back then," I said aloud in a professorial tone, my eyes closed to the tropical sun, and I laughed aloud again. "No lies. No deceptions. No agendas." The worst thing I would have had to confess back then was jerking off sometimes late at night on The Long Island Expressway during the drive back to my parents' house.

"Did we ever speak of fears, Sam?" I asked both of us and the mangrove roots.

Her body was lean, almost bony, yet the skin soft and smooth. Her breasts were small, but nonetheless intriguing.

Small breasts, small hips and a tight round backside, which made her far from voluptuous. In fact, looking back, I think she appeared rather boyish, but she carried herself with a naturally buoyant femininity that had fascinated me then ... and still. Her fine blonde hair was fairly short, and she had an upturned, pixie-like nose. Cute. That was the best word for her. Cute.

I willed her on board *The Do Over* wearing only a bikini, sun glasses, and a smile.

Sun glasses? I flopped my arm over my eyes to keep out the hot Caribbean sun. I needed to move. But the need to be with Sam, with Sam's memory, was stronger, more real.

I struggled to remember: Was I on the cabin roof of my sunken catamaran in an island mangrove channel in the Caribbean or on a couch in Sam's parents' living room in a Long Island suburb? Or maybe on my office couch wondering where I was?

It didn't matter.

Beautiful? No, Sam was not drop-dead gorgeous. But trim and awfully cute and attractive.

The words were gone. Yes, it was a memory. But I remembered how we had planned out every detail of our life of adventure. The best part was that we had talked only of what we were going to do. We never thought of the yeah-buts. We'd fantasized about cruising the world, and neither of us would say anything like, "Yeah, but where would we get the money?" Those minor details hadn't mattered.

The Do Over. That name would have made no sense to either of us back then. Today? I think she'd understand. Would she? Hmmm. Her husband had died, Scott had told me. I wondered.

"Hey, Cap'm." I froze. "Hey, Cap'm." Stolen from my dream, I snapped open my eyes and forced myself to rise on one elbow and survey what was left of my boat. "Hey, Cap'm?"

That was when I realized I was hallucinating. I had to be hallucinating. I kept hearing Kid. Then, through salt-crusted eyes and the glare of tropical sun on blue water, I thought I saw him sitting across the channel lazing as relaxed as could be on a mangrove root. When I looked away and then back again, the apparition grinned and waved. "Hey, Cap'm." I lay back down onto the roof of the boat and closed my eyes. Losing my mind wasn't part of the plan.

THE STATES
Bar Talk

It was a lifetime ago. Still, I remember that hopeless feeling that slammed through me time and time again. Sitting at the bar talking to Scott about it made the pain more sharp, more intense.

My life was over. I knew it. Back when I used to care – correction, back when I thought things mattered, right after Connie left me – I remember hating that my kids, Jamie and Natty, would never have that family home to come back to. As I sat beside Scott, the thought kept stabbing me in the heart.

What about Christmas? I thought, opening that door to my mind just a crack and getting blasted across the room by that full-volume tape that suddenly and loudly kicked on in my head. What about when Natty came home from college? What about the kids' weddings? Wouldn't they always have that uncomfortable mix of celebration, regret, and tension, as Connie and I, strangers sharing the same kid memories, would look across the room at each other from different tables, both knowing that nothing could ever make it feel quite right. What would we do when the idiot emcee at Natty's wedding announced, "Wonderful. Aren't the newlyweds a beautiful couple. Their first dance, ladies and gentlemen. Let's give them a big hand. And now it's time for the parents of the bride." How would we handle that? Awkwardly, I was sure. And grandchildren! What about grandchildren?

It just kept looking darker and darker.

What about twenty years of history, of tradition, of roots? I thought to myself. I settled into self-pity. My total and entire life was a failure. Gone. Nothing. It really looked that bleak back then. Really.

When I looked at Scott again, he cut away, pretending not to have been watching me. His whole expression made me angry, and that felt better. I resented the look on his face and how he had no idea what I was talking about. Then I realized, hell, I had no idea what I was talking about. I was like a dog lying in the road that had been run over by a car, its hind quarters crushed, crying out and gnashing its teeth in pain. People stayed away. There was nothing they could do. If they got too close, they got bitten. No need to bite Scott. He hadn't run me over. The Bitch had. Life had. Poor me.

And here I was blowing it with Scott. Maybe women talked about this stuff with each other. But not guys. We called each other Asshole, which really meant we were buds! Guys didn't do this … at least if they were real friends. They looked away.

I was suddenly so pissed at Scott I thought about decking him. He could see twenty-five years back and twenty-five years ahead, clear as a bell, to Jo and their fiftieth wedding anniversary. He knew where and with whom Thanksgiving dinners would take place. The feel of Jo, the same woman as always, in the middle of the night. Forever. For me, an avalanche had blocked what I had once thought would be a clear and straight road. Not just blocked; the road beyond was gone. And I didn't know which way to turn. When Scott and Jo were celebrating their fiftieth anniversary together someday, I'd be God knows where. That was when I first thought about running away to the islands. The idea kept sounding better and better.

In the meantime, sitting there with Scott in an otherwise empty bar on a snowy Wednesday night, with no home to go home to....

For the first time since just before Jamie was born, when I had made a commitment to be a steady man and a good provider, I now had no idea what tomorrow was supposed to look like. No goals. No purpose. It hurt to look back, since even the best memories were now tainted. And I didn't know how to look ahead. I had lost faith in the future. Nothing interested me. Hell, I didn't even know where I would be sleeping tonight. At the office? I hated it there. A hotel? Even worse. I had resisted renting an apartment. That would have been like acknowledging that this was really happening. So, I'd been living out of a duffel bag for the last two months. I spent some nights on the couch in my office. A few at cheap motels. A few times I'd slept in the guest room at the house, having insisted that this was still my home, too. That had been a mistake, especially when I had heard the door close in the middle of the night and the car start and drive away.

I was scared. Terrified scared. Ask a man to tell you about himself, and he'll tell you what he does for a living. Right or wrong, good or bad, we are what we do. But the whole motivation, the glue that holds it together and what makes it make sense is his wife, his kids, his home, and, yes, even his dog. Take that away and nothing makes sense.

Several decades ago, one of my first jobs was in sales. Big Jim, the manager who hired me, asked more questions about Connie and my home life than he did about me. It really began to annoy me. Several years later, when I left to start my own company, he'd said, "Mind if I give you a word of advice, Joth?"

He had been a good mentor. I liked and admired Big Jim. "Sure, go ahead."

"You're gonna do great, and I've enjoyed working with you these past three years. You'll be managing your own company now. The key is to hire good people. It doesn't matter if they're bright or borderline stupid, if they have a degree from Harvard or just a high school diploma. You want people who will work hard, like you have, people who will put in forty, fifty, sixty hours a week and see it as an honor, not an obligation. So, when you hire someone, make sure he's married, and that he is ferociously in love with his wife. That day I hired you, I kept asking about Connie and the kids."

"I remember."

"I know. And you'd started to become defensive. That's one of the reasons I hired you. That's the magic ingredient in a steady, reliable, dedicated employee. Hire a married man. But more than that, even if he's miserable in his marriage, make sure he's crazy mad in love with his wife. That's you, Joth."

"I'm not miserable," I'd said with a smile, knowing what he meant.

"I know. Regardless, the key is that you're crazy mad in love with Connie."

"That I am," I'd said.

"Oh, and living together doesn't count. It's a red flag."

"How so?"

"Sure, he'll say he loves her, but not enough to want to marry her. They're playing house. He's not committed to her. He won't be committed to you."

After a pause, I'd asked, "What about women?"

Jim smiled. "They're a bit different. If you're looking for a kick-butt female employee, hire a single mom. Don't hire a housewife looking for a career. She'll demand more from you and the job than she'll ever give. And she'll walk the second you frown at her.

"No, find a single mom. She'll work herself to death for you. Actually, not for you; she'll do it for her kids. In return, what she'll want from you is loyalty and flexibility."

"Sort of like Tammy," I'd said, referring to the company's middle-aged bookkeeper, who had just dropped her daughter off at college the week before.

"Not sort of like Tammy," he corrected. "Exactly like Tammy. I do right by her, and she is the most loyal employee I will ever have."

"Loyalty," I'd said, processing the idea.

"And flexibility," Big Jim added. "Don't watch the clock. She'll miss a few mornings with a sick kid and an afternoon with teacher or doctor appointments. Don't ask, 'When did you get in?' Instead, ask, 'How's your son?' Give her that, and she'll be the best employee in the world."

THE ISLAND
Calabash

Jason was swabbing down a table. Coming out from behind the bar, Joanie, slender and wearing short-shorts so short that her cheeks peeked out (once again, good for tips: *Ka-ching*) was bringing my next drink. Just down a few months ago from somewhere around Oklahoma or North Dakota, she still looked clean and wholesome, something you don't see on the island, except for the *touristas*, who tend to buy new clothes before going on vacation. I had bet ten bucks with Calabash that Joanie'd be gone by day 30. He didn't think so. He won.

I had seen that warm, whimsical smile on Calabash's face and had wondered if he maybe had the hots for her. Wrong. That was back before I knew Calabash. Still, for some reason, the girls were all crazy about that old toothless fart. But he was just friendly, nice. No leers, no dirty jokes, not even any vaguely risqué double entendres. I used to think maybe he was gay or just too old to get it up, or a wimp. Again, that was back before I got to know Calabash.

Then I saw him one night go up to a big, bluff guy, one of those perfect fellas with perfect hair, perfect muscles, and a perfect golf swing, with successful attorney written all over him. He oozed arrogance. He was the kind of guy who, when he walked into the boardroom, all the energy was drawn to him. Intimidating. He was holding his wife by the arm, shaking her like a ragdoll, and chewing her out in a loud, snarly whisper. The wife was dressed like sweet eye candy. That was her job … to look good for him. I was sure he gave her everything, and she looked miserable, but not scared. She seemed to be used to this.

"I told you to pack the blue shirt," the man said in a loud, snarling whisper, and it was obvious that this wasn't the first time he'd said it today.

His wife, I suspect, had long since stopped standing up to him. Beautiful and demure, with thick red hair and small, gentle features, she just stood there and looked down, repeating over and over again, "I'm sorry, George. I'm sorry." But she said it without conviction, as if she played this role on a regular basis.

"Well, Miriam, that doesn't get my shirt on this stink hole of an island, does it?"

Everybody in the Sunset was watching, and I suspect that was half of what got this jerk's rocks off. For George, this was probably some kind of foreplay, power foreplay.

Nobody moved. Then, out of the corner of my eye, I saw Calabash slowly rise to his feet, walk over, and touch George's arm. Furious, George swung around, ready to lay out this person who dared to touch him. Again, I got the feeling that this was what he was looking for, hoping for. Maybe this is what Miriam wanted, too. Maybe this was her foreplay, getting turned on by being humiliated and abused, especially in public. I had to admit to myself that her meek demeanor gave me a little pecker twitch. Guys are funny, huh?

"What do you want?" He snarled at Calabash, giving him a withering look, as if he was dirt.

But Calabash just stood there, neither docile nor threatening, with a gentle smile on his face. At first, he was silent, until it was apparent that he had George's full attention. Then he began to talk, very low and quietly, leaning in as he did so, gradually placing one arm around George's shoulder, which first tensed and then began to relax. Then, while Calabash was still talking in a low voice, almost whispering into George's ear, Miriam moved in closer and Calabash gently wrapped his other arm around her. I could not catch the words, but the tone was low and gentle, mesmerizing. The three of them stood in the middle of the tile floor, heads together, for perhaps ten minutes.

Finally, as Calabash gradually pulled back, I could see that George's face was soft, and tears sparkled in Miriam's eyes. That evening, the three of them ended up eating dinner together, drinking coffee and laughing long after the rest of us left.

The next day I asked Calabash about them. He just smiled and said, "I've found that most people are a lot nicer than they give themselves credit for."

He never mentioned it again.

MANGROVE COVE
Do Over ... Again

A s I came around again, I was disoriented, unsure where I was. I could hear the sound of small feet scrabbling close to my head, and I tried to process what that sound meant. Then, without opening my eyes, I realized it was a seagull walking around me on the boat roof. Like a hungry man sizing up how to attack a huge sandwich, the gull was deciding how to best approach this feast he saw in my carcass.

Overhead I could hear other gulls calling to each other, probably waiting for the word that dinner was served.

Was I dead? Nearly dead? Mostly dead? Apparently, this seagull thought the best for him and the worst for me.

I opened my eyes slowly. The gull, jerkily looking around, was within six inches of my face.

He never saw it coming. Swoop! In an instant, I had both his legs in my left hand. Terrified, he fluttered and cawed and tugged to get away. Holding him at arm's length, his wings flapping furiously, I jumped to my feet in triumph. I thought about smashing his head on the roof of the boat, an instinctive reaction. Instead I did a full-body, 360 degree spiral windup and threw him back to the sky.

"Be gone, Angel of Death!" I whooped triumphantly, as the startled gull caught its balance in the air and then flew off to join his now dispersing mates.

Still captain of my sunken vessel, I stood broadly on the roof of *The Do Over* and gloated. I looked down. I had on only the tattered remains of my shorts. But there was something else.

Crossing my eyes, I stared at a red, foam ball on the end of my nose.

THE ISLAND
Universal Man

O f course, then there was our fantasy, the ultimate island fantasy, the one young men talked about and old men still thought about: that the women we met every day really wanted us. Even after we actually quit caring or believing in it – another green flash myth – we still talked about it.

Most went something like this: "Well, I know a guy who knew a girl once. Good lookin', too, with a rich lawyer husband. Still, some nights, when he was either dead drunk asleep or out of town, she used to slip into high heels, garter belt and slinky panties and matching lace bra – nothing else, just that and a coat – and go park the Caddie down at the truck stop." "Oh, yeah, and I know a guy who said .... "

Those stories were legendary. Most were lies. Just myths. Still, we all told them, or at least listened to them, half hopeful that they were true.

Except for Calabash. He told no lies, never bragged. He just spent his time quietly on the island, fishing off the docks, smoking his Camel straights, drinking his Green Label, and seeming to be genuinely having one helluva good, quiet time.

No one seemed to know much about Calabash, starting with exactly how old he was. I guessed he was somewhere between sixty-five and eighty. He always wore a greasy Hawaiian shirt and ratty shorts. He rarely wore shoes, and he almost always carried a beer in his hand, though he never seemed to be drunk, just deep in thought. His hair was shaggy, dirty white, and by mid-December, it was long enough to make a foot-long ponytail. He never worked.

He usually had a cigarette in his mouth, and the rest of the pack in his shirt pocket. He didn't so much smoke those cigarettes as suck them in like a vacuum cleaner hose. His mustache was a blend of white and nicotine tan. His voice was a growling rasp, and you couldn't always tell if he was talking, laughing, or coughing as he hunched over his beer at the bar. It looked like he shaved once a week. Some said it was to go to church on Sunday. We did notice that he looked relatively clean-faced on Monday, pretty scruffy by Saturday night.

He was nowhere to be found around Christmas.

He was beside me the night I got a surprise call from my son back in the States.

"Hello?" Pause. "Hi? Who's this?" Pause. "Jamie?" Pause. "Hey, Son, how are you?"

I had turned away from the bar at Iggie's and spent the next ten minutes roaming around the docks in the moonlight, the phone to my ear. Iggie's was a locals' bar, a wonderfully rundown dump avoided by the *touristas*. That's why some of us hung out there, to get away from the well-scrubbed folks who came into The Sunset in search of an authentic island experience. Iggie's was over in the industrial, less glamorous side of the island.

Jamie didn't hesitate. He'd cut right to the chase. "You know, it's your fault," he wailed at me. Not this, again, was all I could think. When I'd heard his voice, my heart had jumped. I had almost hoped that maybe this was a call that could lead to some kind of reconciliation. No such luck.

The last thing I wanted was a rehash of my who-was-wrong-and-who-was-right divorce from his mother. Jamie sounded a little slurry, like he may have had a few beers.

"Son, it's been more than a year. You need to let it go."

"Like you did, right? Just walk away, go live on some stupid island."

"It just happened," I'd begun to explain, then felt my face getting hot. I resented having to explain anything to one of my children ... or to anybody, for that matter. "You ought to come on down for a visit. How about that?"

"That ain't gonna happen, Dad!" I guess I knew that, too. "It's your fault," he repeated.

"Yeah, I know. It's always my fault."

"That's right, Dad. It's always your fault. You were supposed to fix things. It was what you did. You always made it work. And then you stopped. You just let everything go to hell."

He was right. I was always the driver of the bus, the one who decided where it went and how it got there. On one hand, I was a control freak; on the other, Connie loved not being in control. That meant she was never responsible for anything. Me, on the other hand, I was responsible for everything. It was always my fault.

Actually, it had worked out beautifully at first, until, I suspect, we both wanted something more. I think Connie finally got tired of just sitting back. And I think I wanted more, even though I had no idea what I wanted more of. Doesn't matter. Jamie was right. It was my fault.

But once you got beyond that, what? So what? It didn't matter. Was he going to blame his whole life on me? Why not? That victim mentality worked for some people. It worked for his mother.

On the phone, Jamie's voice sounded plaintive, pleading, childlike, as if he were counting on me to kiss away the boo boo. If only I could.

I looked back at the dim halo of light over the open-air bar. Nobody was watching, but I knew they were all listening.

I stopped and stared at my feet. Then I just blew. I began to shout: "Because your mother wanted out, remember? She divorced me. She had the affair. Remember?"

He came right back at me: "You could have done more. Something. But you just ran away."

"No, son, I couldn't, and you're stupid if you think I could. Maybe it's time you grew up."

After a long silence, he said, his voice now weak, "Well, it doesn't matter anyway. Mom's marrying that guy."

That took me by surprise. That guy was Bob, who Connie had been seeing for months before telling me she was leaving me. He was dull and quiet, a polar opposite of me. The kids called him Beige Bob. A sweater-wearing clerk at a big department store, his greatest joy was getting off an hour early every other Tuesday. According to the kids, his only talent, apparently, was that he could play the guitar and sing folk songs from the 60s. Still, I guess that had been enough for Connie.

"Are you and Natty going to the wedding?" I asked, stupidly.

His voice broke. He sobbed: "Dad, she wants me to walk her down the aisle, to give her away! Like I'm the dad?"

Fix it, Joth, I thought to myself, and I realized that I had held that marriage together by sheer will and determination ... and, yes, some meanness. If I could have fixed this, I would have. Maybe. I had to admit that life was easier, if not better, down on the island. No pouting wife with unspoken demands. No clients who expected me to solve their business problems. And no kids – yes, I admit it – who looked to me for guidance and money. Fix it, Dad. Do something, Dad. Screw it.

I hated this conversation. I wasn't sure what I was supposed to say, do ... or even feel. What I hated most was the aching in my heart. Every time I thought that open wound was maybe healing over, something – a thought or a conversation – would brutally rip the scab off. And there I was, raw flesh, hurting just like it felt the day Connie told me she was leaving.

Yes, I had run away. After months of banging my head against a wall, you bet I had run, finally realizing that there was no way to revive the disaster of my fatally dying marriage, still flopping around like a fish on deck gasping for water. And, yes, in the process, I had run away from my son and daughter who, I had convinced myself, were now old enough to no longer need me. Again, I was wrong. Damn. I was batting zero.

I had circumnavigated the dock and was back at Iggie's. Still holding the phone, I sat back down on the barstool beside Calabash and took a drink of my now-warm beer. "What do you want me to do?" I asked quietly, again stupidly, again acting as if my son should decide for me what I should do.

"Do?" Jamie screamed into the phone. "Do? What I want you to do is go to hell and never talk to me again. Ever!"

The phone went dead. All the old feelings of loss, anxiety, the horrible sense that I was supposed to fix this, but not sure how, all this clawed up through my stomach and into my heart. "Damn," I said aloud.

I looked at Calabash with a wry smile. For a long time he said nothing. He just sat beside me, his head down, dragging on his cigarette, and sipping his Green Label. After about ten minutes he raised his head and looked at me. His expression was beyond sad, dripping with pain.

"You have kids?" I asked.

He didn't answer. He turned to the bartender. "Larry, give me a sixer, and pop 'em all."

The bartender looked at me sadly as he put the six-pack of opened beers on the bar and nestled a pack of unfiltered Camel cigarettes on top. Then, after hesitating a moment, he produced a half-pint of Bushmills Irish Whiskey. Calabash nodded approval. He and Larry looked at each other like pallbearers at the funeral of an old friend.

"Come on," Calabash had said gently as he swiveled off his barstool, tucked the six-pack under his arm and flipped me the whiskey. He padded away on bare feet into the darkness. Larry the bartender looked at me solemnly for a moment and then nodded his head, indicating that I should follow. As I walked after Calabash into the darkness, I half realized that my too-loud, too-public phone conversation with Jamie had dug up and uncovered something not just in me, but in a lot of these guys. I guess we all spent way too much time in this life trying to hide from, run away from, bury, ignore, stab, suffocate, or just avoid the pain of things past … and the fear of things future.

Calabash and I plunked down clumsily on the edge of the dock. He handed me a beer and never said a word. We ended up sitting for hours on the edge of that old, rickety-plank dock. At first, I just drank. Then after an hour or so, I began to talk. And talk. Suddenly, like Blah Blah Brenda, I could not shut up. Calabash listened, sucked down beer, and flicked cigarette butts into the lagoon. At one point, Larry showed up with a fresh six-pack.

I awoke alone, with the rising sun starting to sear through my eyelids, flopped backward onto the dock, my feet still dangling in the lagoon. I had a brown, stuffed monkey clutched to my chest. Staring at the monkey, that same never-alone, Christopher Robin and Pooh Bear feeling warmed through me, that feeling that I remembered from decades ago, when Jocko and I had traveled the known world of my one-block neighborhood back in Ozone Park.

I rolled over as a black man I didn't know put a Styrofoam cup of coffee beside me and, without a word, walked noiselessly away.

Was the whole island watching me? I wondered as I struggled to sit up and be less vulnerable. I sat cross-legged on the dock, Jocko II tucked under my arm, and sipped my coffee as I looked out over the slowly stirring lagoon.

Yes, I realized, at least the men. My former best friend Scott once told me that women would circle around a wounded sister, brush the hair away from her mouth as she vomited after a long night of pain-numbing drinking. They'd do shots, eat ice cream, and hover.

Men? Our version was to stand clear, look away, pretend not to notice. But that morning every male on the island was silently watching, waiting, sharing my gut-shot pain.

My role? It was time to suck it up, take my stuffed monkey, and get back to work.

THE STATES
Falling Back

S itting at the bar that winter night, I started to wonder where I would sleep tonight. I had options, none of them good.

I wouldn't go over to Scott's. I couldn't have stood being around when he told Jo. Or saying good night to his daughter, as she would already have been cautioned not to ask why Uncle Joth would be taking her room tonight, while Jo, battling some hormonal instinct to automatically side with Connie, brushed awkwardly past me in the hall to make up the bed. Or worse, I'd hate listening to Jo ask coldly, "How are you doing, Joth?" Or maybe she'd look at me like I was a pitiful beggar in desperate need of a handout of sympathy. The worst part was that I was just that.

Oh, I wanted it, that sympathy, but I couldn't give in to it. I couldn't surrender any more of what was left of me. I'd surrendered enough. Still, I kept falling back, falling back. I'd try to make a stand, then fall back again.

Like when I told Connie this was stupid and it was time to straighten out, that enough was enough. Take a stand, fall back.

Like when I told her she should get therapy, find out what was wrong. Get help. Take St. John's Wort. And she'd just look at me with cold, blank eyes, stranger's eyes, eyes that used to smile at me. Take a stand and fall back.

Like when I recommended that we get marriage counseling, only to hear the therapist explain how sometimes he counseled in favor of divorce because in some marriages it was the best and most successful outcome, and how Connie had agreed, in spite of my protests that we could get a divorce without this clown's overpriced help, thank you. Take a stand and fall back.

Like when I told Connie that I could forgive her and take her back, that I'd change, that we could start again, that it would be okay, that it wasn't too late. Take another cruise to give us a fresh start. And she'd just stared at me with a sad look on her face that said, Joth, I've moved on. You really need to do the same.

Take a stand and fall back.

Like when I told her, okay, everything is negotiable. I would do whatever it took to save our marriage. Just tell me what you want. Tell me what to do. And she'd give me a half shrug in response, and no eye contact.

Take a stand and fall back.

And, finally, just falling back. She'd just look away. When she did look at me, her eyes were indifferent, and that was a new look, like I was a complete stranger holding a door open for her at a store out of courtesy. And I kept falling back, falling back, trying to find a place to make a stand, only to fall back again.

So, Scott and I just sat. And I appreciated that, while the bartender kept a careful eye on him for any sign of encouragement.

I watched the bartender while she watched Scott.

Can you make a Manhattan, up? I asked her.

Momentarily startled out of her fantasy thoughts, she looked at me with bewilderment and annoyance, and then shook her head, dismissing me. I was getting used to that look, the what's-wrong-with-you? look.

So, I just watched her as she studied Scott. All my life I'd looked at women's eyes. I think it's because when I was a kid, I had heard that the eyes were the windows to the soul. So, I always used to look into a woman's eyes. I'm not sure what I was looking for. Whatever it was, I never found it. I know I never saw into their souls. That was some stupid myth. All I saw were eyes, shiny marbles. Oh, sometimes they were smiling or full of passion, sending a deliberate signal, sometimes hot and angry, sometimes just sad. But I always had a sense that whatever was coming out from them was a diversion keeping me from seeing that that door or window to the soul was shut tight. Or maybe that door never existed. I only saw what they wanted me to see. Just like now, Scott's bartender, she was sending out a come-on message to Scott, but it revealed nothing more than that, not a thing about who she was.

THE ISLAND
Yvonne's Place

Some mornings, when I had two snorkeling excursions scheduled with the cruise lines, I had to scramble to get across the harbor to the pick-up dock by 7:45. Other days, especially in the offseason, when fewer ships pull into port, I often had time on my hands. Some of those mornings, I liked to drop in at Yvonne's Place in town for a cup of coffee. Though she doesn't officially open until 11:00 a.m., I'd walk in a little before eight and help myself to the coffee pot behind the bar.

Then I'd sit by myself and watch the girls – excuse me, the ladies – sitting at the other tables listening to Yvonne. I came not for the coffee, but because this was the only place left on earth where I felt right, where I felt good. I liked being here, at Yvonne's Place. Hard to explain.

Rumor was that Yvonne came up from Guyana and had worked in the brothel on the other side of the island for nearly ten years. That had probably been thirty years ago. Today, big and friendly, she is more like a house mother for a sorority than the owner of a small, well-run tavern. Her bartenders and waitresses are ex-prostitutes.

Women, though truly some are just young girls, who are ready to get away from the brothel, knew they could come see Yvonne. Most had come to the island because being prostitutes at the brothel was better than the life they had left behind on their native islands. Then later, ready to be rid of that life, they would seek out Yvonne. They often would arrive illiterate, physically sick, and emotionally beaten. She would give them a job, a safe place to live, and much, much more.

I don't know why, but the brothel owners leave Yvonne alone; so do the shadow boys. Yvonne and Yvonne's Place are safe havens on a sometimes very unsafe rock.

I think I understand. I also get a safe, peaceful, everything-makes-sense feeling as I sip my morning coffee off to the side and watch.

Mornings promptly at eight, Yvonne would position herself behind the bar and wait for the last lady to find a chair at a table or the bar. Once all were accounted for, Yvonne would offer a loud, joyful prayer of gratitude before cracking open a weathered Bible and reading several verses. The ladies sat in silence at the tables. Most smiled; all gave their full attention, now and then uttering a grateful "Amen." After reading, Yvonne would explain the passages, giving a short sermon, speaking softly. She had only one message: The Lord loves you, and so do I. Then the ladies, some as young as fifteen, others pushing 50, would take turns reading verses, usually from the Book of Proverbs. At exactly 8:30, smiling broadly, Yvonne would slam the Bible closed with a loud bang and announce, "Amen, Sisters." The ladies would roar back: "Amen!"

Then, while Yvonne prepared breakfast on the griddle behind the bar, the ladies would bring out text books and notebooks and pens. That next hour was study time, followed by breakfast. I'd sometimes help her cook.

Some folks call her Saint Yvonne, without a drop of irony or sarcasm. Some of the ladies call her Mom, while some of the islanders call her, well ....

That's because Yvonne is sweet as honey; she is also tough as nails. What she offers comes with a price. There are rules. She makes it clear to every new lady she takes in that there will be no drugs, no drunkenness, and no sleeping around. She keeps that Bible close at hand beneath the bar, and during the mid-afternoon lull, she sometimes pulls it out and reads. She's also been known to use it to knock a foul-mouthed customer off his barstool.

"We don' lawh dat kindda talk in dis stablishment," I once heard her say with a furious look as a surprised customer got off the floor and meekly sat back down, mumbling "Sorry, ma'm."

I once dropped by for a drink and watched a big, bluff Irish skipper – full of himself and full of rum – who had just delivered a yacht across the Atlantic and been paid off. When he got a little loose and a little grabby with the waitress, Yvonne, with lightning speed, doubled him over and booted him out the door with two swift kicks, one to the front side and one to the backside. Everyone knew: Yvonne's ladies were not up for grabs and not up for sale. Zero tolerance. As I said, even the shadow boys, the ones with ganga and nose candy for sale, stayed clear of Yvonne.

She's been the matron of honor, Calabash says, for more than a dozen of her ladies who found good men and got married. "Yo a church goin' man?" she'd demand, as the first of many questions she'd ask potential suitors. They had to get through Yvonne before they got to that wedding bed. No quickie marriages, either. The engagement had to be one year. Yvonne's rules.

The ladies went along. Though the men sometimes complained, they did it with big smiles. In the end, many of these men grew to love and respect Miss Yvonne, as they affectionately called her.

And right before the bride would walk up the aisle, Yvonne would pull the groom aside and make it crystal clear how he needed to treat his new wife. (Word has it that the night before, she would have a similar conversation with the bride-to-be.) Their wedding present was a new Bible and a thousand dollars.

Yvonne also taught the ladies skills. During the morning classes, they learned to read and write. Most finished high school; it was rumored that some even went to college.

She also closes at ten o'clock on Saturday night. I once asked her why.

"Da ladies need a good night's sleep befo church on Sunday," she'd said. Then she looked me up and down, as if assessing me and got very serious.

She reached into her pocket and then held out a closed fist, motioning me to put out my hand. As I did, she folded a small, aluminum cross into my palm and said, "You are a good man, Captain Jolly. Stop trying so hard to foe-get dat."

Then she held my hand in both of hers and looked me in the eye. Her grip was solid and I surrendered to her hold. Her eyes were ancient, and her look was dead serious and yet so kind I melted. This woman had seen more of the dark side of life than I could ever imagine, and yet she was positive and loving.

For once, I knew, I was looking into the soul of a woman through her eyes. In those pitch black eyes, I saw blazing, bright light, and everything made sense, everything came together and had a purpose.

I felt like a jolt of electricity had gone through me, and the blood drained from my face. I tried to think of a smart-ass comeback, but I just stood there, mute. Then Yvonne gave me a light kiss on the cheek and, referring to the cross in my hand, said, "Gi dat to someone who needs it. You'll know who dat person is when you see im."

I left quickly. When I got into my car, I burst into tears and bawled like a baby. I don't know why exactly, but every once in a while, perhaps once or twice in a lifetime, you encounter something true – in a whisper, in a glance – and it haunts you the rest of your life.

I know why the brothel owners leave Yvonne alone.

MANGROVE COVE
Captain Kid

I surveyed the sunken wreck of *The Do Over*. Water bottles and half-eaten packages of tuna, crackers and other dry goods were strewn around where I had been lying on the roof of the cabin. That explained the interest of the seagulls. Rats with wings. There were two blankets, as well as a tarp that had been draped and stretched across the boom, creating an awning.

I looked up, dumbly registering that the mast had been re-set and was ready to sail. All we needed was to get the boat off the bottom of the channel and run up the canvas.

I didn't care about that. Finally, it dawned on me. I spun around. Kid was alive. Where was he?

"Kid?" I yelled. "Kid! Where the hell are you?"

A carton of cigarettes flew up out of the submerged cabin and landed on the roof, followed by Kid, dripping wet, hauling himself up the ladder. He plunked himself cross-legged on the corner, looked at me with a matter-of-fact expression, and said, "Hey, Cap'm, have a good rest?"

He leaned back and dug a lighter out of his pocket and focused on blowing the water out of the top and flicking it until it lit. He pointed to the carton of cigarettes.

"Well, Cap'm, we have fire and we have dry cigarettes. I'm happy. How 'bout you?" He reached over and unwrapped a sealed pack of cigarettes from the carton. Tapping two out, he lit them both and handed one to me.

I sat on the roof and took the cigarette. I began to speak, but decided there was nothing to say. I pulled deeply on the cigarette and tilted my face to the sun.

We both smoked in silence. Just another day in paradise.

Finally, flicking away the butt, I pointed up. "The mast?"

"Logistics. Basics." He shrugged. "Dad was an engineer," he added matter-of-factly, doubling my total knowledge about him.

"What about the rest of the boat? We have this sunken hull."

He became methodical, the first mate reporting to the skipper, focusing on the most serious damage first: "I don't think the damage is all that great. The port hull was nearly torn in half and is sticking way out. It's fixable. We can winch it back into place and patch the break together. We can make it hold till we get back to harbor. The magic of epoxy and marine duct tape."

I nodded, looking over and down at the port pontoon sticking out to the side.

"The rest of the hull?"

"As best I can tell, most damage is above the waterline. We lost cleats, and there are cracks everywhere. But she should sail."

"The four drain plugs?"

"In the cabin, just waiting to put 'em in. The mast survived, as did the sails, though there is a huge tear in the mainsail."

I nodded. "We can sew that closed."

"I agree. As backup, we have the jib, which should make it possible to limp back to the lagoon. The equipment and power have been underwater since Tuesday, so we can't count on them."

"Still, that's good. If they're still under water, that will keep them from corroding."

He looked at me, puzzled.

"Below water the rate of oxidation, rust and corrosion will be significantly slower. If we get her back to port quickly, we should be okay. Some of this gear may only need a good flushing."

Kid nodded, then continued his report: "The radio, radar, and other gear, I suspect, are beyond salvaging. The phones seem to be okay, but I can't get a signal."

"The sat links were probably all knocked out by the storm."

"Plus, the batteries are low. No way to recharge 'em."

"Solar?"

"Gone." Kid looked around the mangrove forest all around us. "The solar generator was washed away."

I nodded.

I stood and looked around the channel. "Now, about the minor detail of bringing her back to the surface."

Kid said nothing for a few minutes. Then he broke into a big smile as he stood beside me and pointed. The eight lines we'd used to hogtie the boat had been moved. Kid had reset the fore and aft anchors. I looked to him for an explanation.

"We're into some super low tides, right?"

"Uh huh," For a few days after a major storm, tides usually ran well below normal.

"Well, maybe we have one or two more low tides left," he offered, and I waited. "I cradled three straps under the hulls, creating three slings." He pointed.

I saw that the straps were on the tops of three roots on each side of the boat, with a come-along winch at the top of each strap.

"I think *The Do Over* has at least one more do over left in her, Cap'm," he offered, sounding awfully grown up and looking off at a pelican sitting on a mangrove root and gulping down a fish.

When he turned back, he looked at me with a ferociously serious expression. "This old gal, this beautiful boat, is our home," he said.

Again, I nodded. Yes, it is, I thought to myself.

"My Dad left when I was a kid," he offered, talking about his past for the first time. "My Mom moved from one cheap apartment to another. She got married last year, and that bastard told me it was time for me to move out."

He paused, and all I could think was that this was another lucky bastard who someone had said needed to get on with his life.

"Mom just stood there and didn't say a word. Nice, huh? So, *The Do Over* is my home, and I guess you'll just have to do for family, you and fragrant Bonita."

I didn't know what to say. Fortunately, before I could speak, Kid put on a red nose and swung over the side to swim out and check the winch lines.

THE STATES
It's a Wonderful Life

For some reason, sitting in that bar with Scott, it suddenly seemed important to me that he understand. I had a sense of how deaf people must feel trying to communicate with those who don't understand signing. Scott had nodded, listened, but it wasn't enough. I was traveling way over the line on our friendship. I should have shut up. It's why men who have seen combat don't even attempt to explain how it felt to guys who had never served. The one who hasn't been through it has no frame of reference. None. "How was it?" "Bad." "Yeah, bad." Everybody nods, but, as the kids say, they haven't got a clue. "Yeah, bad."

That was Scott. He had never lost his best friend, the woman he had adored for more than two decades. He'd never been gut shot. He didn't have a clue.

"Remember, that Jimmy Stewart movie, *It's a Wonderful Life*?" I asked him.

"Where he dies?"

"Where he's never born."

"Yeah."

"The scene that really got me was when he came back and nobody knew him. He didn't belong. He'd never existed."

"Yeah, I remember. And he had an angel that made it right."

"Well, remember when he went up to his wife on the street? She had no idea who he was. She was afraid of him. He was a stranger. And he couldn't make her remember. Whenever I saw that scene, it did something to me. It tore me up."

"I know what you mean. Me, too. What if Jo didn't know who I was? After all we've been through together. Like I suddenly didn't exist."

Scott looked away and got real quiet.

I kept talking. "I was sleeping on the couch in the office last week. And, suddenly, in my sleep, she was there. I was in our bed. My eyes were closed, but I could feel her butt up against mine. We used to sleep that way sometimes, rump to rump. I nudged into her to make sure it was real, and as I was waking, I had this incredible sense of relief that this whole separation and her affair and her not caring anymore, that it had all been just a dream. You wouldn't believe the sense of relief. I woke up and wanted to tell her about this terrible nightmare I'd had. But as I woke a bit more, I realized where I was. In my office. And I was pushing my butt against the back of the couch.

"As I lay there looking around my office, I kept wondering if there was some way I could push back time. To find some way to save what I'd lost. I actually asked God to do that for me. Give me one more shot. Somehow, I'd make it different."

"Like in the movie, Jimmy Stewart says he wants to live again?"

"Yeah. But it didn't work when I tried it."

Scott looked at me, and I could tell by the look that he wanted the conversation to stop. He got tough.

"Look, you dumb asshole," he began.

Now, there's a difference between men and women, I thought in a flash, and smiled. A man calls another guy a dumb asshole, it's like saying, I love you, brother. Try telling a woman that. Hey, Babe, you dumb asshole, I love you.

It was time for the pull-yourself-together lecture.

"Look," Scott started, right on cue, "you're as good as most husbands and better than some. Don't beat yourself up. I don't know why Jo stays with me and Connie left you. But I know what you mean. Hang in there. It's a tough break."

We fell silent. Then he nudged me, hard, with his shoulder. "Shut up and just drink your beer. If I had any brains, I'd be home boinking Jo rather than holding your hand all night. And you'd be out hunting down some pussy. Count your blessings. Hell, you weren't all that happy anyhow, and you know it."

I raised my glass. The conversation had been ended, and I knew I wasn't ever going to start it again. "To dumb assholes," I toasted lamely, not sure what else to say.

"And pussy," Scott added.

And to a wonderful life, I thought to myself, knowing that Scott and I had had a great friendship.

THE ISLAND
Island Whores

Some locals said that island life could be hard for the ex-pats. The natives generally didn't like us, would knife us for a pack of cigarettes; the tourists thought we were lost-soul beach bums, fascinating but unsavory; and the resident Americans who owned successful businesses or were retired with money and lived in gated villas, they had no use for us, unless there was an iguana loose in the kitchen that needed catching.

Still, I felt right at home with that group of refugees known as expatriates, or ex-pats. We lived – or pretended to live – the romantic notion that island life was laid back, easy, and, of course, fun. Many of us were druggies or rummies or fleeing felons, or just mopes who decided that cut 'n run was better than stand 'n fight. And, yes, there were a few of us who actually came down because we were dumb enough to believe the stories about the soft breezes, warm bodies, and easy living. Whatever the reason we all ended up on island, it still generally beat what was waiting for us, or not waiting for us, back in the States.

For people like Squint, his story was good for drinks. Skinny as a rail, he'd sit at the bar, his camera in front of him, stubble on his face, wearing that ratty straw hat, red bandana, and an unbuttoned Hawaiian shirt.

"Take your picture," he'd offer by way of introduction to anyone who sat down beside him. "No charge. Just a drink. I'm your local island rummy. I used to be a stock broker on Wall Street. Now, I prefer the island life."

What an opening line. That was his elevator talk, and it was great. The *touristas* loved it. Who wouldn't? And who wouldn't want to hear more. So, they'd gladly buy him a drink, hoping to hear more of his story. We doubted any of it was true, but it played well with the *touristas*:

"I was one of those fast-track guys, and I had it made," he'd say. "I lived on the Upper West Side of Manhattan. On west 72nd. Just off Broadway. Do you know the area? Had a driver pick me up every morning and drive me down to Wall Street. I had a wife. It was a great life. On vacation, we'd always come down here to the island. Photography was a hobby back then. This island has the best views. The best sunsets. Don't you agree?"

They always did.

He'd finger his camera, a 35 millimeter Nikon F6, a fancy camera, or so people told me.

"I got great shots of the island and of Barb, my wife. Wanna see them?"

They'd always agree, and he'd pull two books out of his backpack sitting on the sandy tile beside his barstool.

The first book was like a family photo album, filled with honeymoon shots.

"These are photos of Barb," Squint would say. "Wasn't she gorgeous?" he'd ask, as he flipped through some pictures that included sun, ocean, and a drop-dead beautiful woman with jet-black hair, a big smile, large breasts, and a small bikini.

Of course, they'd agreed. The wives fawned; the husbands fantasized. In the back of their minds, however, they hoped they weren't going to hear some sad divorce story.

"And sweet. We were expecting our first child. It was gonna be a boy. But then …"

He'd pause, look down at the woman in one of the pictures, and open his hands in a poof-it's-gone gesture.

Then, in almost a whisper, he'd sigh, "Heart attack."

Everything stopped. They weren't expecting this. Now they were really interested.

After a pause, he'd add, "Congenital heart problem. Nobody knew about it until afterwards. She was at home. I found her on the kitchen floor. They say she died instantly. So did Gabe."

He smiled wanly. "Gabe. That was the name we'd picked out for our son."

Then, as if coming out of a reverie, he'd snap the book closed and put it back into the backpack, as if protecting her memory and realizing he'd said too much. Every night, same script. God, he was good.

The tourists didn't know what to say, so they'd sit staring dumbly at the cover of the second book, Squint's full-color coffee table book, *Beautiful Island*, sitting on the bar in front of him. Then one of them, usually the woman, would slowly, hesitantly, slide it in front of her and ask quietly, to change the subject, "Is this yours?"

"Yeah," Squint would admit hesitantly. "I got so burned out on Wall Street. The place has no soul. And nothing really mattered after Barb died."

He'd pause, and the wife would look at her husband, either accusingly or reassuringly.

As if not noticing, Squint would continue. "Our dream was to come down to the island, raise Gabe in paradise, and turn my photo hobby into a business. After ... I decided to do it anyway to honor her memory."

Slowly, always slowly, almost reverently, the tourists would open the book and look at the title page and dedication. Then she'd ask, "Is this you? Manny Donarino? And Barb?"

"Yeah, but my friends just call me Squint," Squint would say sadly and then gesture to his eye. "You know, because you squint when you take a picture."

The couple would nod in understanding and smile cautiously.

Then he'd extend his hand to conclude the introductions, carefully ask their names and ask if they'd write down their address and pose for him, while he picked up the camera and snapped a few shots.

It usually took about 15 minutes to get two free drinks and sell at least one, sometimes two or three, copies of the book. "Will you sign it, please?" they'd always ask, and he'd always agree, acting as if the idea had never occurred to him before. And the tourists would go away happy, books in hand, and they'd have one helluva story to tell about their friend Squint and his late wife and baby Gabe. It was one of those vacation memories they'd share as they showed their friends the book on their coffee table.

***

I think that was why I just didn't like Squint. In the land of whores, he was a whore's whore. No self-respect. Sure, I played the charming buccaneer, Captain Jolly, master of the sailing cat *The Do Over*. It was all a show, and it was good for tips. But I was more like one of Black Mike's topless blonde girls who sat at the bar, flirted a little, and pretended to care before walking out into the tropical night with a stranger who wanted to poke, pet, prod and spread them. Every customer knew what he was getting. No façade, except for, well, a little fantasy. A little dignity. A little, maybe.

Squint? He was like a cheap whore who just spread her legs and said, Hey, baby, want some?

Still, he was awfully good at what he did. Begrudgingly, I admitted to myself, I had to admire that. The whore. Still, I didn't like him.

Of course, he didn't like me, either, but I understood why. When I'd first bought *The Do Over* and picked up the snorkeling excursions contract with the cruise line, Squint used to pull alongside in his skiff as I returned to harbor, and I'd let him hawk his *Beautiful Island* coffee table photo book to my customers. The tourists loved his straw hat, red bandana around his neck, bare feet, camera slung around his neck, and smiling face on the back cover of the book.

"That yours?" someone would always call, pointing to the book, as our boats traveled side by side.

"Sure is. I took every shot myself, well, me and my late wife," he'd call, balancing with one foot on the seat, the other on the tiller of the outboard, and holding up an open copy of his book in both hands. "Filled with island memories. Fifty dollars US. No tax."

While some of my customers thought about it and others scrambled to find their wallets in their beach bags, he closed the sale.

"The beautiful woman in some of the photos," he'd add, sounding bravely cheerful, then pause and lower his head for a moment. "That's my late wife."

Then he'd look away, tear in his eyes.

The whore. *Ka-ching*.

It didn't take me long to realize that, as dollars and books passed across the water, it was my tip money that was heading over the side. So, I started chasing him away, explaining to any of my customers who asked that he was a rummy and a child pornographer.

Funny the things some people will say and do for money.

MANGROVE COVE
Yo Ho Ho

I sat on the roof, cross-legged, eating Ho Hos and studying the tide markings on the mangrove roots. We had winched the damaged port hull back into place and Kid had done his best to create an underwater patch, while I wired it to the still-solid starboard hull. We were ready.

"Yo? Ho Ho!" I called and giggled at our perpetual and childish play on pirate jargon. It was how we called each other to dinner when we had those chocolate rolled cakes for dessert.

"Aye, Cap'm," Kid called from out in the water.

Like most boaters (I hated being called a sailor), I knew the tides that told me how close I could cut it over the reef or the point just outside the harbor bridge. There were a lot of factors affecting tides, but as a rule, the closer you got to the tropics, the less pronounced the tide was.

Still, since the hurricane, the variable of a few feet could make the difference as to whether or not *The Do Over* ever floated again. So, as the tide peaked and began to ebb, I watched the mangrove roots I'd had Kid mark and felt the tide flow slowly through the channel. Meanwhile, Kid kept cinching the winches tighter as the high tide peaked. Then, in theory, at least, we could just sit back and let the tide run out and the boat, cradled in the straps, would be sitting on the surface as we inserted the drain plugs once the bilge water ran out. It made sense in theory.

THE ISLAND
Daily Grind

I like those island myths, mostly because they're good for business. Every day – always, without fail – barely out of harbor on the a.m. half-day snorkeling excursion on *The Do Over*, the men especially would look around, sigh and say how they would love to do this, to run away and live in the islands; that this was their dream. They often said it while looking at the tight, bikini ass of one of the other cruise line *touristas* on board.

Back home, they had perfect, orderly, cubicle jobs, with perfect, slightly nervous, sweet-smelling wives in tow. Hanging on for dear life as we sailed across the light chop in the clear, blue water, they'd say how great it would be to live down here. Then someone would point to the stuffed monkey lashed to the mast and ask, "Good luck?"

"Nah," I'd say. "Jocko the monkey. He's the brains of this outfit."

And we'd pile it on – bullshit on top of bilge water. The men would listen intently as we shared our stories, or at least the stories they wanted to hear: "So, I woke up one day and said to myself, 'If not now, Jolly, when?' So, I sold the wife, left the business, and with nothing but the shirt on my back and a change of clothes, I walked away. Never looked back. Freedom versus security. Give me freedom any day."

Then I'd turn my face up into the sun, study the filling sail and, for just that moment, believe my own mythology. It really wasn't a bad life.

They'd listen, torn but mesmerized. Meanwhile, Kid would hang over the side and watch for an occasional turtle or shark or, more likely, a small school of bright-colored fish. The best part was when dolphins joined us. Sometimes one or two or a small school would swim with us for miles. I never really understood why. Dolphins seemed to like humans, which, in my opinion, made them lousy judges of character. In return, people would capture them, put them in pens and offer tourists an opportunity to swim with them. I've often thought we should put the people in pens and let the dolphins in to visit and swim with them. Ah, but the dolphins didn't have any money.

Oops! Musn't let my happy, Captain Jolly face slip. Dolphins are neat creatures, I admit, and people who see them will talk about them as one of the highlights of their vacations. *Ka-ching.*

So, Kid would point and announce loudly, "Fins off the port bow, Cap'm. Look at that!" And everybody would crowd to the port. Thank God, I'd think, that *The Do Over* was a flat-footed catamaran with two hulls spaced widely apart. It would take an act of God to heel her up, let alone over, even with sixteen *touristas* all rushing to one side.

Meanwhile, I steered *The Do Over* around the reef and into our favorite snorkeling cove. I'd learned how to get the patter down perfectly between the 12 minutes it took to round the point, drop the sail, set the anchor, and break out the snorkels, masks and fins.

Meanwhile, couples exchanged glances, he more convinced than ever that this was the best life. "We could do this," he'd whisper excitedly, "Sell the house, give away the kids, quit the job ... go for it. Just like he did," he'd say, nodding in my direction.

The wives? They'd usually drift away halfway through the conversation and stare blankly out at the water. They were much more practical and levelheaded than the men. Some were annoyed because they wanted the attention; others were afraid their husbands would want to do more than just talk and dream. There was always that risk. They understood better than the men that fantasies were usually best left as just that ... fantasies. As wives, they knew the initial impression rarely lasted as reality set in.

I saw the story as a sales pitch, cashing in on my past life back in the States. That was why I admired Jimmy Buffet. He packaged this myth of the romantic island life bullshit in his songs and sold it in concerts to landlubbers all over the States. It was the myth that sold. Or maybe it was the hope that the myth could be real. Hope and myth.

Every now and then, I'd look over my cargo of cruise ship excursionists and wonder how many suicides I'd helped avoid, or at least postpone, because some cubicle-dwelling wage slave could go back to his job and, while sitting on the 5:35 commuter train in the evening, daydream of sailing *The Do Over* across the reef. Then I had to laugh: It had saved me from pulling the trigger. Maybe some myths are real.

***

Once the sail was furled and the anchor set, Kid would put on a big smile and announce, "Okay, listen up." The guests would then crowd around the bins as Kid explained how to select and use the snorkel gear. "Oh, and be sure to take off all jewelry," he'd add casually. "Might attract the wrong kind of fish."

I hated this herding-cats part of the trip and stayed back.

"Excuse me? Is this right?" "I can't find flippers my size." "How do I keep my mask from fogging up?" "I can't get this snap to work." "Do I have to go in? I'd just rather read my book and watch."

Then some would always end up duck-walking around the deck, mask on, breathing loudly through the snorkel, stepping on each other's fins.

They'd march off the stern and spend 75 minutes splashing around in the water, gurgling oohs and ahhs at the fish they'd see.

Once we had a head count and everyone was back on board and accounted for, Kid would pull out the rum punch, pour it in plastic cups, and snap on some lively island music, either Bobby McFerrin's "Don't Worry. Be Happy," or just about anything lively by Jimmy Buffet or Bob Marley.

I'd stand at the wheel while Kid poured drinks, passed around snacks in a bag, and then rinsed and sorted the gear. Mostly, I was making sure nobody fell overboard. We must have done head counts a dozen times while out of harbor. And, yes, now and then, other boats, not us yet, would come back minus a customer. Not good for business. Contract cancelled.

THE STATES
Boys & Girls

L ooking back on it, I think I went from concerned to anxious to flat-out obsessed, thinking about these things on my couch in my office back in the States. Still, the tape had to be played, and I admit that I became a little psychotic with the topic of men and women. For some reason, I believed I had to get it right. Why? I don't know. I suspect it was because I believed it was all my fault, and I wanted to make sure I got it right the next time. Until finally I quit trying. I just hit a wall. Bang. That probably saved my life.

Until then, though, I had begun to become irrational with the idea of getting it right. And that's a fool's quest, I know now. You see, when it comes to men and women, they will never, ever really understand each other. I think that's God's joke on all of us. Men and women are thrown together, drawn together, always in search of each other. We depend on each other, need each other and, in my opinion, complete and complement each other. But – let me repeat that: BUT! – we also have absolutely nothing in common. Mars. Venus. Yin. Yang. Opposites drawn like north and south magnets pulled together. Maybe that's where the friction and tension that powers the world comes from. I don't know.

We're mysterious mysteries to each other.

I think it's cool. I also think it's funny. Yes, and frustrating and annoying, all at the same time.

It's like I know that most women like jewelry, but most guys couldn't care less, unless it's maybe a heavy-linked, macho, gold chain.

Or take flowers and new babies. Both of those puzzle me, how women can get all funny about flowers and new babies. I remember the first time I saw my son, Jamie, right after he was born. I thought, "This thing is mine? Gross! He looks like a monkey, and an ugly monkey at that." I also knew this event – the birth of my son – was very, very important somehow, but I didn't really know why or how. Connie, however, geez, she got all warm and passionate inside. She'd become instantly focused, all full of some secret purpose. Meanwhile, I was lost. I remember thinking, "Well, I guess that cross country motorcycle trip is off the table, huh?" So, to avoid actually saying dumb things like that, I decided to shut up and take my cue from Connie. I pretended. I faked it.

Jamie was important, but it took nearly a year before that went from a thought in my head to a deep conviction in my heart. Now, I'm crazy about the kid, even though he has the common sense of a toad at times and doesn't like me at all. Connie, though, I think she saw heaven and earth, generations of Thanksgiving dinners, and even her grandkids' weddings the second she touched Jamie. I just saw a wiggly lump with no control over its sphincter muscles.

Most of all, she saw a family, and she knew exactly where she fit into that family. Me? I was lost and more than a little jealous. Jamie and I were instant competitors for time and resources. All of a sudden, I had to share Connie – from her time to her tits – with this little guy. To make matters worse, while I wasn't sure where I fit in in this new arrangement, she seemed, instantly and instinctively, to know who she was, what she needed to do, and where she belonged.

Some people say that kids are the glue that holds a marriage together. I'm not all that sure.

Anyhow, I think women love children naturally. Men have to learn to love them. Come to think of it, men have to learn to love women, too. Of this I am sure. We're really not all that good at it. Maybe we're still in the Stone Age. Or maybe we just love differently than women do.

I have to think about that some more, perhaps same couch, same office, same time, tomorrow night. One more damn thing to add to the highlights tape of the post-game reel.

MANGROVE COVE
The Shark Myth

We were both in the water, on opposite sides of *The Do Over*, working the three winches that were attached to the straps under the hulls. The water was warm, clear and salty. We had agreed we'd do five cranks on the front winch, me following Kid's lead as he called out the numbers.

"One. Two. Three. Four. Five."

Then we'd move on to the rear strap and repeat the process. Then we'd move to the middle strap before doing the whole thing over yet again. After three rounds, we noticed the boat shift as it began to lift off the bottom.

Holy cow, this just might work, I thought. Then I saw three fins moving through the channel. The sharks – and they weren't Threshers – were moving fast, with purpose, and they were heading our way.

When I'd slipped into the channel, I'd scraped my shoulder on some ripped up fiber glass. I hadn't given it a second thought, until now. When I raised myself out of the water, the scrape oozed blood and stung from the salt. I'd heard somewhere that sharks could smell blood up to a mile away. These guys looked like they were on my scent.

"Kid," I called. "Kid!"

He glanced at me and then saw where I was pointing. He knew as well as I that most sharks were not a threat. It was mostly a myth that sharks attacked humans. But these myths, three of them, were closing fast, and those fins were making a straight line for me.

"Get out of the water!" I yelled as loud as I could. "Now!"

The boat, with the cabin roof and mast exposed, was only about 30 feet away. I grabbed my hip. No knife. The first time I actually needed it, and I had no idea where it was. Probably somewhere at the bottom of the channel.

I pulled hard, swimming for the relative safety of the boat roof. Most sharks circled and sniffed around, exploring their prey. These three stooges, I saw as I stroked for the boat, were ready to eat now. No appetizers. No polite pre-dinner conversation. Just gulp and run. Fast food.

Kid was already on the boat. "Come on. Come on," he yelled. He was frantically pacing and jumping up and down on the roof, flapping his arms. "Come on. Just ten feet to go."

As I swam for all I was worth, I saw a dark object go under me. The dorsal fin brushed my chest and kept going, and I realized how big this sucker was, pushing ten feet. And there were three of them. I suspected that the hurricane had disrupted their usual feeding territory, and they probably hadn't eaten since before the storm.

Big and hungry. Great.

I was almost to the boat, but they were circling, one at the surface and two by my feet. The channel was only about six feet deep, and I could bob off the bottom, if I wanted to. But that just meant these sharks had little room to maneuver, so they stayed in close rather than spin and loop.

I was borderline in a panic. This was not how I wanted to go out.

Then I just stopped. This is not how I am going out. Two things attracted sharks, I remembered. One was blood. No stopping that right now. But the other was the flurry of either bait fish or a wounded fish floundering. Like a cat pouncing on your hand moving around under the covers, sharks were drawn to jerky movements like a swimmer's feet kicking.

"Okay, boys, we need to talk," I said, now upright and slowly parrying water with my hands to stay afloat, refusing to bob, while the sharks continued to circle me. Kid had stopped his nervous pacing and, standing stock still, just watched.

"Kid, would you do me a favor, please," I asked quietly.

"Anything, Cap'm," he answered matter-of-factly, as if I were asking him to pass the salt.

"See if you can rip that piece of railing from the roof."

"Okey dokey, Captain," he said and began to pry off the twisted remnant of the aluminum railing. The creaking sound of the aluminum coming off the roof startled the sharks momentarily.

My feet were perfectly still, so the sharks had lost interest in my lower half. All three of them now were on the surface, circling.

One nuzzled my shoulder, knocking me almost two feet to the side. "Stop playing with your food," I said, more irritated than scared. He seemed to like what he smelled, because he swam away faster, excited, wiggling his body, and then he turned sharply around.

THE ISLAND
Night Sweats

Bonita never asked for anything, which is why I remember that late night I found her wrapped in my too-large T-shirt, sitting, curled against the silent coolness of the December Caribbean darkness on the stern deck, tears in her eyes, watching the sleeping lagoon, so silent that, as I noiselessly approached with a blanket, I could hear the tires of a car humming on the far side of the water as it crossed the steel mesh of the drawbridge, the rigging of the dark boats gently, rhythmically slapping their masts, and, without moving or seeming to even know I was there behind her, she asked me, in a whisper, to please, please not ever make love to her again.

Suddenly, swimming in Mangrove Cove with the sharks, I understood what she meant. I understood her.

MANGROVE COVE
Shark Myths

In the water, with three very interested sharks circling tightly around me, I found myself thinking, "What's the worst that can happen?"

I thought of the movie *From Here to Eternity* and the one line I remember from it, and I started laughing. Kid, who was busy ripping off the aluminum railing, turned and looked at me. "Cap'm?"

"Remember, Kid," I called to him, still laughing, as one of the sharks brushed by my side, "They can kill you, but they can't eat you."

"No disrespect intended, Cap'm, but these boys are gonna gobble you up like popcorn."

He looked at the fins, as the sharks circled faster and tighter, and I was trying to inch myself closer to the sunken hull of *The Do Over* to get on the roof of the cabin. I imagined panicking and getting half way up, and one of these behemoths taking off my leg as I swung out of the water.

Hmmm, I thought. A peg leg would help the whole Captain Jolly mystique. Good for tips. *Ka-ching*!

Kid held up a five-foot section of the railing.

"Want me to harpoon those big boys?" he called.

"No. Not yet. Okay, now take that whiskey bottle you have stashed in the sail and smash it in on the side of the boat."

Kid looked disappointed at the thought of wasting good whiskey. So, he first uncapped it and took a swig before breaking it in half on the edge of the roof. It took three tries, and that spooked the sharks, but only momentarily. Becoming increasingly skittish and excited, they returned, moving faster and seeming more in a hurry. They were cutting between me and the boat, preferring to dine out in the channel.

"Good. Now stick it on the end of the railing pole and pass it down to me, please. Nice and slow."

Kid inserted the end of the railing in the broken, jagged end of the bottle and passed it to me. As I took it by the neck, all I could think was that I'd be damned if I was going to just let these bastards eat me without a fight. It felt good to have something resembling a weapon, though it would probably be of little help. Still ….

"Now, hang onto that railing and get ready. When I start yelling, I want you to do the same, real loud, and bang that thing for all you're worth on the mast. Then if you get a shot, Ahab, stick that thing as deep as you can into one of those sharks. Go for the eyes."

"Aye, aye, Cap'm. And who's Ahab?"

"Later, Kid. Later."

With the broken bottle in one hand, I was having trouble inching my way to the side of the boat. Plus, the sharks seemed to want to herd me away further out into the channel. It was getting dicey.

The biggest one passed and brushed my chest. Then, as he turned to pass by again, I plunged the bottle as hard as I could into his eye and started yelling. I let out a deep, wild primeval howl, the kind that would have made Rocket, my old dog, proud. I must have done some serious damage, because the shark thrashed and turned, confused and disoriented, a thin stream of blood trailing from his blinded eye. The idea was to make him more focused on his own pain than on me. It seemed to be working. Energized, I ducked beneath the surface and let out another full-lung, underwater scream.

I came up for air right as Kid aimed his aluminum spear at the big shark's other eye and plunged it in. Adrenalin running at full bore, we were both screaming as loud as we could. There was something primitive and downright joyful about those full-lung screams.

Kid's aim was dead on. The railing piece went deep into the shark's eye socket, and he kept shoving it in as hard as he could.

The other two sharks swam off to get their bearings and were hovering about 20 yards away. The big one, however, now totally blind, was thrashing around and gnashing his teeth, way too close for me. He turned again, so I shoved the jagged bottle toward his nose. It hit his teeth, and he clamped his mouth shut, barely missing my hand. The bottle shattered. Kid kept pushing with his aluminum spear. Finally, the shark began to slow down, and I hoped he was dying. The water was rich with blood.

"How's that feel, you son of a bitch!" I bellowed in triumph as he began to sink to the bottom. Then he came back – second wind, maybe? – swimming wildly about the channel. He slammed into the mangrove roots. Blind and insane with pain, he began attacking them, ripping and tearing at the roots, pushing himself deeper and deeper into the tangle of steel-hard roots, until he was hopelessly tangled, with no way out.

"We got 'em, Cap'm!" Kid hooted, jumping up and down on the roof. "We got 'em. Now, please stop playing with the fish and get back on board."

I began to swim back to the boat and the twisted piece of railing pole he was holding out for me.

That was when the other two sharks returned, moving fast, and one of them plowed into my ribs like a pile driver, knocking the wind out of me and sending me a good three feet across the water.

Myth, my ass, was my last thought, as I curled up and began to sink to the bottom.

THE ISLAND
The Real Thing

Referring to Calabash, Chicago Mike once asked right before the hurricane hit, "Why do you like that old bum?"

I thought about it for a minute, then said, "His eyes. Did you ever look at his eyes?" Mike gave me a blank stare. I continued, "They're pale and clear, a light sea blue."

Chicago grunted dismissively.

"And they have a sparkle to them. They're honest. And gentle."

Calabash didn't have a job. I'm not sure how the subject came up, but one night, sitting at the Sunset Bar eating his rib dinner, Black Mike mentioned to me that Calabash had a wife who lived back in the States.

"Calabash?" I'd exclaimed in a voice way too high pitched, almost a whoop. I guess I'd never really thought about that possibility. I supposed that Calabash had always been part of the island: no history, no past, no future, a pleasant, decent island bum.

"That be right. Calabash. His wife, she a big-bucks financial planner. Good lookin' too."

"Well, why'd she leave him?"

"Who say she leave him?"

"Really? So, he left her?"

"Who say he left her?"

"They're still married?"

"Long time. They crazy in love wit each utter."

"Really? Well, why'd she stay married to him? Why not leave him? Or him her? Do they have kids? Why'd they split up?"

"Shhhh," said Black Mike, slowing me down. "Yo talk too much. Axe too many questions. If Calabash wanted you ta know, he'd a tole you hisself."

Black Mike paused, picked up a spicy jerk rib from his platter, and munched on it. He seemed distracted, as if debating something with himself.

Finally, he said, "Jus for da record, dey ain't split up. Dey very much togetter."

I sipped my whiskey and waited. Dropping a stripped-clean rib bone on his plate and wiping his hands on a napkin, Black Mike looked at me. He saw I wasn't about to let this go, he continued, dropping the island accent. "Have you ever noticed how you don't see Calabash with any other women?"

"Yeah. I guess," I said cautiously. "Now that you mention it."

"That's because he only wants one woman. Sandy. And have you ever noticed how he disappears for about a month in December into January?"

I'd never really thought about it, but it was true that Calabash was never around for any of the Christmas celebrations on the island.

"Uh huh. I guess."

"That's when Sandy comes down. They go off island together."

I frowned skeptically.

"Oh, he cleans up when he wants. And Sandy, she's the sweetest thing on two legs."

"How do you know so much about them?"

He paused, frowned, and looked at me. "Look, Jolly, I like you. You are a good man. So, I'm telling you this because, well, I don't know. Like I said, you're a good man."

I cocked my head and waited.

"Sandy and I went to school together in England. I introduced her to Calabash more than forty years ago. The day they met, they fell wildly and totally in love." Gazing back at some wondrous memory, Mike's face broke into a gentle smile. "They still are. They have the perfect marriage, not because they live in different countries, but because they respect each other. They are both good people."

After another rib and another long pause, Black Mike added matter-of-factly, "I officiated at their wedding."

My eyebrow went up. "I'm sorry, what? You did what?"

"I officiated at their wedding." Still living partly in that memory, his warm, tender smile broke over me, enveloped me. "Like most people who are blessed, and my life has been nothing but blessed, I have had the good fortune to be many things, to play many roles. One of them is that of an ordained minister in the Church of England."

My jaw dropped. "And now you …" My voice trailed off and I looked at the blonde girls in their usual seats at the bar. One of them saw me looking; she smiled and wiggled her fingers in greeting. I smiled, nodded, and turned back to Mike.

"There are many noble professionals, Jolly."

I just shook my head. I wasn't sure which questions to ask first. "So, why aren't they together?"

"They? You mean Calabash and Sandy?"

I nodded.

"She is most comfortable in the high-powered, high-heeled life. And he respects that."

"And he," I added, starting to understand, "loves the shaggy-haired, greasy Hawaiian shirt life."

"And they each respect that in each other," Black Mike added, as if that answered everything. "Oh, and there's no great tragedy to tell here. No drama about jealousy, lost love, dopey, deliberate misunderstanding. No artificial plot for a formula book or movie. Just life. Oh, and from everything I can see, they're happy with themselves and for each other."

I stared and smiled. "And you introduced them … and officiated at their wedding?"

"That is correct. And, no, he is not my long-lost half-brother, and she is not some once-upon-a-time lover I'll always pine for. Sorry, it's that simple. Those, in my opinion, are the best stories of all, don't you agree?"

Black Mike looked down at his plate of food, shook his head and got back into character. "Yessir," he said loudly. "She be crazy 'bout that ol fart. An he be crazy fo her. She unnerstan him, take care a him in her own way. An he her. He da real ting. She da real ting. Mos folks I knows would kill foe dat, Mon."

MANGROVE COVE
Captain Blood

I was vaguely aware that I was curled up on the bottom of the mangrove channel. I knew there were sharks around, and they were not happy. I was also processing that I could not stay here much longer, since the shark had pushed all the air out of my lungs and probably cracked a rib, maybe two. So, I held my breath as long as I could, savoring what I suspected were my last seconds of being alive.

Did my life flash before my eyes? Nah, not really. I'd spent the last few years doing enough of that on my own, analyzing, reviewing, wondering, second-guessing. I had done enough belly-button gazing for ten men. The only thing that flashed through my head was that I had spent enough time pondering the past and trashing the present. It had been one humungous, drunken pity party. Enough.

I tucked myself into a ball, planted my feet on the sandy bottom and, my lungs ready to burst, pushed off toward the surface as hard as I could. At that moment, I also heard a muffled "Yee Haa!" followed by a loud splash. I broke the surface and gasped in the sweetest, deepest lung full of air. At the same time I almost passed out from the pain in my side.

Ignoring the ribs, two strokes and I was holding onto the cabin railing of the still partially submerged *Do Over* and let myself drift onto the deck. I pulled myself upright with the help of the wheel and, still up to my waist in water, turned to see Kid. For a second, I thought I was hallucinating again or still. He was straddling a shark with his legs. All I could see of the shark was its fin. It was swimming wildly around the channel, and Kid was jamming his knife into its head again and again. Blood was trailing behind the two of them, as Kid hung on and kept stabbing the shark. Kid was laughing and laughing, and it sounded maniacal.

Finally, the shark stopped thrashing and swimming. It slowly began to sink to the bottom. Kid slipped off its back, put the knife between his teeth, pirate fashion, and stroked for the boat, swimming into the open cabin. He swam up to me and pulled himself up by the wheel.

Our noses almost touching, we stared at each other for a moment, both breathing hard, standing on the deck in three feet of water. Then he slowly took the knife out of his mouth, lowered his head onto my chest, and started sobbing. I put my arms around him, kissed him gently on the head and said, "Son, thank you for saving my life."

"Cap'm," he said, his shoulders shaking as he kept sobbing, "Please, let's go home."

THE ISLAND
Homeward Bound

I t was late at night when we limped back into the harbor, guided home on a quiet sea by a full moon in a clear sky. It had taken two more days to get *The Do Over* fully afloat and, though she was a bit leaky, she was ready to sail. The batteries were ruined so we had no running lights, electric bilge pumps, or any power of any kind. We hadn't even tried to get the engine operational. We'd sewed the hole in the mainsail. We hoped it would last for the short voyage around the island. Even Jocko II was still there, though there was pretty much no stuffing left inside him. I know how he felt.

The boat, with one cracked hull, was sluggish in the light breeze and pulled to port. We were making only about three knots, even with the wind at a good angle off our stern and the sail in tight. That was okay; too fast and I was afraid the sail would split and we'd shake apart.

Kid had been working the big hand pump on the port pontoon, which was taking on water, but not as badly as I thought it would. And as he cleared it, he patched a little more of the broken seam. By now, the hull was barely leaking.

Kid was standing beside me, looking up and smiling. I followed his gaze to the top of the mast. There flew the Jolly Roger, the pirate flag, tattered and frayed, but still snapping proudly in the light breeze.

Turning to him, I asked quietly, "Well, Peter," referring to what he had once told me was his favorite story, "do you think it's time to grow up?"

"What about the other lost boys, Wendy?" When I didn't answer, he lowered his gaze down to his bare feet and said nothing for a while. When he glanced back up at me, the look in his eyes was unsettled.

"We almost died out there," he said slowly.

"Several times. Thank you for saving my life."

"Several times," he repeated, with a cockeyed smile, that unsettled look dissolving into an impish grin. "I definitely do not get paid enough to be your babysitter."

"Thinking you might go home?" I asked after another long silence, as we watched a school of flying fish skip across the water.

"I could go to school," he said, almost to himself. "Get a degree in accounting. I'm good with numbers. I could go to Ohio State."

"Go, Buckeyes," I offered vaguely. Another long pause. "And then what?"

In the silence that followed, I suspect he plumbed for an answer. He said nothing, so I guess that was his answer.

I looked at the sail. We were on an easy tack. "Prepare to come about."

Kid swung into position. In thirty seconds, the boom had swung overhead, the lines were tight, and we were heading on a smoothly executed change of course.

"What about you, Cap'm?" Kid asked, returning to my side.

Me? I took a deep breath and something didn't seem right. No, it wasn't the pain in my side from the broken ribs. Something was gone, something was missing. It was that uncertain ache, the vague pain of loss and anger that I'd been carrying around inside me like a bowling ball. It was gone. I was no longer angry at Connie or even reluctantly regretful about losing the house, the business, the family, the dog. Well, maybe the dog. I still missed

Rocket. Most of all, I was no longer angry or disappointed at myself. What's wrong with me? Absolutely nothing. Thank you for asking.

I started to laugh before the hitch in my side made me think better of it. For way too long, I had been a prisoner to old memories and lost dreams, to those irritating and endlessly looping tapes. Perversely, I decided to try running a few; they wouldn't play. Again, I breathed in deeply and, for the first time in ages, it was just a breath, though a physically painful one. There was no tell-tale memory or bitter emotional hitch. No self-pity or arrogance.

Kid saw me smile. "What about you?" he repeated. "Ever think about going home?"

"Right up to just now, pretty much every minute, Kid. Pretty much every minute."

"And now?"

"And now ..." I said, letting the words hang. Then I stepped back from the wheel. "Here, take the helm," I said, and went below to get a pack of cigarettes. I came back up a minute later, lit two cigarettes and gave one to Kid. He was standing, legs spread, both hands on the wheel, a faint smile on his face.

As we smoked and watched the sea, I explained, "Kid, I was grown up once. I gave it one helluva shot. Parts of it were fun."

Kid just listened.

"Parts of it sucked."

Kid nodded. "Down here?"

"Down here you have guys like John/Candy, who kill themselves and bums like Chicago Mike, who never knew how to live and never will, no matter where they go or what they do. But I knew too many guys and gals like that back in the States, too. I didn't know enough people like Calabash, or Bonita, or Yvonne, or Jason, or Black Mike ... or you, Kid. Good people."

He stared at me for a moment, uncertain why he would make the list. Then he went back to watching the sea, his eyes scanning slowly from port to starboard and up into the sail.

***

As we approached the island, Kid and I stared silently at the cameo of the mountain. It was mostly dark, except for a few compounds where the owners had generators. We sailed close in along the shoreline, close enough that we could hear the gentle surf, tacking lightly. A few dogs, heads down and scurrying quickly across the sand, scavenged along the beach.

Kid and I switched off at the helm. He pointed at a twisted building and flattened trees. I nodded. The Giggling Gecko. All that remained were a few of those silly three-foot flag poles on the beach, one with a white pennant flapping lazily in the breeze. A dog barked and a man came out of the pile of debris that had once been the restaurant. He held a pickaxe handle loosely in his hand and watched us in silence for a moment before waving and disappearing back into the shadows.

I touched my ribs and winced. Kid had guessed I had two broken ribs, which were now snugly bound by strips of what had once been the jib sail. He had wrapped me from nipple to navel. I felt okay, as long as I didn't bend or breathe too deeply.

We rounded the inlet, adjusted the sail and approached the drawbridge leading into the lagoon. Half of the bridge was up, and I saw no sign of the bridge master. There was also no traffic. None. We eased through, neither of us saying a word as we scanned the harbor.

As we looked around, Kid muttered, "Holy shit!" My heart froze, as I saw it, too. Heading in slowly, we were surrounded by what looked like a forest of leafless, branchless, skinny tree trunks. Boat masts. Dozens of them sticking up out of the waters of the shallow lagoon. Not a single boat seemed to be above water.

I whispered, "Let's pull up the skegs, Kid."

"Aye, aye, Cap'm," he answered, also in a whisper, like one does while passing a cemetery, either out of respect or fear of waking the dead. I wondered how many people had died. We'd never know. These kind of statistics were bad for business.

Kid went below to pull the swiveling keels up into the base of each hull to avoid snagging any debris below the water.

Good bye paradise I thought. *Nah, maybe it's just home,* I answered, giving the automatic response. I also thought about the cruise lines. All full of kind words and condolences, they would likely cancel their contracts, screw their island crews, and cut a deal with another island.

I searched for what had once been our marina. No sign of it. Gone. Kid, returning, pointed to a pile of splintered docks. Boats were tumbled all over the shore and a hundred feet or more inland, lying on their sides, upside down, piled one on top of another. There was no pier to tie up to. I was thinking that it might be best to drop anchor and moor just off shore. Normally, there were perhaps a hundred boats attached to mooring buoys in the lagoon. Every one of them was either on the bottom, sunk where it was tethered, or part of the pile of junk along the shoreline. We'd made the right decision to sail away to Mangrove Cove to weather the hurricane. That gave me a wondrous feeling of self-satisfaction. Nice to do something right now and then.

"How much water are we taking in?" I asked Kid.

"Almost none. She's super-glued together tighter'n a drum."

"Good work." I nodded to a clear piece of beach. "Over there."

He adjusted the sail without a word, and I steered *The Do Over* toward a small strip of fairly uncluttered white sand. It was, or had been, Skipper Bud's launch ramp, which had been partially cleared, so I knew the marina was at least attempting to be operational. No buildings were recognizable, though. I could not tell where the store, laundry, fuel tanks, or snack bar had been less than a week ago. Nor could I tell where Gloria's cleaning and supply shed had been. Except for the light breeze, the island and the marina were totally still and silent.

Then I saw someone on the beach, staring at us, hands on hips. It was Gloria dead ahead, and I heard her sweet, lusty laugh. "Crap," I thought, "Now I have to go to church on Sunday."

We came about, dropped the sail and Kid tossed out a front anchor while I struggled to lower a stern one. We were within 30 feet of the shore, in about four feet of water. Gloria deftly tossed a line over the bow, and Kid scrambled to secure it to the one remaining front cleat. We were still in the post-hurricane calm. We would be fine with three lines out.

Gloria was gleeful. "Ah knew you'd be back in time fo church ta day, Cap'n Jolly. Ah knew it. Das what I tole her. You be back, an you be back alive."

"Told who?" I asked, laughing at how Gloria could be so cheerful standing amid the debris of the island that looked like a six-day, back-and-forth battle had been hard fought on rough terrain. Childless

Kid hopped out with a splash, and I eased over the side, being careful not to further injure my ribs. We were up to our waists and quickly waded to the beach. Once ashore, I looked back and studied the boat. "Oh, my God," I thought. She sat heavy in the water and was in rough shape, all beat up, not much better than the boats piled on top of each other all over the shore. But she was afloat.

"Jus look at yo," Gloria said. Grinning, she grabbed my arms and turned me into the moonlight to study my face. I guess she was over her fear of my evil eye. My hair was ratty and salt crusted, I hadn't shaved in a week, my torso was wrapped in a make-shift bandage, I had no shoes, no shirt and a pair of shorts that were little better than a rag. I also realize I must have lost ten pounds.

"Only the good die young, Gloria," I said and, seeing the frown on Gloria's face, instantly regretted it.

"Doan you start again. Yo a good man, Cap'm Jolly. Yo a truly good man. Like ah says, you and me, we goin to heaven. Das a fac. But we ain't goin yet. Firs, we goin ta church."

The sky was growing lighter as night slid abruptly into dawn. Gloria turned to the lagoon. There was very little that had been left undamaged. People began to appear out of makeshift shelters, little more than lean-tos, built out of the debris. Most wore cheap, plastic flip-flop sandals, and some had white masks over their faces. With quiet determination, they resumed digging through the debris with their bare hands. I suspected they were looking for personal possessions and loved ones.

I could only imagine their fear. With a single storm blowing across their island, their entire culture, their whole world had been knocked back to a subsistence existence. Thank God the waters around the island still had an abundance of fish.

The hotels were surely shuttered and shut down, the airport closed, the cruise lines probably had already re-directed their ports of call to islands that had been spared. I also suspected the banks and ATMs would still be shut down. I wondered if the desalination and electric plants were up and running. I doubted it. So, there was probably no fresh water, no electricity, and very little food.

Good-bye, good life. One good blow, and it was gone. Poof!

Gloria said, "I tink yo *Do Ova* da only boat that made it, Cap'm Jolly. Yo done smart."

That's me, I thought, looking around. Smartest damn guy on the island.

As the light grew, I was able to see more of the devastation. Boats piled on top of boats on top of buildings, with cars and docks mixed in. And bodies, I strongly suspected. As the sun rose, so did the tropical heat. Even in the open air, there was a heavy smell that wafted over me intermittently in the breeze. It was a bitter, hard, head-ducking odor that mingled with the sweet smell of ocean breezes. It reminded me of the time back in the States when the basement freezer had quit, and we hadn't discovered it for weeks. I had cracked open the top and the stench of rotten meat had knocked me back and made me retch. No, I guess there are some things you will never get used to.

But here I couldn't slam shut the door and walk away. The odor wasn't spoiled meat. It was bodies. There had to be hundreds of bodies in all that debris – men, women, children, as well as cats, dogs, and rats and fish. I thought about Bonita. I hoped she'd gotten to high, safe ground.

I looked around and saw the wreck of a large mega-yacht sitting upright about fifty feet above the waterline. I could read the name, *She Monster*, on the stern. That was the boat that had had the berth beside mine in the marina.

"Has anyone seen Gary and his wife?" I asked, turning to Gloria.

Her lowered eyes and silent head shake told me that nobody had even thought to look. I suspected – no, actually, I knew – they were still on board the wreck of that once beautiful cabin cruiser.

I looked over at the boat and then down at my bare feet. Anticipating what I had in mind, Gloria stepped out of her sandals and nodded. I slipped them on and picked my way slowly through the shattered boats and building debris toward *She Monster*. I climbed up the stern ladder and crossed the main deck. The entire top of the boat was missing. The cabin door was open, partially torn off its hinges. By the time I got within five feet of the door, that sickening odor hit me. I stopped, unsure what to do, and then climbed slowly back down the ladder and off the boat.

Bracing myself against the hull of *She Monster*, I stared dumbly onto the water at my boat sitting at anchor. She looked frail and battered. My heart began to ache, and then I shook my head. *The Do Over* had saved my life in many ways. She had given me purpose and focus and, most of all, a wondrously romantic myth. But, I told myself, startled at what I was actually thinking, she is just a boat. I rolled that thought around in my head while I picked my way back down to the shore line and returned Gloria's sandals to her, steadying myself as I slipped them off by holding onto her arm.

The Do Over had become my life, my love, my home, my friend, my Holy Grail, the vessel of my salvation. And, yes, she is a beautiful structure, I thought, and she sails like the wind, or at least she once did. I stopped and stared at her. But she is only a vessel, only a boat, made of wood, fiberglass and aluminum. In the end, she was like the Corvette insecure men drove to make them feel cool and studly. Yes, this beautiful boat had become a myth, and a wondrous one at that, but a myth, nonetheless.

Just like me. Just like Captain Jolly, a fantasy that made men envious and women dream. And it had allowed me to be Johnny Depp playing Captain Jack Sparrow. Or maybe just Peter Pan outsmarting Hook and trying hard not to grow up, or having grown up, found the experience lacking and decided to turn back and slip again into Never Never Land. Oh, and by the way, it had worked just fine. I could not muster up a single regret.

Still, "She's just a boat," I mumbled aloud, as if revealing a revelation handed down by God. Kid, standing nearby, turned and began to say something, but seeing the quizzical look on my face, he just nodded.

Finally, cautiously, he added, "A fine boat."

I smiled. "Aye. A fine boat indeed."

In the distance, I heard a sound that made me think of war movies. Looking out beyond the drawbridge, I saw a U.S. military transport ship sitting offshore, with two helicopters starting to warm up on their pads. Also pulling hard away from the ship was a small fleet of tenders, each maybe 30 feet long. They were sluggish, filled with boxes, and were wallowing slowly, making their way to beaches outside the lagoon.

"Thank Ga fo America," Gloria said. She pointed to a case of bottled water just above the water line. "We be in big trouble if dese supply din come in."

Beside the bottled water was a stack of heavy, white plastic bags with zippers down the middle from top to bottom. Most were just over seven feet long. Some were smaller.

"Have you seen Bonita?" I asked Gloria.

"No," she said flatly, and then smiled again. "But she be smart and she be tough. Maybe we hear sometin aah church. She be glad to hear you back and 'live."

"Candy?" I asked.

Gloria shrugged a vague I-don't-know.

"Calabash?"

Apparently not in the mood for this Q & A, Gloria walked away. I didn't pursue it. I was studying the helicopters, hopeful that Bonita was safe amid this carnage. I could only imagine the press release headlines from the island Chamber of Commerce: "Island Survives Close Call with Hurricane Olive. Some Damage. No Fatalities."

Keep the myth going.

Gloria returned a few minutes later with two lightweight, blue dress shirts from what I suspect were relief supplies collected in the States. She gave me one and handed the other to Kid. She also tore open a large bag and handed us each a pair of plastic flip-flops, explaining that the ground was a mess, with glass, jagged metal, and splintered wood and nails.

"Yo ready fo church? It be Sunday," she said firmly and matter-of-factly before turning and heading up a narrow path that had been cleared between two piles of devastation.

Kid shrugged into his shirt, put on his flip-flops. "Got anything better to do, Cap'm?" he asked. "Besides, they may have something to eat besides Ho Hos."

He followed Gloria. Well, I did not have anything better to do, and would love a meal that wasn't a processed, cellophane-wrapped chocolate mini-cake washed down with warm beer or water, so I shrugged into my shirt and shoes and tagged along.

HOME

Kid and I shuffled into church behind Gloria.

The roads had been partially cleared, with the debris not picked up but pushed to the side of the road, I suspect by bulldozers. Small fires smoked everywhere, as people burned debris and cooked meals.

As we drove along, the scene looked like something out of a World War II newsreel, with the American forces occupying a town after weeks of artillery shelling. People were everywhere, some wearing white masks and digging through the debris; others, Bibles cradled in their arms, were marching up the road to the church.

Big, green, roll-off trash bins had been placed every few hundred yards or so along the road, and people were quickly filling them up, tossing the broken remnants of their lives over the tall sides. My only thought was mild appreciation for the government, which was actually doing something right. Except for the garbage trucks that carted away the bins, everything was being done by hand. The trucks would haul the roll-offs to the docks and loudly slide them onto barges, which would then be towed a few miles off shore and dumped into the sea. Mother Nature, a strong and powerful female, would do the rest.

Higher up the mountain, bright blue tarps were spread over the roofs of the homes of the walled villas that belonged to the more prosperous residents, often the ones who could afford to visit the island for a month or two in the winter. The walls had either barbed wire or shards of glass cemented onto the top to keep the shadow boys and other riff raff out. It would be a while, I suspected, before repairs would be made, even to these homes, even with the owners waving cash.

I had heard that, after the last big hurricane a few years before I came to the island, an entire four-star resort had been blown away – trees knocked down, windows exploded out, everything ruined. The investors, at first, had not been concerned, however, since they had purchased top-of-the-line insurance coverage. There was only one problem: The agent had never bothered to file the policy or submit their premium payments to the insurance company. There was no record of coverage at the European-based insurance company. After the hurricane hit, the agent had quietly slipped off the island, along with several million dollars of premium payments. The roofless, gutted condo villas still stood, like ghosts scattered around the golf course, which was the only thing back up and running even years later. It was eerie.

While Gloria maneuvered the car slowly along the road, she paused periodically to offer a cheerful greeting or word of support to those working to clear up the debris.

The church was still standing. The walls were made of coral blocks and stone shipped in from one of the larger islands. The walls were covered in mortar and painted bright white, though some of the coating was now missing. The entry had been cleared, and a big, heavy wood door, painted bright red, hung off to the side by one hinge. I looked at that door as I went inside and thought, *this church has been here several hundred years*. Inside, I could see white, plastered walls and rows of well-worn, straight-back pews. It was as bright inside as outside, and when I looked up, I saw the reason: Half the timbered roof was missing. Still, the inside had been swept clean, mostly by women using palm-frond brooms. It apparently had seemed important to them.

The church was filling up fast with mostly black men and women and a few clear-eyed, smiling children. In spite of the carnage around them, the boys wore clean, freshly pressed, white shirts, dark long pants and black, shiny shoes. The girls were in modest, pleated skirts, anklets and loafers or sandals.

The older adults wore modest, out-of-date suits and dresses. It was hot, and a stifling aroma of moth balls mixed with the smell of sweat filled the crowded church. I felt out of place, not so much because Kid and I were among the few whites present, but because we were in shorts and plastic, flip-flop sandals. Most everyone else was dressed up in heavy, decidedly non-tropical garb. The women wore dark dresses and old-style hats; the men were in black, shiny, often ill-fitting suits, white shirts, ties and black dress shoes. I noticed a frayed cuff on one man's shirt. He saw me looking, smiled and tucked it back into the sleeve of his suit coat. I wondered how old that shirt was, and then I looked away, suspecting I had embarrassed him. But he touched my arm, and when I looked up at his dark, black face, he smiled at me and said, "Welcome, Brother. Awfully good ta see ya here, sir."

I smiled, nodded, and turned away. I puzzled over their clothes. They were old. The style made me think of the 1950s, right down to the women's hats. I suspect these Sunday clothes had been handed down for several generations. But it made no sense. Most fabric barely survived a year or two, at most, in the tropical humidity before falling apart. That was also why houses, even those up the mountain, had tile floors and no carpeting. It would mold up and begin to rot within weeks.

That wasn't all. How did these clothes withstand the hurricane carnage? I suspected that many of these people had lost their houses. Everything. Then I realized that these were their treasures. These clothes were packed away, along with their Bibles, each Sunday afternoon in special trunks, sprinkled with moth balls – that kept away everything from mice to mold to the ravages of brutal weather – and these trunks were the first things the people dug out after the hurricane.

But here's what puzzled me the most: I expected to see a somber bunch of humble, beaten down, angry, downtrodden worshippers begging God to please, please stop cursing them with so much misery and suffering. After all, God had wiped out their island. Most were destitute. So, I was surprised that the mood was like a party, a big and festive family reunion. Many had not seen each other since the hurricane had come through, and they were genuinely grateful to see the survivors. They were joyful, laughing, hugging and calling to each other, commiserating over a loss, but celebrating the lives of family members who had survived.

I smiled in spite of myself and then shook my head. I was thinking, "What are you all, nuts? Happy as if you had sense."

I couldn't help but smile. They seemed okay. And, no, it wasn't some simplistic, innocent, native joy. These folks had little before the hurricane destroyed their island. Now they had even less. These people didn't have bad hair days, or become frustrated because they couldn't book a reservation for Saturday at their favorite restaurant. Blessed with next to nothing, they were grateful just to be alive. I couldn't help asking myself, "James Robert, when was the last time you were happy … or grateful just to be alive?"

I thought about the days my children were born. Pretty happy then, I admitted. When Connie and I had gotten married. That was fun, a good day.

A woman brushed my arm and handed me a bottle of water.

Thank you, I said, as she moved on to distribute bottles to others.

"Happy?" I thought of the night, decades before, when Jocko and I had run away for the first time. That had come close.

"How about grateful," I thought. "When was the last time I was grateful to be alive? Today," I thought, a bit surprised. I stuffed my hands into what were left of my pockets and grinned to myself. "Before today? Never. Wow."

The church was filling with people, all standing and greeting each other and shuffling past each other. I bumped into a big black woman with huge, matronly breasts, and an equally big smile. She started to throw her arms around me.

"My ribs! My ribs!" I yipped in surprise, jumping back and lifting my shirt. Then I recognized her. Yvonne, ancient and strong, like a pillar, stood before me, her arms frozen in mid-embrace. Behind her, like baby chicks following the mother hen, were half a dozen young women, some still girls, in clean, pressed dresses, Bibles in their hands. Dark, with hair combed and, in some cases, braided, they were smiling like innocent virgins. If I didn't know their stories, I would not have ever suspected that they'd done time being paid for and pawed over at the brothel across the mountain before being rescued by Yvonne.

One of them glanced over at a young, broad-shouldered man in a suit who was smiling at her. She quickly lowered her eyes, and the other girls giggled, and they all turned their backs away from him. Yvonne, still looking at me, took a second to shoot a menacing glance at the young man. He gulped, smiled back, looking her straight in the eye, and said, "Good morning, Miss Yvonne." Yvonne slowly nodded the slightest of approval and then turned back to me. Yvonne made it clear that she liked men who had the courage to look another person in the eye.

Seeing my rib bandage, Yvonne gently placed a hand on each of my arms, looked me in the face and smiled fiercely, almost shaking. "Oooh, Cap'm Jolly, Ga bless ya, Chile. We bin prayin yo be safe, and we bin prayin fo dis day."

"This day?" I asked, confused.

"Dis day dat Ga brought you to His house. So glad yo here."

I began to protest that I was here only in hopes of a meal. Suddenly joyful, she shushed me, threw back her head and laughed. It sounded like a howl of triumphant joy.

I just stared at her. Yvonne was a good woman. She cared. No games. No gimmicks. No sleight of hand. No myth. And nobody crossed her. I'd seen men twice her size end up on the floor of Yvonne's Place for just patting the backside of one of the women who worked for her.

Now, I'm a grown man, far from innocent, and I've seen more than many people would want to. And I suspected that, if I stayed on this island, I would see even more horrible things. But as I stood there, in front of Yvonne, the strangest feeling ran through me, a feeling I hadn't experienced in ages, if ever.

I felt safe.

It wasn't just because of Yvonne. These men and women here in this half-destroyed church didn't just believe in something. Even if it was just a myth, they were sure about it. I didn't understand it, but the energy of all that joy was starting to overwhelm me. When was the last time I'd believed in something beyond shallow slogans like, "Unless you're the lead sled dog, the view never changes"?

When Yvonne lowered her eyes and looked at me, I stared dumbly back and then muttered, "Thank you." I think it was the first time in a long time I'd said something I'd actually meant.

Then she looked down at my shirt, lifted it again, and studied the wrapping. "Ya know, two thousand years ago, sometin happin that made a bunch a people not jus die, but die fo what they believed. Dey died fo da trute. Das all we got."

"I broke two ribs," I explained dumbly. She nodded. Then she kissed her fingers and placed her hand on my side. Loudly, almost singing, she prayed. "May da Lore, in His swee time, heal you," she declared forcefully. "Lore, dis be a good mon. He doan know it, but he be a good mon."

Instinctively, I bowed my head and closed my eyes. As she prayed, people all around me placed their hands on my head, shoulders and arms. Yvonne, looking up at, through and past the half-missing ceiling, prayed loud and joyfully for my healing, and I realized it had nothing to do with my ribs. No, I didn't feel the power of God go through me. My ribs took another two months before they were right. But in that hot, sweaty, moth-ball smelling, half-ruined church, something did begin to heal that day. All those hands, all that praying, it felt as right as when Sam and I used to hold each other and innocently, gently, rock back and forth in each other's arms. In my heart, I felt years of walls, defenses, suspicions and fears disappear. They didn't so much crumble as just dissolve. Gone. On one hand, I felt as if energy were pouring into me and over me. But at the same time I felt drained, heavy-limbed, like when waking up from a deep, deep sound sleep.

I felt still, like there was no place I had ever been, and no place I would ever need to be.

On the elevated altar at the front of the church, I could hear a man begin to sing, a cappella, an old hymn, "How Great Thou Art." I recognized the song from my past as one that starts out in a gravely, non-melodic, almost monotone, sing-song awkwardness.

As the man half sang, half recited the opening lines, people slowly removed their hands from my body and moved to the pews.

"Oh Lord my God ... when I in awesome wonder ... consider all the worlds ... Thy hands have made."

I slowly opened my eyes and noticed that one of the hands on my arm was that of a white man. I looked up and saw Calabash. He was clean-shaved, neatly dressed, his hair in a ponytail. He was staring at me with that gentle, warming smile and those deep blue eyes.

"I see the stars ... I hear the rolling thunder ... Thy power throughout ... the universe displayed."

Without saying a word, I felt compelled to wrap my arms around Calabash. He hugged me back gently around the neck and whispered in my ear, "Welcome home, Brother. Welcome home."

Then the music crashed over me, as every voice in the church roared the chorus: "Then sings my soul ... My Savior, God, to Thee ... How great thou art ... How great thou art."

The hymn went on, the man at the front chanting each verse, and the people just waiting for their opportunity to roar the chorus: "Then sings my soul ... My Savior, God, to Thee ... How great thou art ... How great thou art."

When I looked up, over Calabash's shoulder, I noticed Black Mike sitting on the platform, off to the side, wearing a white cassock, rope cincture and deacon's stole. His large black head glistened with sweat in the heat. As he sang, he locked his eyes on me and gave me an almost imperceptible nod. I glanced around and saw three of his topless blonde girls in the pews. They were fully dressed, in demure skirts and blouses, Bibles in their laps.

Calabash stepped back and watched me for a few moments as I looked around. Then he whispered into my ear: "You're not the only one who gets a do over."

I just nodded, and a woman I didn't know took me by the hand and guided me to a seat beside her. I sat in silence and let the words from the hymn pour over me. To my right, several pews away, Kid, who seemed to know all the words, was singing and clapping and laughing and smiling, tears pouring down his face.

I just sat in my own peaceful silence among the roaring singing. There was no past, no guilt, no nagging memories, no anger, no fear, no angst, no what-ifs, no relentless tapes playing of how things could have been, should have been, would have been. There was only the now, the present, with nothing to run from and nothing to run to.

Even Sam, the mythical, idealized memory of first love lost, stopped haunting me. I wished her well, and I wished Connie well. Maybe I would look up Sam when the phone service and internet came back online on the island. Yeah, I think I will. Just to see how she is.

My kids? I would need to reach out to them, but even that I knew would be okay, no matter what happened, though I had no idea how. Eerie, but not spooky. No more myths.

I wanted to sit there with my eyes closed forever, listening to the music and the service, sitting hip-to-hip and shoulder-to-shoulder beside these black, wondrous, sweating people.

I opened my eyes when I heard Black Mike's voice. What startled me was that his voice was usually booming and gravelly. However, as he stood at the front of the platform, it was soft, gentle: "I'd like to read to you from Psalm 18, verses four through six."

He paused and looked around. A few Amens-with-conviction came from the pews, and some people fluttered their Bible pages to find the reading.

Then he gently, lovingly read:

"The ropes of death entangled me;

floods of destruction swept over me.

The grave wrapped its ropes around me;

death laid a trap in my path.

But in my distress I cried out to the Lord;

yes, I prayed to my God for help."

Heads nodded as a chorus of Amens rose from the pews.

"We have had our share of the floods of destruction this past week," Black Mike offered softly, and then paused.

The words went into my soul. Somebody was speaking for me and to me, finally. For the first time, I thought about how much I had survived. I thought of my time clinging to the roof of *The Do Over* and the sharks that had tried to eat me. Amen, I mumbled.

"I am not talking about Hurricane Olive," Mike continued, his voice suddenly rising loudly. "I am talking about the ropes of death that bind and hobble and stunt our souls. I am talking about the floods of destruction that drown our hopes and that keep us from truly enjoying and appreciating the gifts God has showered upon us … and continues to shower upon us each and every day."

He paused. In the silence I could hear his breathing. He looked strongly and lovingly around the church.

He continued slowly, now in a low voice: "How many of us walk around acting like everything's fine on the outside? But every day – ev-e-ry day – we struggle with the ropes of death that are wrapped around our hearts, our souls, and our minds? We are entangled in fear, in guilt, in regrets, in self-hatred, in self-doubt, in self-loathing.

How many of us in this church this morning truly believe that we are good people?"

Mike paused and looked around. No one moved.

"How many of us believe we are truly blessed far beyond what we deserve?"

A roar of Amens filled the church.

"How many of us believe we are frauds? Frauds that others – even our spouses and closest friends – have no idea how messed up, how broken, and how hurting we are? How many? Please stand."

Almost everyone in the church rose. I looked over at Kid, who had lowered his head. Tears flowed down his face, as he pushed purposefully to his feet, took a deep breath, and bravely looked up at Black Mike.

Sweetly, gently, Mike continued: "The ropes of death are the darkness in our own hearts and souls that hold us down and that do everything they can to destroy us. I'm talking about the grave of darkness we let rule our hearts, our minds, and our souls, that imprisons us and keeps us from truly living and fulfilling God's plan and purpose for our lives."

I stared dumbly at my feet and listened as Mike spoke: "I speak of forgiveness, not just of others, but of … ourselves," and I thought about what Gloria had said that one morning: "Yo a good mon, Cap'm Jolly. What eatin' you ain't gonna kill you. I know. We all got tings eatin' us."

I rose slowly to my feet. As I did, one thought struck me, screamed at me: I'm tired of running. Running to, running from, it doesn't matter. I'm tired of running. Maybe it's time to cut loose from those ropes of death, I thought as I straightened up and smiled.

***

Goin' home? I asked Kid later, outside of church, blinking sheepishly in the sunlight.

He paused and shrugged. "I guess I am home," he answered, with that big, goofy smile.

I just nodded. That's another myth about paradise. Sometimes it is just home.

EPILOGUE

After the service, over a cup of black coffee and a shared, stale biscuit, Calabash filled me in on what had happened to our friends. Chicago Mike and Patti the Beast, always smarter than anybody else on the island, had refused to leave their low-lying ramshackle apartment. It had taken the full force of the hurricane. They'd found her in the rubble, alive but badly injured. There was no sign of Mike. Calabash and I agreed that he probably had found a way to survive and escape.

French Tony and Blah Blah Brenda had sat out the storm in their store, one of the alcoves in the old warehouse. High water had flooded the place up to their waists. However, neither of them had been hurt. Brenda said she's had enough, though. The last Tony saw of her, he had dropped her off at the airport. She had insisted on going, even though the airport was still closed and no flights were expected to go in or out until next week. Tony barely came to a rolling stop, never even gave Brenda a kiss, and sped away fast after she got out, probably concerned that she might change her mind. Jason and Joanie had headed up the mountain, where some wealthy couple from the States had taken them in. The Sunset Bar is gone, though it will probably be rebuilt.

"What about Candy?"

Calabash shrugged helplessly. "No one knows. I suspect she is with John."

I nodded and thought to myself: Best.

"And Bonita?" I asked, saving the best for last.

"She's fine. She sat out the blow with me in a shelter. Hideous place. Couldn't get a beer. Have you ever eaten SPAM? They say it's meat, but God only knows what animal it comes from."

I nodded. Compared to Ho Hos, I thought, a freakin' feast.

"Bonita came back with me to my place afterwards. The cottage had some water damage, but not so's I really noticed. She'll be pleased to know you're back."

Calabash paused. "She did say, though, that she figures it's time to move on. Most women complain that a man doesn't give her what she needs. She told me that what scared her about you was that you gave her everything she needs … and more. She said it frightened her so much that she'd wake up some nights in tears."

I nodded, understanding. "She's a good woman," was all I added, and Calabash agreed.

***

Kid and I stayed. By the way, his name is Louis Albert, but I promised I'd never tell anyone. He likes being Kid. We'll see how well it fits when he's eighty.

We came out of church that morning and shared in a sparse spread of sad looking vegetables, a case of cold SPAM, a few tins of tuna and sardines, stale crackers, and bottled water. I wished I'd brought some of those left-over Ho Hos for the children.

Most of the adults held back, letting the children gorge themselves. If they were like me, they went away hungry.

Afterwards, Kid told me two of the men knew where there was some fishing gear that had survived the storm.

I thought for a moment about poor old *Do Over* and how much work she needed. Then I looked back at the meager crumbs remaining on the table and the kids still hovering hopefully.

"Well," I said, "I guess we're going fishing, Kid. Grab a can of SPAM for bait. Let's go."

The End

CPSIA information can be obtained
at www.ICGtesting.com
Printed in the USA
LVOW13s0532240817
546205LV00031B/214/P